Thank you for the support! I hope you — my tale. Sincerely,

SHREDS

OF

BY

M.J. HANGGE

Also by
mjHangge

Penalty of Pride: Dispersive Ground

Thanks to Becky
You are the love of my life.
You are the reason I live.
You are what keeps me human.

This book is dedicated to:

Our incredible BooBerry Jones
Our little Brown Bear

And, as always, to:
—JJ—
—TG-RJ-PJ-CT-JS—
NSDQ!

"If you turned into a zombie,
would you eat your own family?"
~Jessica Hangge

PROLOGUE

I was sane once.

Sane?

That single word seems like such a clean and tidy word. It wraps my whole mind and body in a thick blanket of normalcy which no longer seems possible.

But I *was* normal once, just as I was once sane. That sanity is gone now, though. As gone as my wife and child. As gone as everything normal.

That word keeps ringing in the emptiness of my skull. *Sane.* Seems to chase my very soul, or what is now left of it, and I have to wonder if I was ever sane. And if I *was* sane, then what am I now?

Crazy?

That word was even tidier than the other option, but just as incorrect. If I was crazy, would I know that I'd driven my mental bus past the right exit? If I was crazy, would I *feel* the loss of my sanity just as I felt the loss of my family?

No, I wasn't crazy any more than I was sane. My brain bus was just stuck in neutral, unable to shift into drive or reverse—forever stuck on the psychological highway without the ability to simply unbuckle and step away from the bony cage surrounding it.

These wandering thoughts and images were all that was left of my mind now. They were the wisps of imaginary smoke trailing from the ethereal crack pipe of reality and, no matter how hard I swatted at those hazy tendrils, they simply evaded my mind and left me grasping at the nothingness before me.

Nothingness. That was a better word for what I was left with—the nothingness of a soul trapped between sanity and insanity. Like an empty balloon so full of nothingness that it has to burst, I am an empty vessel which could never be filled again. Everything that I had once known and loved was gone now—my child, wife, job, life, mind—all gone like a screwdriver in the junk drawer.

But that left only me in this great mental wasteland; unable to form complete and rational thoughts, yet just as unable to completely bend to the comforting quilt of insanity.

CHAPTER ONE

As lonely as my mind might have been, my body had joined the rank and file of an army so immense that it nearly enveloped everything in the world now surrounding me.

I hadn't signed any enlistment papers for this army. Nobody had ever asked me if I wanted to join, nor had they ever given me a choice. I had been an unwilling draftee with no options to dodge.

At first.

The unwillingness had quickly evaporated and this army was now my own. I had been indoctrinated into it and had eventually become it. I was a soldier now, though I wasn't part of any organized army. This army had no commander to guide us or ranks to manage. This army had no rules and only one purpose.

To kill.

And we were good at killing. We hunted our prey in packs. We hunted them in large waves. We even hunted them alone. We killed our prey for food, yet our bodies no longer needed that food. We killed them because we had to; because that was what we were now wired to do. And we did it without thought and without sympathy. We didn't fight for our families or our fellow soldiers. We no longer cared for the soldier beside us or even the families we had once cherished. We cared for no one—and that was our strength. The inability to care for others gave us a power that the uninfected could not possess. The uninfected—the humans—still cared for each other and still died for the ones they loved. Such a silly concept—love—yet the humans seemed to value it above all else, cherishing the sickening fragrance of devotion enough to lay out their own skin in ridiculously futile attempts to save their families and friends.

I had once felt that need to protect. It had flowed through my veins like smooth Kentucky whiskey and the sense of duty to my own family had once been as strong as the pull of gravity upon my tall and mighty body.

But those feelings were gone now. I no longer suffered from the weaknesses of humanity. I was no longer one of them, only a mere shade of my former self—I was *infected*.

Infected was another simple word, but this one did fit me now. Once, that word had brought visions of simple colds, sneezes, and runny noses. Yet it meant so much more now—to both sides. The *un*infected feared us, feared becoming one of us. We, the *infected*, were driven by some unknown hand to feast upon those still free of this cursed disease which slowly rotted our minds and killed our souls. The infection had stripped me of everything I once considered strength. I knew it was tearing me down, possibly even tearing me apart. But it wasn't weakening me. Even as it broke down my muscles and my mind, this disease had also built new muscles above the others and thick rings of semi-consciousness around my psyche.

This disease had made me strong and made the humans weak. They were our prey and we were the greatest of predators. That made us strong; that made us the kings of this new world.

At least at night.

The night belonged to us.

The days were still the time of the humans. We couldn't risk the sun's touch. That light, which had once fed our bodies with nourishment and our minds with sanity, now burned through the pale skin stretched across our thinning bodies and drove us even closer to the precipice of total insanity. Or maybe we had already jumped off that cliff and it only reminded us of our few weaknesses. Both armies—human and infected—had long adapted to the laws of this new war. They controlled the days and did whatever they did during those long and hot hours, but we ruled over the nights and did what we did then.

And what we did at night was...

death.

That was the only word that could fully describe what we did, but even that word fell short of capturing the true horror that we inflicted upon our enemy. It did little to explain how we tracked the humans through the darkness and took their lives without remorse or mercy. Those were human emotions, built upon the cornerstones of culture—we didn't suffer from those obstacles, though, and were free to feast upon the humans' flesh without emotion or conscience.

Imagine what a perfect army I had been dragged into—singular of mind and purpose with no leadership to guide us astray and no emotional baggage to hold us back. Thousands, millions, maybe even billions of soldiers united by a single disease, a single thought, a single cause, a single appetite.

We were united against the humans, as we feasted upon their flesh and sought only to extinguish their kind.

We were the perfect soldiers in the perfect army.

CHAPTER TWO

Darkness was beginning to fall upon the world outside. I liked the darkness now. The cool rays of the moon seemed to soothe skin burnt by the heat of the sun. I was glad for the blackness of night, but I was even more excited for the blackness of mind that came with it.

The days were slow, bright, and dangerous. They were filled with the footsteps of the humans and the scent of their flesh. We hid from them in huddled and panting masses in the dark recesses of abandoned buildings as they hunted us as if we were diurnal coons. I hated the days now, as I was forced to squat silently and allow my mind to retake lost territory within my skull. Questions pelted the emptiness of my soul during the day. Was I sane? Had I gone over the edge? What was I now? Who was I now? Who were these twisted creatures that surrounded me like sand on the beach? Was I twisted like them? These thoughts ruled my days, torturing me with their continuous barrage as I squatted in the sea of infected flesh and waited for night.

Thankfully, the days were mere flickers of sanity between the long and vivid flashes of my new reality.

The nights.

That was my new life.

That was what I lived for now.

The nights were our time—my time. We ruled over the blackness—as mindless and soulless as the moonless night. The night offered the humans no quarter as they were forced to fear every sunset and scream in terror from every shadow. The night made us gods as we listened to the humans' fearful prayers for sunrise and sniffed deeply at the scent of their fear. But it was the taste of their blood that strengthened us the most. We could smell it—even as it coursed through their tender bodies.

And night was nearly upon me now. As the hot day began to give way to the stillness of night, I could feel that familiar hunger and insanity beginning to overwhelm what little mind I was still left with. Each night, my mind seemed to shrink back, the rational portions overcome by what I was driven to do during the short hours between the light. My mind became more primitive as the heat of my curse burned as brightly as the day's sun. I could feel the knowledge once stored within me slipping from my mind as if someone were using sharpened knitter's needles to stir the soft tissue of my brain through the twisted tunnel of my nose.

The sanity scurried out of my body as I prepared for the darkness. Bob's beams of light were disappearing quickly as he fell below the horizon. The Bright Orange Ball had once been my friend, but Bob now sapped the strength that the darkness willfully restored. I could feel the excitement building in my chest as the dwindling strings of light marked the final moments in my day's coffin. I would soon be free to run the ruins of the city; to search for the uninfected just as they searched for us during the day. I craved the thrill of the hunt; the taste of the flesh. I thrummed with excitement as I listened to the others stirring from their own crouched positions within the shadows.

The nightly spark was being struck within the darkness now—a spark which would soon become a flame that would light a fire within us all. That fire could be heard in the creaks and moans of the others as they slowly rose. Like weeds growing through hard-packed soil, we crept upwards and straightened our painfully twisted backs. It was an impressive sight that was lost on my thinning consciousness as the thick crowd of infected climbed higher in unison. I didn't know those around me. I couldn't speak their names nor describe their faces. I didn't care what they had once been; who they'd once liked; or where they'd once lived. I would never ask those things, even if I knew how to ask them. Their eyes were dead now, just as mine surely were, and I didn't know if there was any part of their minds still hiding from the sickness as mine seemed to be. I didn't know how many of them would return from the hunt tonight, nor did I care about that either. I didn't even care if I came back. I didn't think about what would happen in the next minutes or the next hours of darkness. The only thought running through my thin skull was the thirst for flesh, blood, and brains.

Human flesh, human blood, human brains.

Groans and shouts rose as the infected called out like crazed roosters. The nightly calling was as ritualistic and timely as Bob's first rays. My own throat joined the chorus, though I couldn't understand or control it. I felt the sounds spilling out, but it wasn't the sound exiting that seemed so intriguing to me. Even as my throat clutched and coughed out the sounds, it also pushed something down. It was my humanity—what little still remained—that was shoved aside as my rational thoughts were trampled by the big, black boots of my disease until it squealed out in surrender. Thought abandoned me and strength bolstered me. The well of strength was unseen, but it felt full and unending.

I was transformed.

Strong.

Powerful.

Divine.

CHAPTER THREE

I burst from the thin opening of the doorway, knocking others aside with the force of an overgrown bully. Still strong and powerful, I was different than many of the twisted wretches whose bodies were literally eroding away with each hot day. Their bones crackled and their skin tore away as I pushed my way to the door.

I didn't notice them.

I didn't care about them.

Night was nearly upon me now, cool and free.

I pushed through the doorway as the last of Bob's light disappeared behind the high-rise horizon. My nose sniffed at the air as my eyes searched the streets for those tasty human treats.

There were none.

The humans had already hidden themselves away for the night. They knew what monsters owned the night and they knew their only hope to survive the darkness was to blend into it and to cower behind walls and guns.

The hypnotic thrum of hunger rose in my head, overcoming the small and useless portions of my mind which still gathered and developed information into cognitive thoughts.

My mind was along for the journey again. My legs moved and my nose followed the scents of humanity. I could see that the mass of diseased flesh running beside me was similarly guided. We were a school of fish swimming through the darkness searching for our next meal.

I had walked these streets as a human. That familiarity confused me for a moment. The high walls of Nashville's inner city felt like a home now lost. The smoothness of buildings and the clean streets were gone, though. Cars, bodies, and trash littered the basin of the walled jungle like a third-world country in the grips of a civil war. I had gone to shows here. I'd watched games here. I'd even walked with my family through the crowds and feared only the occasional homeless person. Those had been the 'infected' before the disease had hit. Their infection was simple poverty, but I could remember the horror of their touch as if it could have caused all of this. Those fears seemed ridiculous now, the shelter of civilization had blocked out the true horror of the world as it made simple 'disgust' and 'fear' nearly synonymous.

My conscious mind settled back into the shadows of my skull as it braced for the horrors of the night which I now both dreaded and craved. My eyes seemed to be locked open as my soul was forced to watch the depravity of my new world.

The scent of humanity was growing as I waded through the slower throngs of infected. I sucked in gulps of the scents of the humans who had walked these streets only hours before. Their smell lingered on the trash-littered streets—thick, heavy, and tasty.

The scents were pulling me forward, but a scream twisted me backwards. The scream shook me from my chase and the smell of freshly spilled blood changed my course instantaneously.

Fresh blood.

Thoughts gone now.

Foot followed foot.

Nose followed scent.

Gunfire above me.

Tall building. Door open. My body never stopped as it pushed through.

Bare feet pounded hard on smooth floor.

It was a shotgun. Several floors up. The knowledge of guns was not my own any longer, but mere remnants of an earlier life.

The concussion of the blast was only another floor above. The air of the thin stairwell shook as the shotgun barked out again and again.

The smell of burnt flesh tried to fill my nose, but it couldn't overwhelm the fresh blood that was dragging my willing body forward. Piles of diseased bodies disappeared under my feet as I leaped and climbed. They were not human—I didn't need to stop to know that.

The grey walls of the stairwell climbed high above me, now black and red with the reckless mixture of fresh and dried blood. I turned the corners without slowing as my body clawed upwards, nearly on all fours as I scrambled over the multitudes of my infected army.

Doors broke open above.

More screaming.

More blood.

I needed that blood. Needed to taste it. Needed to allow its warm flow to coat my fingers and chin.

A sharp sniff stopped me. Others continued upwards as they rushed past me and then through the door above.

Sniff...

I sucked in the tiny smell. I wanted to rip my own nose off to allow more of that scent into my head, but my hands were already too busy clawing through the bodies that clogged the stairwell floor.

It took my full reach to wade through the tall stack, but I quickly felt the warm slickness of fresh blood. I took full breaths of the bloody perfume before dipping my head into the pile. My coated fingers pulled back small pieces of flesh as I continued to wiggle deeper. Feet stepped on me as more infected climbed up the stairwell, but my personal banquet was buried deep below the dead and diseased.

The night's first taste of human blood soothed me almost instantly, but my hands never stopped dipping down and digging out more flesh. I could feel my lungs dragging for air beneath the pile I had burrowed into, but I only dug deeper to get closer to the only drug I now needed. My bottom was now at the top and my top was near the bottom. My whole body shook as my heart beat faster and my hands ripped even harder. Human flesh didn't normally pull easily from bone, but my fingers were clawed talons now—their bony extents suited only for one purpose, to rip and feed.

The stairs of this high-rise building were piled thick with the dead bodies of the diseased. Though the layers had probably built with each night, the freshest layer of bodies was nearly waist high. I cupped the human flesh upwards through the blanket of dead. The air was so thick and heavy that I couldn't breathe it in, but I couldn't pull my body from this small banquet of flesh I'd discovered. I would die from asphyxiation before I drew my head out.

A fresh flood of infected were clawing their way up the stairwell above me. I ignored them, my only thoughts were of the tasty bits of human flesh I'd found. Half of my hand was still pushing the chunks of skin down my dripping craw when heavy feet pounded over my protruding legs and ass. I felt the infected feet smashing my baby maker, but it was my gnawing teeth that truly hurt as they closed over the meat of my hand.

Grunting and crying out with disgust, I pulled my nibbled fingers away before spitting out the cocktail of my own infected flesh and diseased blood. The taste of that infected flesh was bitter and rotten, though my sane mind might have argued that everything around me was now bitter and rotten. The flavor of my own disease gagged me and its texture tainted the wondrous taste of humanity. I spit and vomited as I pulled myself back towards the surface.

My head swirled and my stomach wrenched violently as I popped back out of my tiny cave.

Back on my feet, I could feel my body swaying dangerously before being shoved over by the rush of more infected. The world slowed, blurred, and then tipped as the taste of diseased flesh coated my innards and toasted my mind.

I toppled to the side and then dropped down the stairwell, my limp body rolling and falling as the stairs passed above me.

CHAPTER FOUR

What remained of the night passed as I lay at the base of the stairwell. Bob was already beginning to light the sky outside, but my body didn't want to obey its simple commands. The stirring light lit the grey walls and black, metal stairs. I could remember landing here, but everything before was a chaotic blur and everything after was just gut-wrenching darkness. The tumbling fall down the stairs, the pained weakness, the rotten taste of my own flesh—it all played through my scrambled brain, a bad movie stuck in rewind.

The taste of human flesh, mmm... that memory perked my mind like stiff coffee. My eyes drifted over the stairs again, this time seeing the dead, diseased bodies clogging the utilitarian stairwell that hadn't been used much during the time of humanity.

Bob's light grew brighter as the silent struggle ensued within the span of my skull. The noises—maybe they were voices—in my head seemed to fill the quiet of the staircase now. There were no more shotgun blasts; there were no human screams; there were no more diseased monsters rushing up or down the stairs. Only the quiet of a dawn breaking upon the remnants of a great battlefield; the ghosts skittering back into darkness as the low fog hung thickly over the scarred landscape. I didn't see the battlefield until Bob's brilliance climbed up the first step, but I couldn't ignore it once the first casualty had been lit. I was at the base of Little Round Top, looking up at the bloody remains of Chamberlain's victory. Every stair was covered with the bodies of the damned, their black blood drying to an oily crust upon the stairs beneath them.

Memories flooded my skull before I could push them away. I had climbed over those bodies during the darkness. I was disgusted by the visions, even as I was inspired by them. I had been strong as I'd climbed that death hill. No, I'd been more than strong—I'd been divine—I'd been a god as I tore up those stairs. An animal god—powerful, hungry, and deadly. I hadn't crawled up those steps and I hadn't feared the death above or below me. I had clawed my way upwards, using the dead and diseased to thrust myself even faster.

But my strength was gone now. I was weak, even weaker than the humans who I feasted upon. I felt a new disease running through me like cold mercury slowly working through my black veins. Every ounce of my body seemed to pool across the blood-stained floor as this new disease fought for control. I didn't know what *new* disease I'd caught, but I could feel it in me just as I'd felt the rash of measles covering me as a child—a full lifetime before. But this new disease seemed to be in contest with my other disease, the two only agreeing to kill their host before each other.

Pin holes along the walls, reminders that I actually *was* lying among a battlefield, allowed small glimpses of the world outside. The holes, bullet holes, streamed light like a thousand tiny flashlights into the dark and stagnant stairwell. Rational thought began as I lay silently in a semi-comatose state and Bob's light burned at my eyes and skin. I was burning up, a strange mixture of disease and sunlight baking me from every angle. There was no pain any longer, just the apathy and disgust that came with most deadly infections. I burned with a cold heat that seemed to freeze my intestines and evacuate my bowels. I could feel the liquid running down my legs and the smell made me vomit again. Clumps of flesh and hair barked out before me and I could feel my head swinging back before falling onto the bloody mixture underneath it.

I felt the comforting warmth of unconsciousness soak through me again. My heavy lids clicked open for only moments at a time before slapping closed. I sank deeper into the blackness of my own soul; deeper and deeper until I felt my emotional feet hit the bottom of the black tube of nothingness surrounding me.

Hours passed, maybe even nights, but I was frozen still. I probably wouldn't have woken again if not for the smell of human flesh passing within inches of my bent and broken nose. I heard the footsteps and the whispered voices as they stepped over me, disregarding my prone body as the dead creature that I was.

I felt their presence like a cool breeze moving in off the coast, filling my lungs with the salty freshness of another life. I watched their steps above me, my dead eyes tracking them in the harsh light. I couldn't move, couldn't reach out to grab them, but I could have feasted on the flesh above me if my body were still my own.

But it wasn't.

I tried to move, tried to grab at their heels as they stepped over me. The three adults and two children passed over me like ghost ships in the fog and I could do little more than lie there and watch. They bounced and jumped down the stairs and over the tallest piles, but barely even noticed when they stepped over my flaring nostrils and hungry lips. I could have nibbled on the youngest child as her heel landed only a fingertip from my hungry mouth. I heard the smoosh as she stepped into the bloody goop that had been in my belly only hours before.

"Yuck!"

I heard the girl's disgusted utterance, but couldn't decipher it. I no longer understood the humans' words. The sound of her voice was nothing more than grating across my ear drums which triggered no thought or emotion.

The scent of the girl's flesh filled my nose and bolstered my strength enough to allow me a deep breath. I grunted out in pleasure as a second breath filled my lungs.

"Daddy!" The girl screamed as she jumped away from me. The word was familiar and filled my mind with a strange warmth that seemed to thaw my icy insides a few degrees. I didn't understand the word, but I knew I'd heard it before and that it had once meant something to me. What the word meant to me didn't matter, though, as one of the human men pushed the barrel of a shotgun into my face. I couldn't move to defend myself or even to shrink back from him, so I simply lay still and watched as his finger tightened on the trigger.

Something within me welcomed the blast that would soon come. My life, if that was what it was, meant nothing to me and I suddenly found myself wanting it to end. I was trapped somewhere between humanity and death, hovering above the hot fires of an unending purgatory.

"No!" Another human pulled away the shotgun and I could see the two turn to face each other. There was anger in the man's eyes, but I watched it settle into the folds of the dark orbs as he nodded. They talked, their words a strange, alien language as they prepared to leave my grey casket.

But the man's eyes never left mine.

There was hatred in his eyes, but I felt only hunger in mine. It was a hunger that I'd never felt before, my gut finally settling from the wretched taste of my own flesh. Each breath of the human flesh made me stronger and it would only be a few more minutes before I could push myself off the floor to chase them away. I grunted out a snort of laughter as I found the strength to lift my head. These humans were so tasty, but so weak. They feared everything and I laughed again, as if I myself had not feared everything when *I* had been human.

I made it to an elbow when I heard the girl's shriek and felt the hard sole of the man's boot as it came down on my head like a hammer flung from the roof of a skyscraper. My arm collapsed and I fell back into the puddle of vomit again. I didn't struggle as the toe of the boot reached out again. I didn't even fight off the blackness that overwhelmed my mind as unconsciousness took me.

#

I woke angry.

I wasn't sure if it was the pain in my head or the fact that I was still able to feel that pain which made me the angriest, but I was angry and ready to take that anger out on the man who owned the boot. Everything else blurred as I remembered that boot.

I would punish the booted man. I would hurt him for what he'd done to me. I would kill him. I would *eat* him.

And I would smile while I did it.

I would relish his pain. I would bask in his cries.

Sunset was fast approaching, the many beams of light seemed to tell me the hour better than my expensive wrist watch once had. My time was fast approaching. My time to hunt. My time to feed. But my body didn't quake with excitement this evening.

I felt weak.

I felt scared.

I felt human.

It was a disgusting feeling. Fear, pain, and weakness seemed to melt through my body and every ligament seemed to be loosened by the effect. I could feel the shaking in my hands and the quivering in my belly as every nerve cried out in mutiny.

The beams of light changed to deeper oranges and reds as they danced up the dull grey wall. Bob was diving lower as it fell towards the western horizon. The lights dimmed and I waited for the familiar excitement.

It didn't come.

I waited for the hunger. Only nausea filled my belly.

I waited for the strength. I found none.

Night settled onto the streets of Nashville and the cries of the other infected bounced through the valleys formed by the high-rises. I felt my voice lift in response and it bolstered me enough to push myself up and onto my feet, but my stomach emptied again as soon as my throat finished the familiar cry of the infected.

As chunks of flesh and hair billowed out, my head circled heavily on my shoulders. The human flesh chunked out, but I could only taste my own flesh—metallic and rotten. The rage was gone, replaced by disgust and nausea. I couldn't imagine eating again—ever.

But the taste of human flesh would revive my strength. Somehow I knew this was the truth, more truthful than any truth left to me now. Though the thought of filling my gut nearly emptied it again, I knew that was the only medicine for the nastiness of my own taste.

Walking through the door and into the open night, my mind was reeling along with my body. I couldn't think. I couldn't control my body any longer. I couldn't control *any* thing *any* longer.

Foot followed foot, but my destination was no longer clear. I tried to listen to the cries of those around me. I heard them, but they were muted by the thunderclouds that seemed to be building within my skull. I couldn't feel the humans' fear. I couldn't taste their blood. I was a devil no longer. I was merely a simple lost soul with no hope for redemption.

A pistol's sharp report rattled through the tall buildings. Its sound was muffled by the distance and the ringing in my ears, but I knew it was my last chance for life. I was dying now, an especially dramatic statement for the dead to make. I knew that I would soon wilt in the darkness if I didn't find human blood to strengthen me. My bare feet pushed forward faster. There was still some life in me, but I knew it would soon dim into the surrounding darkness if I couldn't move faster than the others now around me. They ran like demons possessed. They ran like I had only nights before. I felt myself elbowed and pushed aside as the stronger ones rushed past. I'd been the one pushing the weak aside, but now I was one of the weak and I could only push myself off the brick and glass walls as the others stormed through the streets of Nashville like an advancing army.

I shuffled through the streets, my body struggling to keep moving forward. I knew these streets; knew these buildings. We'd walked these streets together, my family and I. We'd eaten in these restaurants and shopped in the stores.

Strange that I recalled these streets; strange that I remembered such odd facts. I hadn't thought of such things since the infection—the original infection—had taken hold of me. Nausea was replaced by curiosity and something else. Something that I couldn't describe. Something that I couldn't feel. Yet I was feeling it, not just feeling it but being torn apart by it.

Loneliness?

No, not exactly loneliness.

Longing?

Closer, I longed for my family and for my life, but longing still wasn't right.

Emptiness?

That was it—emptiness. My unfelt feet stumbled as my empty mind stumbled over that explanation. I was empty now. Everything within me seemed thin and empty as I tripped, bounced, and stood again. I was the empty vase without any life in it. I was the blank pages with nothing to be written on them. I was a void now. A black and soulless hole that moved through this black and soulless world with nothing that could fill the void within me.

My mind rolled inside my head, working hard—too hard—even as my body struggled just to keep the air moving in and out of my rotted lungs. I would have enjoyed pondering the small nuggets of knowledge further, but the pistol reports were getting louder and I could hear the screams of fear gathering power above me. Maybe those screams would be the flowers to my vase; the story to my pages.

Or maybe they would just lead me to a meal that would fill the void in my gut.

A whiff of a familiar potion passed my nostrils. My legs shook and nearly let go as I stopped to breathe in that smell. It was a familiar scent, but I couldn't place it until I was pushed aside and nearly trampled by the infected army coursing through the dead streets. My head struck the unyielding concrete hard enough to split that empty egg open. I didn't crack, but I could feel my golf ball brain bouncing from one side to another as I lay facedown in the mud and muck of the streets that had once been clean. My nose sniffed and sucked at the small trail that was already growing cold. I could smell the boot, the man's husky filth mixed with stains of my own blood. But it was the girl's blood that sent gobs of thick saliva coursing through my mouth. I could smell her heart pumping that crimson potion even as my head swooned from weakness. The scent firmed my knees and granted me the strength to push myself back up.

Across the streets of Nashville, a battle for power rocked the darkness. The humans fought for their lives and my brethren fought to take them. Every high-rise seemed to quake with a different battle within. Some screamed out in victory, but most only shook with the humans' pain.

Below those buildings, I pushed on through the thinning crowds of infected. With each building, more of the infected pool seemed to funnel out. I didn't follow them, though. I tried to steer around them as my nose followed the thin scent of my prey. The streets of my family's hometown seemed to disappear around me as my mind focused intently on the scent. The miles of wrecked cars, burnt buildings, dead bodies, and broken glass faded into the blackness around me.

The girl's scent powered my lungs as I began running. I wasn't the strong and vicious killer I'd been only nights before, but I was passing the weaker beings once again. It wasn't just the scent of her blood that propelled me, though. I was spurred on harder by the desire to be the first to find the little girl again. I wanted to find her and then to kill her. More than that, though, I wanted to find the man whose boot wore my blood. I wanted to kill him. Or maybe I wanted him to kill me. I didn't know which was more exact, but it no longer mattered. We were tied together by the ribbon of the girl's scent and we would meet soon to find out who would be the first to die.

CHAPTER SIX

The night passed as I chased the girl's weak scent. There were humans around me in the darkness, sweet and tasty morsels that would have brought a hot spittle broth to my lips only days before, but I was no longer interested in just *any* human meal. My gut hungered for only one meal now, the tender cosset's meat of the girl and the aged leather of her father. My eyes searched the night, but I was following my nose and not my sight. Buildings passed, their facades unlit, but somehow recognized. This had been my home before the sickness. I didn't know how I knew that or why I even cared now. My home was now the night and my life was filled only with the desire to feast upon the booted man's flesh.

An image of a long-toothed cat adorned the wall of a long building under human words which meant nothing to me. The symbol did mean something, though. My eyes guided me towards the beige building while my nose fought to keep my body on the path to vengeance. The scent, which had faithfully followed the middle of the wide road, was suddenly forgotten as long-lost memories pulled me to the building. Blue glass rounded the end of the building and stretched into the sky until glass gave way to steel-framed antenna that nearly touched the night's low clouds.

Brilliant visions of a lost life shattered the darkness around me. My family was with me in my mind's hallucination. The visions were so vivid that the battle-strewn streets were gone—replaced by the lights of a living town. I could see the colorful cars and hear the roaring pipes of the motorcycles. I could smell the beer in the open-front bars. I could taste the salt of the pretzels on my lips. Mostly, though, I could *feel* two hands in mine. They were warm and loving—one grown, the other small and swinging with excitement. We were going to a game, a Predators game, and this long building was our destination.

I stared into the sky, my eyes following the blue glass upwards. I saw it as it had been—bright, busy, and exciting. I could see the bustling crowds filing up the long escalators and hear the roars of the fans as they cheered on the Preds.

But all of that was gone now. The girl's scent pulled me back to the deserted streets and I finally saw the stadium as it was now—burnt, broken, and empty. Few blue panes had survived into this new world—a world where the true predators didn't play with pucks and the losers were killed and eaten.

I was one of those predators and I felt the memories of my other life drift away—a small balloon on a strong wind. My nose tugged me back into the street, over the thick piles of dead and rotting flesh, through the confusing maze of abandoned cars, and back to the girl's trail.

My mind was gone again, replaced by the predatory lust for blood.

Yes, I'd been here before.

Yes, it had once meant something to me.

No, I no longer cared.

What I did care about was that scent; that lovely and familiar smell that had so entirely enraptured my soul. It was disappearing, though, melting into the cacophony of dead scents filling this dead city.

I couldn't waste any more time. I couldn't afford to ponder my thoughts or search for past lives. Those lives were gone, if they were ever there at all, and those people were dead. I was in this life and this life was full of only one thing—the need to kill.

My bare feet gripped at the burnt hood of an old sports car. Unfelt glass from the missing windshield cut through my soles as I continued onto the roof. I surveyed the wide street below—a king over his kingdom. But I didn't rule over all that

I saw, rather I belonged to it—was one with it. Nashville, a town that had survived a war between men, hadn't survived this war.

And neither had the men.

The town was full of ghosts and demons now. The building blocks of humanity still remained, their tall steel and rock structures stretching into the black clouds above, but the humanity itself was all but gone from the town. Those who did remain had to scavenge from the carcass of the town during the days and had to fight for their lives through the nights. The town now belonged to us—the infected—and we didn't bother with the power or the water, we didn't need those things. We didn't sweep the streets or park the cars and the beautiful town was quickly beginning to look like Nagasaki circa August 1945. The stench of death and the shrill screams of dying didn't disgust me, though, they made this *my* town. It belonged to me and I to it. The town belonged to all of us infected now and we *all* belonged to each other. We were a collective mind—without thoughts or emotion, yet with all of the same thoughts and feelings.

But the girl's scent was disappearing even as I dawdled at my memories and I couldn't waste any more time. The booted man hadn't. My mind was roughly shoved into its small lair again as my nose did the thinking for my loose limbs. Nearly dropping to the ground to regain the scent, I rushed forward with every ounce of strength left to me. I passed a tall building to my left, a single word, *Batman*, passed with the building, though I knew not what it meant nor cared why it filled the emptiness of my skull. I ran on, my feet pounding the littered streets until I finally broke free of the flat-faced red buildings on either side.

There were no others around me, though I could smell the signs of humans in the buildings I passed. I couldn't see them at the windows, but I knew they were there, and I knew they feared my footsteps. Their fear empowered me; the smell of their nervous bladders propelled my feet and begged me to find them. Though I needed the strength their flesh would provide, my teeth ached for only one flavor now.

The road ended abruptly as the buildings stopped on my left and right. Before me, a circle of flags was half-collapsed where several vehicles had piled upon each other. To my left, the tall guitar of the Hard Rock was tilted at an odd angle and...

A name?

Strange that such a small recollection should shake me so violently, but my human memories were now as foreign to me as the I's and O's of computer language had once been. This memory didn't comfort me, though. It only made me angrier. I had eaten there. More than once. Maybe it was a regular hangout. I couldn't tell, but I knew that life was gone and, with it, the memories of what I had enjoyed as a human. I wouldn't eat there now; there was nothing inside that I would enjoy. But outside, there *was* something I wanted to eat. All I had to do was follow the aromatic breadcrumbs of the girl's blood to collect my meal.

Her smell was strong here. Perhaps they had tried to decide which way to go, for the river ahead now funneled them either left or right. I didn't have to stay more than a moment to tell which direction they had chosen. The girl's scent clung to the road on my right as the trail weaved back and forth. I could almost see where she had stepped, I was that close now.

But daylight was coming soon. The openness of the river showed the light to the east. I was closing on my prey, but they would survive another day. A feeling, strange and foreign, worked at my gut. My mind was detached from my body, but this feeling somehow connected the two. It was happiness. But why I might be happy was a thought I would have to consider in the shelter of a dark building with the long and hot day quickly approaching.

CHAPTER SEVEN

Bob was beginning to peek through the shattered windows now. The day would be hot and miserable, but I was happy to be hidden in the back rooms of the Hard Rock. A strange calm had overtaken my feverish body as I passed beneath the large fresco and through the revolving doors.

I was alone.

That wasn't unusual during the nights, but I hadn't been the sole infected soul during the day in some time. It was a strange feeling to be alone in the shadows now. Though we didn't talk or even acknowledge others, there was a strength in numbers that I had come to depend upon. During the nights, I was strong and I was happier without the others to eat my prey or to slow my chase, but during the day I huddled in the shadows and felt secure knowing that there were others around me.

Hunger ached within me, that dull and painful twisting of my gut that made me want to lie down and pull my knees tightly to my chest. I couldn't sleep that way, though. I couldn't let my body recover if I lay on the floor like some damned dog—like some crippled human. Dropping to my haunches in a perverse kimchi-squat, I willed away the distractions of my weakened body as I tried to regain my strength.

My body loosened with each passing moment and I could feel the passing of my illness as the strange sleep overcame me. Every ligament and muscle was so slack now that my butt rested against my heels and my armpits held my chest firmly between wide knees. Sleep—hot and restless—came quickly as my stomach emptied beneath me. The gut-wrenching smell of my own feces wafted up, the scent was comforting and it was the last thing I noticed before my eyes slammed shut and my mind was freed back to dream.

CHAPTER EIGHT

There was something in the darkness with me. It moved through the restaurant around me.

I could smell it.

I could taste it.

It was human.

Mmmm, the sweet smell of human flesh woke a desire within me that overpowered the need to sleep. The human's blood and breath were aphrodisiacs which excited me to edible orgasm. I could taste its flesh upon my tongue. I could already feel its fat and sinew upon the sharp edges of my teeth.

The human moved through the shadows. He was cautious. I could sense his movements, yet I couldn't see or hear his footsteps. With every step, he came closer to me. My lips quivered with excitement and my stomach ached for his blood.

But I stayed silent.

I stayed hidden.

I was the silent killer who hid in the shadows and awaited my prey. I would not move, would not breathe, until my unsuspecting meal was close enough to touch.

My silence and stillness hurt, though. Daylight had taken over the restaurant and the tables were topped with sunlight that angled sharply downwards through the many broken windows. It was late afternoon, I could tell by Bob's steep angle. The restaurant was a sieve of light that let through more than it blocked and it burned at my eyes, strained the remains of my mind, and made me wish for the sanctity of darkness.

My prey was moving towards the back rooms. I could feel his desperation and hunger. I could see that he was alone. I could sense that he was scared. The humans didn't venture into the darkness alone unless they were scared, desperate, and hungry. They knew that the shadows were our territory.

I could see the long rifle in his hands as he moved slowly through the dim light of the restaurant. He clutched it and it comforted him. He believed that the weapon would save him.

He believed wrong.

I watched as the man edged through the restaurant. His heavy feet lifted and fell, rustling the thin carpet and bumping aside the broken plates that were the final memories of humanity in this forgotten restaurant. The guitars above our heads rattled in their cases with each step. Stillness overwhelmed me as I waited for the man's approach. I could feel the calm take over and knew that the man would wander closer as he searched for food. The feeling of happiness edged into my head again, its peaceful touch soothing but unwelcomed. I didn't like this feeling, even though the soft serenade of content blanketed me as I awaited my meal.

But why was I so happy now? I'd lost my wife. I'd lost my child. I'd lost my humanity. Yet I'd never felt so alive before. I barely even remembered my family or my life, but some string of consciousness told me that this new life, this new reality, was what I'd struggled through my other life to achieve.

Calm happiness.

The man was moving even closer now. Through the small opening before me, I could see his feet slipping closer. The restaurant's kitchen surrounded me, a stainless steel trap that seemed to have been set for this man alone.

Every nerve in my body was tense as I waited for the trigger. I could feel the jaws of the trap tightening with each wary step this human took.

He was hungry. I knew he was hungry because he was gambling his life in the darkness. He must have known that I was here. He must have smelt the nauseating stench still dripping from my torn pant legs, but the man continued forward still and my heart pounded with impatience.

My lungs filled with the silent rush of air.

My pulse beat faster.

My legs tightened.

The man's face peeked over the stainless counter and our eyes locked. There was a recognition in those eyes that pleased me. It was an acknowledgement, a silent and barely perceptible realization that he had doomed himself to death.

I could feel the smile cracking across my face as if I'd carved it across a great pumpkin. I could feel myself nodding in agreement—yes, you screwed yourself! Welcome to death.

My legs released.

My body sprang upwards. I felt the force unclench as I leapt upwards and my hands reached towards the man. He never even tried to bring his gun up; he knew that he was dead even before our bodies met.

The battle lasted only a moment as my powerful hands ripped at the man's throat. I could feel my hands thrust and pull. I could see the blood splatter across the room. The smell of fresh blood filled my nose and drove my hands even faster. I was a god again. A god of pain and death as I ripped and tore. My fingers were iron claws; my hands steel hammers. They rained down on the man's body as my mind entered a state of delirium.

I could taste the blood now. So delicious; so soothing. It coated my fingers and rolled down my throat like a delicious honey. His body was still twitching and his heart still beating, but his head had already rolled under the counter.

My fingers searched for the muscle which powered the human's body. His ribs cracked beneath the force of my hands. I could feel the beat in my palm as I yanked the man's heart from his chest. It tried to fight against the death as if it could release the man from my grasp by its own desire alone.

It couldn't.

There was a moment of divine pleasure that coursed through me as my loose teeth entered into the tough muscle of the man's heart. The blood within was divine.

I was strong again. The uninfected blood warmed me like a sensuous candle and I could feel the pull of sleep coming again. I could barely find the strength to drag my kill deeper into the shadows before crouching again.

What had I become? My eyes showed me the kill and my body soaked in the human's strength, but my mind still questioned my new existence. Stuck somewhere between painful consciousness and restless sleep, I had to wonder how long I would survive. It wasn't my body that would soon die, but my mind. My body was strong and my instincts were dangerous, but my mind was endangered. Both a blessing and a curse, the blanket of ignorance draping itself over the small remnants of my humanity coaxed my eyes shut against the vision of my latest kill.

I would miss my sanity.

I would miss my humanity.

I slept with the knowledge that I was no longer sane; no longer human.

I was dead again.

But I was finally alive again!

Night was coming. I could feel the excitement within me building again as the bright light streaming through the front windows began to temper into darkness. The smell of my latest kill only furthered my anticipation for the nightly race to begin. Like a world-class runner eagerly awaiting the firing pistol, my body was tense and my heart was thrumming. My feet were locked into the starting blocks between the ribs that had protected the man's organs only hours before. Those bony extents were useless now, my own ribs were now protecting his organs as my stomach busily tried to digest the banquet. There was still so much to eat, but I couldn't make the night's chase if I did.

I was ready for the race again; I was strong again and ready to chase down my little rabbits.

I couldn't smell the girl's trail inside these walls. I feared I wouldn't be able to pick it up outside either, but I could still smell her footsteps inside the rotting walls of my nose. If I closed my eyes and breathed deeply, I could still taste her fear and disgust.

In the silence, my mind began wandering again. How long had I been whatever I had become? What had I become? The small portion of my mind which still guarded the smallest nuggets of my humanity seemed to ache for those answers, as if the answers could unlock some door that might regain control again. But I didn't want to release my body back to humanity. There was power in what I'd become. There was something greater in the strength I now possessed. Compassion, integrity, kindness—those were mere words which meant nothing to me any longer. I had no need for those emotions. I had no desire to possess those qualities.

Without those hindrances, I was free from the rules which still trapped the humans.

I liked that freedom.

I needed that freedom.

And I would take that freedom from others.

But my mind's questions seemed to demand answers. How long? I didn't know, I no longer owned a ruler to measure time which now seemed to boil down to simple visions of daylight and darkness. I *could* remember that the sickness took some time to overcome my defenses. Even as a human, I had been strong. Tall, powerful, and handsome. I had taken pleasure in the gifts I'd been born with, just as I now enjoyed the power I'd been reborn with. I was important, too, though my importance was based upon a scale which no longer existed.

The restaurant was once a busy and tasty stop in my busy day. A lifetime ago, I'd eaten well here. I liked it here; liked their food, their service, their recognition of my importance.

But what and who I had been only frustrated me now.

The illness had been here for some time. I couldn't say the days, but the dust covering the restaurant's tables was evidence enough that it had been more than a mere moment. The desperation and disappearance of the humans also seemed to point to a great span of time. I could remember the earlier days of the disease when the humans were plentiful and the infected were not. I didn't have to fight the others for my meals then. I could stand in the remains of my own capture while others did the same around me. We were weaker then, yet I was stronger.

It hurt my head to think of such useless facts and I wanted for nothing other than my mind to clear for the chase. Shallow breaths absorbed the scents around me, but I could only smell the body beneath and my own feces beside me. My breathing deepened and my mind disappeared again as Bob continued to dip lower. I sounded like a well-ridden horse as big puffs of blood and snot shot out of my nostrils. I could smell the girl's steps again. Even through the distance of time, I knew where she once placed her feet. I could almost see the steps outside and I could sense her confusion. I could practically taste her fear now.

She would take me to the man with the boots.

She would betray him, though she called him father and loved him.

She would watch me eat his insides.

Bob was finally gone and I rocketed through the broken windows. Shards of glass tore at my skin, but I didn't feel the pain. I was the hunter again. I had been recharged by the blood and I could feel the horror of my prey in the distance.

On the streets, my body didn't break stride as I leapt from roof to hood and back down again. The girl's scent was nearly gone now and I had little time to waste as I avoided the maze of cars below by jumping from one to the next. I barely noticed as the call of my kin carried over the death of the city. My lungs exhaled with the cry, but my body never slowed.

Other infected joined the hunt behind me, but their feet were not as graceful and their focus not as keen. They were distracted by the chase for *any* human, but I was looking for only one. It focused me and kept my feet limber and quick.

The trail took a sharp left turn under a tall bridge that I'd once driven over. The girl's steps widened as the humans had broken into a run. They turned right on twin railroad tracks at the river's edge and raced away. I stopped to sniff a small patch of dirt that smelled of piss too cold and deep to be less than a day old. They'd moved quickly while I'd been weak, but I would soon be gaining on them.

I followed the tracks, both the girl's and the railroad's, for some distance. They left the river's edge and crossed under a highway now silent of traffic. Standing under that highway, I realized that everything around me was silent. I hadn't heard that kind of silence ever before, even when I'd been human. It was a silence that seemed nearly deafening in its quiet. It was maddening. It was driving me mad.

In the silence, I also noticed the total lack of scent beyond the trail I was now tracking. I couldn't smell any humans, I couldn't even smell any infected. There were dogs, cats, rats, and birds; but there were no humans—uninfected or otherwise. Signs of humanity surrounded me—cars parked and crashed on the road above, buildings lining the streets to my right, and a boat floating lazily downstream with the current, but nowhere around me were the creators of those items. Nowhere was there anything to indicate that a human, other than my prey, had been in this area in a week. A month. A decade.

In a rush, the small edge of my consciousness was recalled and it fought for control over my animalistic impulses. I wanted to know how long it had been. I didn't know why, but something inside me wanted to know.

The railroad tracks disappeared behind me as I climbed up the steep hillside. A long, low warehouse stretched out before me as I topped the grassy hill. Its bottom half was white, the upper blue. There was nothing more than a few street hounds occupying its inside. I could smell the emptiness without even opening a door, but I needed to know more than just the state of the building. My feet were slowly plodding along as I rounded the corner to find several of the large roller doors cracked open.

I dropped low, almost crawling on all fours, to enter silently. The dogs heard my approach, but they merely barked and whimpered to acknowledge that I was more dangerous than they. The warehouse smelled of mildew and rot, but it was the smell of death and disease inside the long, open building, that interested me. The smell was old and withered. I pushed past a litter of pups cowering under the warehouse's machinery and growled menacingly at their mum as she tried to protect them. We both kept our distances—she in fear, me only because they weren't of any interest to me.

The smell of death grew. I could see the source behind a broken window. A man lay on the floor near a pair of wooden desks inside. I pushed through the door and leaned down to sniff at his body. His body was tight and posed in death, half his skull missing. He'd been infected, I could smell it on his decomposing body, but it had never taken hold completely. I could see a shotgun lying beside the desk and remembered that I'd almost done the same thing when I'd become infected. Human weakness had nearly driven me to end my life just as this bastard had done.

The man's body was dry, withered, and blackened but what that meant and how long he'd been dead was a mystery which I no longer cared to solve. I was suddenly done with my science project as anger flushed my body.

I rolled out of the warehouse and looked to the sky for signs that Bob would soon be climbing. I still had some time and I used it to continue my chase. The girl and her boot-wearing father were somewhere in the distance and I wanted to find them before Bob rose again.

Sprinting down the hill and back onto the tracks, I ran until my lungs burned and my body quivered with weakness. Still I pushed myself on; running when I could, stumbling when I couldn't. I could smell every member of the girl's party now. Their footprints were distinct and I followed them like an old beagle on the track.

The scent left the railroad tracks and climbed onto the streets before turning into a wide cemetery. Grass grew unkempt to my knees and I could actually see where my prey had marched. My feet pushed on as my body tried to keep pace. I ran through the high weeds and grass, passed hundreds of unnoticed gravestones and then stopped at a small building.

They were daywalkers and, even in the totally abandoned sections of this sprawling city, they couldn't risk being out after sunset. Like me, they were captives of t' clock. This area was so empty of my kind that these five have lit the greatest Independence Day fireworks show last night and they would have been safe through the night. There was only one monster chasing them at the moment and I hadn't been in any position to find them. But they'd hidden, scared that they wouldn't survive the night in the open. They were right to be afraid, they couldn't survive the night when I finally found them, but they could have survived last night. So they'd hidden from death, surrounded by the history of death. Their tracks surrounded the building which lay upon the once-manicured fields of the cemetery; their feet passing only inches at times from the blocks that marked the death of their kind.

The humor was not lost on me. I might have been a monster, a killer, a diseased cannibal, but I still saw the ironic twist of these human's pitiful existence.

They weren't in the building any longer, but my instincts told me that I would soon need to be. I was a nightwalker and I could see that the night had only a few degrees of darkness left. I entered the building and could smell my prey in every corner. They hadn't left until this time yesterday and I knew I would find them early the next day. I was getting closer and their blood would soon be mine.

But, for the day, I would enjoy their smells as I crouched in the darkness only inches from where the girl had slept through the night.

I would soon find them.

I would soon kill them.

I would soon enjoy my feast.

I would soon relish in my revenge.

#
CHAPTER TEN

The day was hot and humid. Bob beat down upon the thin roof of my cemetery hide-out. The building was filled with delicious scents that should have lulled me to sleep and filled my dreams with tastes of the booted man's blood.

It did not.

My rest was fractured by visions of the dead man in the warehouse. It was strange that such a body would affect me when the multitude of deaths I had either witnessed or caused did not. But the man's half-missing skull reminded me of my final days as a human. Memories flooded my own half-missing mind and I fought to push them away; fully aware that they would only leave if they could take the splinters of sanity I still retained with them. But I thought that I was whole now, even without the encumbrance of my mind, and had no need for things such as memories, thoughts, or reason. My body was a fully-functioning tool with no need for a hand to guide it.

But, even as I tried to argue the uselessness of my mind, I knew that I'd be incomplete without it. My psyche seemed to keep my body company like a mouse riding along in a man's pocket. Did that make sense? Would a mouse ride along? Would a man take a mouse with him? This was the dead-weight that my brain took with it. Questions. Demands. Orders. It made me want to know; made me want to discover.

I didn't want to know; didn't want to discover. I merely wanted to eat. Even as the remains of the man's body spilled from my ass, I wanted to eat more. The revolting scent that emanated from my insides only fueled my hunger and made me want to pull the curtain over the day's light faster. I couldn't eat if I couldn't catch my prey and I couldn't catch m prey if I couldn't run the streets behind them. Impatience tortured my mind and made me shake with frustration. This would not happen if I no longer possessed my mind, if I could somehow shake these thoughts which plagued my body and filled my head like some drive-in movie. They must leave me.

But they did not.

I was cursed by these thoughts which grew and filled my head until they were too large for the emptiness within.

Memories of the man's decomposing body echoed in the darkness surrounding me. I could see his body—withered and blackened. How long did that take? How long had I been *this*? How long had humanity been banished from the darkness? How long had the infected hidden from the light? Why couldn't I stand in the light of the day any longer? Why would I want to?

Questions pelted the insides of my skull. Pain filled the darkness of my head as the mental waves crashed around within. My hands tore at my head now. I couldn't control my own talons as they ripped at my ears and nose to get to my brain. My brain bombarded one side of my thin skull while my hands tore at the other. I was at war with myself and there was no treaty to be signed.

Pain finally shocked my body into stillness as shards of my ears and nose flew across the room. I could feel the pain, though it was like the distant hammering of a thunderstorm on the horizon. Complete exhaustion overwhelmed me and moved the two warriors into separate corners to continue the fight in another round.

I'm not sure who would win this battle—the sickness or my mind—but smart money was on the sickness and I welcomed the payoff—a final release from my consciousness.

CHAPTER ELEVEN

Darkness was upon me again. I welcomed it with the cries of my kind, but the others were distant and nearly unheard.

I was totally alone now.

Yet I was not alone. I had my prey and their path to keep me company as I erupted from the building and into the quiet darkness. Their scent was still strong and my nose, now ripped and torn wider to absorb more of the air, easily followed it.

The footrace had begun again. The starter pistol had sounded. The humans had gained the lead during the day. I would close that gap during the night. I would find them and feast upon them before the light crossed this sky again.

My lungs were burning and my limbs were pumping, but I never paused as I chased my prey. I ran without thinking. I bounded fences, slugged through tall grass, and climbed over the remnants of humanity, but I never thought about any of it. I didn't have to think, my body knew what to do—it would chase and it would kill.

The trail climbed onto the highway and moved through the thousands of vehicles still occupying the wide band of asphalt. I skittered left and right through the maze, ignoring the stacks of bodies piled higher than the cars they'd been attacking. A battle had been fought here in some far forgotten time. I didn't care about the battle nor did I slow to ponder who'd won it. I simply didn't care. Nothing mattered to me but the girl's trail and the man's life.

The scent trailed on for a few miles, but their target was apparent to me even before their fragrance left the road. My instincts were in control and my body followed them in total obedience. What had once separated me as a human from an animal was now gone, I couldn't control my instincts any more than I could fight them. My animalistic lust for blood was in control and my mind was merely along for the curiosity of it all. I felt my body leaping over a chain-link fence, my hands grasping barbed wire at the top without any thought of the flesh it might rip away. Flying over the fence, my feet were moving again even before I landed on the rough road beyond.

The hill was steep and slick from a thick mixture of burnt soil, oil, and blood. An airplane's carcass sat upturned near the peak and the bony remains of its passengers lay strewn haphazardly on the slope.

I chased the scent through the rib cage minefield and sprinted up to the crest. Many days ago—maybe weeks or months, I no longer knew—this place had been thick with humans. I had been here. I could recall chasing after the departing airplanes like a dog on the mailman's bumper. It had been good eating here, too. The humans had been panicked and unorganized as they tried to escape in the many airliners. We—the infected—had no organization either, but that was how we worked best, without planning or guidance.

Those days were gone, though, as far gone as the airplanes that had once clogged these ramps and waited for their humans to pack inside.

My prey had moved through the airport near midday, I could taste the freshness of their steps now. I was only hours away from them. Every step that I ran took me a foot closer to their blood.

They had moved across the runways, obviously hoping to find an airplane to make their escape in. There were planes still parked on the aprons, some tilted on their sides and others burned to the ground, but all were surrounded by large piles of dead bodies.

The girl and her family had searched each plane, their hope dwindling with each discovery. I could smell their growing terror as they moved to the other side of the airfield. I could taste tears on the ground behind their steps, the salty remains only hours old now. I was so close now that I thought I might soon see them scurrying ahead of me.

I did not.

Their aroma stopped in another puddle of piss still tepid in the early night air. It stopped as twin tire tracks led away from the airfield and down a steep grassy hill.

Damn it! I could feel my body clenching as I cackled out in frustration. The sound was strained and so animalistic that I barely recognized it. Like a wolf bred with a whale my screams were loud, high-pitched, and long.

My hands shook with fury as my feet began chasing the car's tracks. The humans had used their one advantage—their minds. They had outsmarted me, but that would only keep them alive a few hours longer. Anger propelled me faster as I chased the tracks away from the airport as they joined a smaller road that was nearly barren of abandoned cars.

Though the family was pulling away from me, I could still smell them ahead of me. Little wisps of their skin and blood seemed to dot the dark ground before me. I followed those small breadcrumbs as the night's sky began to lighten and I realized that they would survive another day. Rage filled my body again and I let out another animal howl.

But my howl was echoed by a scream.

It was small and muffled, but I had heard it. In the near distance ahead of me, the girl had replied to my angered call with her own terrified cry. My feet moved faster, so fast now that my lungs burned and my stomach sprayed out vomit like a bloodied mist before me.

I didn't stop.

I couldn't stop.

I could hear their voices now. I could hear a motor. I could hear water lapping upon land and smell the moisture in the air. They were so close now that I could hear their hushed words.

There! I could see them now. They were on a boat. Cement turned to rock and then to wooden dock beneath my feet. I didn't notice.

I could see them.

I could taste them.

The booted man pushed the boat away from the dock ahead of me. I was only seconds from them now. The girl's eyes were wide with fear. She knew I was here to kill her. She knew I was here to eat her dead body.

I was in the water.

I was in water?

Why was I in water?

The boat was only inches from my palm. I could hear its engine. I could feel its propeller just beyond my outstretched hand.

They were getting away. I swam, my graceless limbs chopping at the surface as my meal pulled farther away.

Could I swim? I *was* swimming, but it was an ungainly push through the water that covered my head more than my head covered it.

What do you call a man with no arms and no legs in a pool?

Bob.

What did that joke even mean?

Bob?

Why did that word mean something to me now?

Bob?

I swam harder. I could still see the girl's fearful eyes as the boat skimmed across the water. I could chase them. I could still catch them.

Bob?

No arms, no legs. The man was bobbing. The man was called...

Bob?!?

Why did that word keep repeating within my skull?

Bob!

Whose voice was screaming out that word?

Bob!!

The word seemed as familiar as the voice.

Bob!!!

The word was so loud now that I could barely swim with the pain of that single word in the vacant space between my twisted ears.

Bob.

It was nothing but a whisper, but I finally understood. Bright Orange Ball. The sun. Bob was coming!

I looked up.

Bob wasn't coming, Bob was already here.

Bob had pried himself from the horizon and was already soaring high above it.

Pain.

My mind cried out to my body.

Stop!

My body ignored my mind. Yes, my body was finally free of my mind. The link was severed, my body had won and my mind was merely luggage now. My body chased the escaping boat even as my mind screamed for it to turn back. They would both die soon if I couldn't reach across the torn connection to turn my body back to the coast.

Stop!

Stop!!!

My body slowed, but didn't stop. I could no longer see the girl's face.

Stop.

It was a mere whisper that finally stopped my body.

The sun.

Bob.

Turn around.

My body obeyed.

It took me several long minutes to swim back to the docks and several more to pull myself up to its wooden surface. The morning sun boiled at my flesh as I flopped exhaustedly onto the dock. My fingers were filled with pain as my body began wilting in death. I would soon die.

Get up.

Get up!

Get up!

My body obeyed and crawled on pained knees. It pulled itself over the transom of a small boat and across the fiberglass floor.

I was only minutes from death now.

Unfelt hands opened the cabin door. I was pulled through the door by my own dead arms. The door closed and I toppled down the short wooden steps. I collapsed in the semi-darkness of the boat's small cabin. I didn't even possess the strength to pull the loose curtains completely closed.

Unconsciousness took me away.

CHAPTER TWELVE

Daylight soaked back into night as the water lapped at the boat's hull. I lay on the carpeted floor like a human—feet splayed to the sides, weak and vulnerable. Death, true death, would soon take me.

I didn't care, let it.

Unconsciousness licked the edges of my skull just as the water did the boat. Let the mental darkness take me. I was done. I was ready for it to take me. Please let it take me.

In the distance, I could hear the cries of the infected. The sound caressed my body and stroked my hair. I didn't have the strength to join the cry, but I could feel my lungs expand. The rush of air leaving my mouth was moist with blood but devoid of sound.

I was dying.

It was about time. I was ready for death. I was beaten. I had lost.

But nothing was ever that easy. Death did not obey the orders of man—infected or not. It would allow me to lie here waiting for it, but it wouldn't take me until it was truly satisfied, though I didn't know what would satisfy its hunger.

Time passed and I was left to lie like a pitiful human as I awaited my end. The night had taken over now. I should be out there. I should be sprinting through the darkness in pursuit of my meal. I should be striking terror into the human's souls. But I was here, my burnt body soaking into the boat's carpet like a melting popsicle.

I no longer had any drive, no reason to rise. I had been beaten. The girl's eyes, so filled with terror, had changed in the dementia of my mind. They now glistened in victory as her father drove the boat away from me. She laughed at me now.

I could hear her childish giggles and I could see her pointing at my drowning body. I knew these were not the events I'd witnessed only hours before, but it was now my truth, my reality. I was bested by a simple child. She had tricked me into chasing her, then left me to drown as she slowly drifted away.

Anger welled within me. It began slowly as if I were being warmed by some small candle deep inside my body. I found small banks of strength that I hadn't discovered before. They combined slowly, a few breaths or twitches here or there, each compounding upon the others until they were limb movements. The twisted memory of the man's cackling voice filled my head and pushed me to my feet. Slowly at first, but soon I was pushing past the cabin door and back into the night.

It felt good, the coolness of the night's breeze and the gentle rain that swirled downwards in the darkness. There was no moon, nothing to light my steps, but I could feel my path as my feet stepped forward one by one. I stumbled and fell more than I walked, but I was moving. Death had not taken me; it was saving me for something. I didn't know what, nor did I care. Vengeance filled my mind again. I would eat those smiles from their faces. I would suck at their repulsive eyes and nibble at their vocal chords. So much anger filled me now. It steadied me and kept a firm hand on my back—pushing at times, shoving at others.

Trees passed my body. Thick undergrowth tore at the few remains of my human clothing. Rocks ripped through the bloodied stumps of my feet. I was a robot in the darkness; my dead eyes useless as my feet merely plodded out of the forest and into another town.

I smelled human flesh. The scent was weak, but I could still smell it. It was hidden somewhere in the town. I turned away from the lake, knowing somehow that the girl and her booted father had passed upon those waters, but also knowing that I needed to find that unknown human heart still beating in the darkness of the town.

There were other infected in this small town. I could hear them. I could feel them. They clung to the shadows and hunted the human which I also searched for. They were few. They were hungry. They were desperate.

I was one. I was starved. I was weak and nearly dead.

But I was once strong and I was driven again. Anger drove me now. Rage made me dangerous. Vengeance made me strong again. Not strong enough to race the other infected for the kill, but certainly strong enough to meet them there.

The small road turned into a quiet road which eventually ended in a cul-de-sac. I followed the short road to its end. Puffy green trees lined the road, it had been a peaceful suburban area before the disease had hit. It was quiet no longer. I could hear the crowd of infected tearing at a two-story brick home near the edge of the turn-around.

The infected growled, hissed, and howled.

The human screamed and shot.

I merely walked. I didn't have the strength to run. I barely had the strength to stand. But I marched on, watching with pleasure as the infected fell before the human's pistol blasts. She was putting up a fight. That was good. The more infected she dispensed, the less of her remains I would have to share. I needed her body; needed her blood.

I plodded on, my feet dragging heavily as my head lolled drunkenly.

The front door was now open. The battle had moved upstairs as the woman's last defenses were raised. She didn't have a chance, but I wished her the strength to stand against a few more. My peers would eventually prevail, I knew that, but there were still too many of them. They crashed against the walls and clawed at the door upstairs. The woman was trapped, they had her locked in the final room of the small house.

But she wasn't trapped.

I was on the front step, but I couldn't move any further up. The woman wasn't even in the house now. I didn't know how I knew she wasn't, but something within me was convinced that she wasn't and wouldn't allow me to move any further. I was back outside before I even questioned the proof. Turning the side of the red brick house, I saw the proof.

The woman had shimmied out the second-floor window and was making her way across the steep roofline just outside. I watched in amusement as I listened to her pursuers tearing at the door inside. She was smart. She was ingenious. She was desperate.

And she would be tasty.

I sidled up to the building silently. I could smell her moving above me as I shrunk into the thick darkness below the roofline. I didn't have to wait long as I saw her long legs stretch over the edge of the roof. She was trying to lower herself, but I didn't give her the chance.

Reaching out, I grabbed her ankles and pulled with what little strength I still had. The woman screamed out and clutched at the gutters. I yanked down again and she fell quickly. Her body hit the ground hard and I heard the air leave her lungs with a loud 'ummph'. I didn't give her a chance to recover as I leapt forward and bit into her neck.

Blood instantly rushed into my mouth as her artery burst beneath my sharp teeth. I bit down again and again, my strength returning with each pump of blood-honey that quenched my dried lips and throat.

She struggled and kicked, but the dead weight of my body was too much for her dying throes to push away. I bit down, feeling the air of her screams filling my mouth as I collapsed her larynx. Her voice box tickled my tongue as her final whimpers vibrated through her body.

The others arrived. I knew they wouldn't take long to smell my kill. They would take her from me, there were just too many of them to fight. Yanking at the woman's head, I tried to fight for control of the body.

I curled around her skull, my teeth still buried deep into her throat as the others pulled and kicked. They were ravenous and I was still weak. But I wasn't helpless or hopeless any longer. The crack of the woman's spinal cord was followed by the rip of skin and I was thrown aside, still cupping the woman's head to my stomach.

The head was only a small trophy, but I picked it up and limped away with it. The others piled upon each other as they fought for their share of the scraps, but I would not fight them for it. I needed the strength this woman's blood would give me and I wouldn't get it if I stayed there to fight for her innards.

My teeth ripped into the soft tissue of her neck. I sucked at the blood still dripping from her arteries and chewed on the flesh of her face. Slowly stripping her skull of the tastiest of morsels, I never stopped moving away from the others. They would soon smell what I was trying to hide and they would take her away from me.

They were still strong and I was still weak.

CHAPTER THIRTEEN

Memories, like aged home videos, played within my head. I watched the films in pained silence. I didn't understand what they meant or who they depicted, but I knew that they were once important to me.

I watched football fields and felt the ball in my hands. I saw white dresses and heard 'I do'. I saw baby diapers and smelled their contents. The videos tugged at my heart, even as withered and blackened as it was now.

What did it all mean?

Why did I care?

None of it mattered any longer. Those private moments were gone now. Those human emotions no longer existed. I was not the man who had made the winning catch or loved my wife or cherished my daughter. I was not that man. I was not *a* man at all; I was not human.

Tears stung my eyes. I didn't know that I could still cry. I didn't know that I could still feel. I didn't even know if I *was* feeling. I was lost within the darkness of my own skull.

But I did feel.

I did cry.

I *wanted* to feel the pain of those memories again. I wanted to feel that ball in my hand again. I wanted to feel my wife's touch again. And I wanted to watch my baby girl take her first steps again.

But they were gone. All of them were gone now. I was gone now. There was no way to become that boy again. There was no way to touch my wife or hold my baby again.

I was still weak from the sun's exposure and these emotions were nothing but the byproducts of that weakness. They plagued me as I squatted in my own shit; they teased me with a life that I had once loved. I hated the memories, even as I longed for them. They were nothing to me, yet they were everything. Visions of a baby stumbling across an open carpet blurred my vision with more tears. Her first words bent and broke the thick coating around my heart.

But there was nothing beneath that covering now. I was a monster. I did not feel the heartbreak of a love now lost. I was too strong to cry and too powerful to be floored by the soft touch of my lover.

CHAPTER FOURTEEN

The day was already disappearing, but I didn't even recall it beginning. I was lost in the darkness of a strange house, but I was not afraid. My strength was returning. I could feel it flowing through my veins as I dug at the woman's decapitated head. It sat upside down between my legs and I pulled small bits out as if I were pulling chips from a tall bowl. The soft tissue inside was delicious, though it was drying faster than I could eat it.

I was nearing the bottom of the bowl now. The second eyeball pulled from its socket with a soft plop and I dangled it before my mouth. I watched this with interest, knowing that my mind was still battling with my body. My mind held the juicy orb mere inches from my snarling and biting teeth. My head yanked at my neck to get at the eye, but my hands just pulled another inch away. It was a strange power play which only I could see.

Everything within me was at war now. There was no truce between the millions of parts which tied my being together. Each part found ways to combat the other, none trying to incur the sole wrath of the others while still trying to anger all of them. I was falling apart now. I could feel the pieces breaking away as if they could just abandon the whole and squirm away.

I did not will my being to peace. I did not care. Disband, I begged. Go away! Leave me alone. My psyche screamed at the pieces as if it could survive without them all. I wished them to leave; wished them to pull at the single string which bound them all together. I could imagine my body unzipping and disintegrating into dust.

I enjoyed the thought.

I dreamed of the physical mutiny, but I awoke again as a whole. Nothing had disappeared, none of the parts had left the sum.

Fever burnt through me now. It was my body's weakness, but I knew it would eventually burn away the remnants of my mind. Again, I welcomed that total departure from sanity. It would be better to be either wholly crazy or wholly sane than to live in this strange between-world where my body threw my mind on its back like some well-worn pack.

CHAPTER FIFTEEN

The cries of the infected dwindled in the distance behind me. The other infected would stay in the town, searching for the final human remains. There weren't many humans left in the town, though, those who still survived had escaped and abandoned it.

The humans I chased had never entered the town, though, and that meant that I needed to leave it to get back on the chase again. I hadn't waited for the cry of permission to begin hunting through the darkness, though. I was different now or, at least, I was becoming something different. What had changed and why I was changing were thoughts that my predatory brain never pondered as I left the dark sanctity of the house and rushed into the semi-light outside.

I chased those who had escaped. I chased the girl and her booted father. They had gone beyond me, but I would find them again. How, I didn't know. It wasn't even a thought that I worried about as my feet fell before each other. My thoughts were not in the details. My thoughts weren't in much of anything. I was an automaton now, a fleshy robot built only to track and murder the booted man. He had angered me, for what I could no longer recall, but he would surely die for his mistake.

I skirted the lake's shore, tacking back and forth across the straight line to their ultimate goal. I didn't know where they were headed or if I would have to circle this entire lake to find them, but I *would* find them and I *would* eat them.

The night was nearly half-gone when I climbed onto a tree-lined road. I rushed down the road and soon found myself upon a straight bridge that crossed the wide lake. They were not out here, but some unseen hand pushed me nearly half-way across the abandoned bridge. I felt the hand lift and then I smelled the scent again. It was light and carried effortlessly on the gentle wind, but it was there like a brief flicker of a sensuous perfume.

They had passed below the bridge sometime during the day. I could feel their passing just as easily as I could detect the girl's scent. I stood at the edge of the bridge, my head so far over the edge that a strong wind could have sent me over, and sucked in her scent. There was fear in that smell. The fear coated my tongue. It buzzed in my ears. It blurred my sight. But, mostly, it made me mad.

Her fear angered me because she shouldn't be *able* to feel that fear any longer. She should be rotting at the bottom of my belly and waiting her turn to evacuate my bowels. It enraged me that I had allowed her to escape.

My feet beat the pavement beneath as they pulled me back down the bridge and then over the side as they tracked the rocky beach. Green, bushy trees hung low over me, their leaves a dark within the darkness. Water splashed as I ran, warm and loud, but every bit of focus I still retained was sniffing for that bouquet of aromas. I rushed over the coastline, ignorant of the small inlets I was backtracking along. She would *not* escape me again and I would not leave an inch of the beach unsniffed.

This lake would not hide her from me.

Most of the night disappeared as I ran past houses and marinas. There were other humans in those houses, but they would be meals for others. I hungered for only two humans now and I didn't smell them again until the lake narrowed far enough that I could nearly throw a brick across. Their scent was carried in the waters along the shore. It floated like small chunks of flotsam, but it no longer carried with it the fear I had smelled just hours before.

The girl's fear was gone?

Somehow, that made me even more enraged.

How dare she not fear me!

I nearly dove into the water to wring the death from the liquid itself. Every sinew in my body was ready to kill these humans now.

Rather than wasting my time and dwindling energy upon the water, I pushed my body even harder. I cut the corners of the small outcroppings of land knowing that I could catch their scent if they had beached the boat. I moved fast, knowing that I still had enough night to find and corner my prey.

A shotgun blasted in the distance. It filled the quiet night with hope as I pushed my body as hard as I could. I had heard that blast before, it was the booted man's shotgun.

The boat was beached ahead of me. There were no humans on it, though, they had left it like discarded luggage. I passed their boat without stopping, it held nothing that I wanted.

Howls filled the night as the blasts of several shotguns joined the fight. My prey! They were being attacked! My anger turned from the humans to the infected now attacking them. Those were *my* humans to attack. That was *my* flesh to eat. Like an abusive, but defensive, brother, I would defend my own. I would protect *my* prey!

Only steps from the water's edge, my feet met asphalt and I was immediately surrounded by the wings of airplanes again. My humans were trying to fly out of another, much smaller, airport. Smyrna—a town of Tennessee, an airport, and a church of the bible. Some hidden nuggets of knowledge filled my head with those trivialities, though I didn't care about any of them. My prey hadn't made the safety of the skies—that was what I cared about. They'd been forced to hide in the airport to wait for next light.

I followed the screams, both human and infected, as they filled a hangar near the edge of the airport. The tall doors were broken wide by the hands of the infected. There was a strength in the hole they'd created. It was a brutish and violent hole ripped through the thin, but strong, metal wall.

There hadn't been any thought in the attack, just the straight forward assault of a hundred bulls staring at a single red flag. There was an eloquence in the simplicity, an elegance in the singularity, of the attack.

I stepped through the hole, the razor-sharp edges tearing at my skin. I didn't notice. The darkness wasn't as complete inside the hangar and I could see the airplane, still intact and presumably ready to launch, just inside the doors. Near the back of the wide hangar, steel stairs led to a small office that sat on top of another. The office was near the top of the tall hangar and it was the focus of every movement within the hangar. Two bright lights wavered across the multitudes of infected trying to climb those steps. Two men stood at the top of the inner staircase, their shotguns barking down the steep incline of steps. Dozens of infected climbed and died upon those steps as they fought to get to *my* humans.

Rage echoed through my head, bright red and burning. I could see the booted man at the edge of the door. His hands were pumping more shells into the shotgun as the other blasted away with his own. My body sprinted across the empty floor.

I would not make it in time.

Even before I made the first stair, I watched as the shorter man's foot was caught by an infected's hand. Screams, some human but most not, resonated through the wide expanses as he was ripped down the stairs. His body fell from the steps and collapsed on the tall pile of dead already lying there. I saw him struggling just before the infected cascaded over the edge of the steps like a waterfall.

Though the man's death angered me, it wasn't him that I was after. That man meant nothing to me, the booted man was everything I was after now. The other's death merely made it easier for me to pass my peers as they emptied the steps.

I reached the middle landing of the stairs just as Boots backed into the office. I took the steps two at a time, but I was still behind a long line of infected as they ripped through the flimsy door.

Screams floated out of the office and I ripped at the creatures' backs, throwing several down to the concrete floor below. Absolute fury—honest and pure—tore through every inch of my body. Shrieks of anger shook me, their sounds so foreign and terrifying. The infected could not be allowed to reach *my* humans! Those were my meals. I had chased them for nights. They belonged to me alone.

The shotgun went silent above me and I saw a boot fly through the doorway. I was only an arm's reach from my prey, yet I was still miles from him now. I smelled fresh blood as another boot flew out above me. I'd lost my booted man. I'd lost the chance to right the wrong he'd done to me. Rage filled me even further. I felt it burn at my insides and tighten every inch of my body. Everything I lived for now had just been lost. Without the booted man to devour, my life—as pitiful as it already was—seemed vacant again. Without him, I could simply die right where I now stood.

I reached the doorway just in time to see a dozen infected tearing into the man's hide, their talons sharp and their eyes full of the devil that now possessed them. More rushed by me, but they were merely fodder for my disappointment.

Then I remembered the girl.

I could smell her in the office. I could smell the lamb's blood coursing through her veins—so salty and warm with the innocence of youth. Her father was gone, my reason for killing him was forgotten, but my revenge would not be lost. I would kill her for her father's mistake. I would savor her blood for her father's sin. Renewed vengeance filled my soul and I was now even more determined to eat the little girl myself.

All by myself.

The mother's cries filled my ears. I ripped at the creature between me and the mother. His skin peeled back, yet he never turned as he tackled the woman. Bones crunched and blood flew as he ripped into her body.

My vision filled with red as I tore the two apart. I could feel the infection that heated his body as I hurled him away. I stood and turned towards the others rushing through the door. Every piece of my body joined in defense of the three humans behind me as I stood and fought off my own kind. The infected attackers kicked and bit, but they were driven by mere hunger and instincts.

I was driven by hunger and *vengeance*.

Though I was obsessed, their numbers were too great. I could feel them pushing me back and I watched in anger as they overwhelmed me and took a young boy from his mother's hands.

Rage filled my soul. These were *my* humans! Did they not understand? Did they not respect my vengeance? My fists flew and they fell. Infected bodies filled the doorway, yet they fought on.

The woman's cries filled my mind. I didn't understand her words. I didn't care to understand her words. She meant nothing to me. But the girl she protected with her body was everything to me now. I had chased that girl's scent across the miles and I couldn't allow these animals to take her. She was mine! I would be the *only one* to taste her blood. I would be the only one to digest her innards. Cries of rage exploded from my mouth as I yanked and swung. My fists were sledgehammers that connected over and over again.

"Zoe!"

The woman's word escaped as she was pulled from behind my feet. I grabbed at the woman's clothes, but I couldn't stop them from taking her.

Again, she screamed that word. *"Zoe!"*

It was her final word.

And it was a word that I understood.

Though I no longer spoke the language of humanity, I could understand that single word. It was a name. A name that had meant something to me long before I had become the monster that I now was. I could hear the fear and sadness in those two syllables, they shocked me into a crazed state that filled my soul with cement and my fists with steel.

I had heard that fear and sadness in those two syllables before. That word had been screamed before. *I* had screamed it. I couldn't tell if it was my final word, for I didn't know if I was now alive or dead, but I *was* sure that it was the last human word I had uttered.

The fight blurred into a mist of arms and bodies as I defended the girl from my own kind. My only thought, if that's what the activities within my fever-riddled head could be called, was that I must keep this 'Zoe' safe. I didn't know what I would do after I fended off the infected; I didn't know anything beyond the forward motion my fists were now making.

I created a protective bubble of fists as the throngs of the infected kept pushing forward. Their small and feral bodies were strong, but I was now stronger.

I heard two other human words that I recognized as I continued the fight. The girl's small and terrified voice was screaming out the words. One was for the woman who had given her life and the other was for the man who should have been protecting it.

The first word did little to me, but the second word tore at the strings of my dead heart. I remembered being a '*daddy*' once, though it was a lifetime and a humanity ago.

CHAPTER SIXTEEN

The day drifted by slowly, painfully. The hours were mere hellish visions of a nightmare that teared my eyes and emptied my gut. The pain in my skull centered on my forehead and then moved across the crest to the base of my skull as if someone had split it with a great axe. Every inch of scalp along that path hurt, every hair seemed to scream out in pain.

I remember very little of those hours. They were brief snippets of a body—my body—twisted and dying in the semi-darkness of the hangar's office. I could remember the piles of dead surrounding me, but they were mere backdrops to the girl. I saw her in the corner. I heard her tears. I felt her pain. I sensed her loss.

I felt my own loss.

I wanted to eat her. I wanted to make her suffer for what her father had done to me.

I wanted to protect her.

To protect her?

I could feel the dichotomy within my own skull.

The girl, small and scared, hid in the corner. She looked like a girl I once knew. She looked like a girl I once loved. She looked like my own daughter, my own little Zoe Jane.

They looked similar, some fragment of memory seemed to tell me, though this Zoe was ashen white with fear and mine had been a dark and rich, burnt sienna. Between shades of unconsciousness, I saw her moving through the office. Her face was filled with fear, shock, and loneliness. She worked her hands on her lower lip, she cried, she begged for her mommy and daddy.

I could feel a familiar tug pulling harder with each vision of this terrified little girl. I could feel her uncertainty as she looked out the windows. She was a sheep without a shepherd and the wolves would have her before this new night even fully darkened.

But what did I care? She wasn't *my* Zoe. I didn't even know if there ever *was* a Zoe Jane. My mind was playing tricks on me, I was suddenly sure of it. Even if there was a Zoe Jane, why would I care? My Zoe was long gone. *I* was long gone. There was no *me* anymore. There was no Zoe anymore. It was *all* gone now.

Anger welled up within me as I watched the girl's fright. She *was a human!* She was my enemy! She was my meal! I didn't care if she was merely a mini-meal, her blood would taste sweeter for her youth. Her flesh would taste as tender and succulent as expensive veal and her bones were perfectly formed for a toothpick I would no longer bother to use.

The smell of death was heavy in the office air. It tainted everything with its pungent and metallic taste. There had been a great battle fought here. I knew I'd been in the middle of the battle, though I couldn't recall any of it now. The dead bodies surrounded me, yet not one was human. But I did not fight on behalf of my infected peers, I'd fought against them. Strange that my final battle would not be at the feet of humans, but rather at their side.

The girl paced the office floor. Her movements were slow and sad. She knew that her parents were gone now. She knew that everybody was gone now. She knew that she was alone. Totally and utterly alone. Her feet padded the floor as she tried to find someone to protect her. There was no one. Everybody who had once protected her was now dead, their bodies rotting in the bellies of the dead surrounding us both.

She cried.

Her heart broke.

I cried.

My heart broke.

I closed my eyes and begged for unconsciousness.
My body obliged.

My Zoe Jane appeared in the darkness. Her smooth and simple features were lit only by a small orange flame. Beautiful brown skin soaked in the small light, reflecting nothing but the smile that made my eyes tear up. There were no teeth in her mouth, which was filled with the littlest pink tongue that stuck out of her brown gums as she giggled. Cheeks, round and cheery, flittered slightly as her laughter rattled them. Her eyes, pupils so dark that they were nearly black, stared at me with love. Small, loose curls covered the back of her head, but the hair on her forehead was straight and angled.

She was beautiful.
She was my Zoe Jane.
She was gone.

The girl eyed me as I stirred. I was unable to move, I felt the weakness in my body. I felt the pain. I felt the lack of motion. I was not myself, though I hadn't been for some time now. I couldn't push myself to my feet, couldn't even push myself to my elbows. Unconsciousness enveloped me again.

I woke to find the girl wiping at my brow. Her tasty features were only inches from the gaping hole in my face. I could smell her sweat, her fear, her uncertainty. She wet the towel and moved it across my face, dabbing like a mother does her child.

It felt... nice.
It made me mad.
I didn't want her to comfort me. I didn't want her near me. She was my enemy. She was my *meal!* I didn't care if she lived or died.

I did not care!

But I *did* care. I didn't know *why* I cared or even what it meant to care. But I did. It was a strange feeling, this tender sharing of emotions that fell far short of warming the freeze-dried muscle now pumping my black blood.

What should I do? How could I protect this little Zoe?

My traitorous mind questioned what I should do, but never seemed to question why I should care or how I could care. Those were the more important questions. Those were the questions that demanded my limited facilities, not the ridiculousness of planning my next move.

Blackness took me again.

I woke to find the ceiling walking towards my feet—inches at a time. Why was the ceiling moving?

It's your body moving.

Why was my body moving? What was causing the movement? I felt the tug at my shoulders. Small hands were pulling me. There was strength in those tiny limbs as the girl used her arms to pull me away from the door. There was power in her arms. They made me hungry. They made me want to nibble on them.

"Please!" The girl's voice cried out above me. There was fear that soaked her words; terror that trembled her voice. "Wake up! Please wake up!"

I didn't understand her words. They had meaning to her, though they passed nothing more to me than if she'd been using snaps and claps instead of the rising and falling tones of humanity's chatter. I once understood the words. They once meant something to me.

But that time was now gone.

I was infected now and we didn't speak any language that the humans might have understood. We still communicated, though we used simple grunts and sighs that spoke little more than hunger or anger. But those grunts and sighs were all that was necessary for we cared little for much more than hunger or anger. We didn't care for each other as the humans still did. We cared not whether the others understood if it was a tough day at work or if we'd seen a good movie, for there were no longer movies or jobs for us. There was now only hunger or anger and those grunts and sighs were sufficient to pass our thoughts, as deep as shallow puddles, on to the others.

"Get up! Please get up." The girl stretched out her words as she pulled my dead-weight away from the door. "They'll be coming soon. You need to get up."

But the girl didn't understand my lack of depth any more than she would have understood the shallow thoughts of a fevered pup. And that was what I now was—a fevered and dangerous pup. She seemed to think that I was her protective and trusted canine because I had come to her aid, but she understood little of the shallow pool of thoughts and feelings which spilled through my head. She had no more clue that I could not be trusted than she understood that her words meant nothing to me—no matter how slowly and carefully she spoke them.

 CHAPTER SEVENTEEN

The cry of the infected.

It filled my head and I felt my body trying to repeat it. I was still too weak to cry out in reply, but I felt its strength soothe me.

The girl's eyes popped open. I could see the fear in them. I could smell the fear on her. She'd been sitting in the corner, her arms crossed around her body and hugging herself tightly.

Our eyes met. Mine filled with anger, hatred, and hunger. I could feel the emptiness of my gut and it gave me the strength to roll onto my side. I wanted to see her eyes as they searched for an escape. But she did not look away. She only stared back at me—not challenging me, but not wandering from me either. They held fast upon mine as they filled with hope.

I wanted to taste the hope still swinging in her eyes; to feel it warm my belly as her blood soaked my craw. The hunger pushed me to my knees. Our eyes never left each others. We spoke through that connection. I told her that I would soon eat her small body. She told me that I would protect it. Our wills battled in the semi-darkness of twilight.

Back and forth, our spirits fought for control of the others. I was weak from the fight and the hunger, but she was small and fragile. I thought that my will would overpower hers.

It did not.

She won the silent stand-off.

Her small and beautiful features melted my hatred and somehow suppressed my hunger. I could remember my little Zoe Jane at her age. Full of spit and vinegar, she had been her own woman at that age. Six, maybe seven, but she knew everything and wasn't afraid to let everybody know it. Everything was a journey with my Zoe Jane then and every destination was a dream. We had so much fun then. She had been my baby, even though she would have hated me for saying those words.

How could I eat that button of a nose?

How could I rip the life from her body?

Easily.

The animal within me could have torn her body into small strips of jerky to pack with me on my journey, but something within me could not. Something human inside fought against the animal that usually controlled my actions.

My knees pushed upwards. I moved slowly, careful not to tip to the side. I knew that I couldn't fall, that I was too weak to make this climb again.

Yet our eyes never wavered. There was a brave soul trapped in that little body. I wanted to find that bravery, taste it, and suck it down.

But I couldn't.

My hand found a desk and it pulled me to my feet. I searched for my other hand, but couldn't find it.

Our eyes separated as I nearly fell over. She had given me the strength to stand. She had willed me upwards, but I had to do the rest myself.

I looked for my missing parts.

How could I have lost them? What had I lost?

It wasn't my car keys I was searching for, it was my left arm?

I could remember having it just the other night.

But it was gone.

Did I lose it at a party? Did I forget to get it from the coat rack?

A thousand maniacal questions filled the cavity of my skull, but there was only one answer. I had lost everything below my left elbow in the fight. I had given my arm to save my meal.

And you'll lose more if you don't leave this office soon.

I stood tall, taller than I had since losing my humanity. It made me feel strong again. Made me feel powerful. Made me feel human.

A small hand dropped into my remaining claw. Looking down, I could see her staring up at me. I had been wrong. I was not the frightening rabid dog that I'd tried to imagine myself as. I wasn't the vicious man-killer that had tracked his meal across the miles.

I was just a pup, a protective pup that would lie down to save this little Zoe—my pale little Zoe Jane.

CHAPTER EIGHTEEN

Run!

I screamed the word, though I knew it never left the cavernous expanses of my skull.

The girl obeyed my silent command, though. Her feet charged the hangar door with the knowledge that her very life depended upon her speed.

It did.

I ran behind her. Not to protect her as she ran, but because my left foot drug the ground and left a deep furrow behind. I pushed harder, my beaten body limping and jerking like some pitiful B-movie monster. My life was in jeopardy as well, but I didn't run for my own life. I ran to save the girl sprinting away from me.

I didn't know where the girl was leading us. I didn't care. She ran out of the hangar and down the long taxiway. We sprinted over the asphalt surface and past several airplanes that had been upturned and burnt to their rubber tires. Zoe's feet were quick and light; mine tripped on the cracks and flat spots of the airport parking area. But we both ran with every ounce of strength we had left.

We had to.

They were after us. I could smell them behind us, fast and deadly, their stomachs tight and their teeth sharp. I could feel them beginning to surround us, even as our bodies pumped through the air like angered locomotives on broken tracks. The infected moved so fast; so fast that I wondered if it was my own imaginings. I tried to convince myself that they only lived within my damaged skull, but I couldn't believe my own lies. I knew those creatures existed in the world around me and not within the lunacy of my mind.

"Hurry!" Zoe stopped to turn and wave me forward. She knew they were after us, too. Her nose couldn't sense them, but her body could feel their deadly appetites.

I didn't understand her word. I didn't have to; the word was filled with fear. I understood *those* emotions. I had seen them in the humans I'd chased. I had tasted them as I ripped the humans' flesh from bone. They were delicious emotions, tainting the meat of the humans with tasty adrenaline. Her word made me hungry. It made me wonder why I tracked behind her like a guard dog when her words were filled with the fear of a dog in Korea.

Kagogi.

Mmmm.

Come here little puppy!

The creatures around us were forgotten. They would have to kill me to get to my meal. I would taste her flesh. I would taste her adrenaline.

No!

My mind was twisted into knots. I wanted to eat the small girl. Every ounce of my body reached out to crush her bones and rip out her heart. Only the small pebble of my humanity fought for her now. I could feel my brain knocking about in my head as it went to war with my body again. I was strong, but my psyche wasn't scared. It had faced me down before. It had also lost before. But it was still there, small and feeble, but still there.

And it would win this time.

I pushed my body harder. My lungs swelled and burned, the inside of my left foot bled where it was already being drug to raw hamburger.

We ran off the airfield and through the parked cars.

The screams of the infected were getting louder behind us. They would kill us both if we didn't move faster. They wouldn't attack me to eat me, though. They would attack and kill me because my damned traitor brain would force me to fight for the girl's life and they would trample me in mere seconds as they reached her and ripped her into small and tasty morsels.

The drumbeat of bare feet was getting closer. I could feel it in my gimp foot, could hear it in my soul. They chased us in a frenzy of hunger and anger. That was all that was left for them now. Fear was all that was left for me.

But it wasn't. There was more to me. There was that tiny gnat of humanity buzzing through my airy skull now. I could picture it as I ran—a small and pesky little creature winging its way across the wide and empty expanses of my soul. Did the others still have that bit of humanity? Was there a voice in their heads that cried out for them to stop? Or was I the only one? Was I all alone now?

No.

I was not alone.

I now had the memories of my Zoe Jane. I could see my little bronze Zoe Jane in my mind's eye. She was so perfect when she'd been born. An angel spreading her wings upon me. I had held her only minutes after she appeared into the fresh air of the hospital room. I'd thought that she was such a small and perfect little being. She made me know love. I hadn't known it before that very moment. I had *thought* I'd known love, but she showed me all that I didn't know. She'd been so perfect and I was so imperfect. My Zoe Jane had changed my whole world. In that moment when I'd held her, the tiny angel had allowed me a brief vision of heaven. It was just a snapshot, barely even that, but it was all that my simple mind could comprehend.

But I wasn't holding my brown angel now, I was chasing after her pale namesake with the last shreds of my humanity. Trees passed and asphalt turned to gravel, but it all blurred around me. All that I could see was this tiny white angel before me, but I could sense the vision of heaven she held within her. She was not mine, I knew that, but she had been given to me. She was perfect and I was so imperfect. I would die for her. It was not a statement of desire but of knowledge. I would soon die to protect her, but the thought didn't scare or anger me. It somehow comforted me.

I had purpose.

I had life.

I had humanity.

The trees opened in front of us. She knew where she was leading me and I was only just realizing that this little creature was not just guided by fear. She had a plan. How ridiculous it seemed that such a young girl could know how to escape the multitudes behind us, but she did.

I could smell the water near us now. Moist and moldy air surrounded us, the smell became stronger with each step, with each drag, but it was only slightly stronger than the bloody air behind.

I could see them behind us now. There were hundreds of them. They tripped over each other, the strong ones throwing the others to the side as they fought for the little morsel running ahead of me. I could turn on them, but I wouldn't slow them even a step.

Zoe was screaming at me, I could hear her in the distance as she climbed onto the boat. We had both been here recently—prey and predator. But now we were both the prey. It was a terrifying feeling. I didn't think I could still feel fear, but I did. It filled me with cold, both icy and hot at the same time. It sped my feet even as it slowed my brain. It made my hands shake and sweat.

The boat's motor cranked over. Zoe was trying to start it. I was still a dozen steps from the beach, but I wasn't many more than that ahead of the raging creatures behind me.

Go!

She couldn't hear my thoughts, though. Nor would she obey me. She wouldn't leave me.

It angered me.

It scared me.

It lightened me.

This little creature *cared* for me. Why would she care? My mind pondered those thoughts even as my feet hit the sand and rock beach.

I dove forward; my one hand grabbing onto the boat's front cleat as the powerful motors churned the water hard. The boat creaked and shuddered, but didn't move. Zoe's tearful voice was screaming, but the sounds disappeared below the engine's growls and the angry shouts of the infected behind me.

We weren't going to make it.

The boat was caught on the beach and wouldn't budge.

They were only steps behind me.

We wouldn't make it!

She cared for me!

You'll die if they catch you!

She'll die!

My hand let go. I could feel the muscles pop open and the cleat disappear from its grip. I dropped back to the angrily swirling water that covered my ankles.

Digging my feet into the beach, I pushed my shoulder into the boat's bow and drove upwards.

I was strong once.

The monsters were only steps behind me now.

I was strong now!

The boat moved—one inch, then two. I pushed even harder. My already destroyed shoulder popped, snapped, and broke. I ignored it. My feet stepped deeper. The water covered my knees.

Water splashed behind me. They were on us. My muscles compressed and the strength funneled through my arm. I pushed the boat away as the prop finally grabbed the water and the boat rocketed out of my grip.

I fell into the water. My head was under as the creatures stepped over my body and dove for my pale little Zoe. They trampled my unseen body as they dove further into the water. I could hear the boat's powerful engine grunting and the fuming propeller pulling away.

The air was escaping from my lungs. I didn't fight the death. I couldn't fight it. My body was broken and trapped by the heels of the infected mass above me. They churned at the water, but they wouldn't catch her. They couldn't catch her. She was an angel that couldn't be taken by these monsters.

Darkness surrounded me; darker than the dark water in the dark night. It was my end. I was ready.

But I saw a small light. It pranced in the darkness and I tried to reach out to grab it. I couldn't grasp it, but it came closer. I saw my Zoe Jane in the light. Her chocolate frame stumbling and bumbling across an awful Berber beige carpet. I saw her arms reaching out to me; could feel my human tears welling hotly as her giggling form stumbled forward. *She's walking!* I remembered those steps; remembered the pride and love of those steps. How amazing was that simple event? How simple was that amazing event? She had walked; something that nearly every human eventually accomplished. So what? Big deal, she'd walked. Yet it was a big deal, the biggest deal of that day. The biggest deal of that week, even. Success at work didn't compare to those simple steps; games won or deals made were just foolish games and folly deals compared to *those* steps.

I cried now. Hot tears in the warm water.

The light disappeared and I fought for one more glimpse of my little Zoe Jane. I reached out, I pushed up, I grabbed, I gripped, but I couldn't see her face now.

My head popped above the surface. Air rushed into my lungs, wet and hot, fresh and welcome. I could see the boat driving deeper into the darkness of the lake. Zoe's cries bounced across the water. I could feel her terror; it weakened my knees and stooped my shoulders. But she was safe.

Godspeed, little Zoe.

Drive on and stay safe, my little angel.

CHAPTER NINETEEN

My body rolled with the gentle rising and falling of the lake water, with only my head and shoulder propped above the murky water. I hadn't moved in hours. I didn't have the strength to move. I was dead. Only the cavity of air in my head kept it floating above the water like some broken and bloodied bobber.

Bob.

Yeah.

No. Bob!

Yeah, yeah.

Bob!!!

I didn't care.

And I really didn't. I was ready for death. Damn it, I wanted death. How many times must I edge to the precipice before I was finally allowed to jump off? How many times must I lay my body out in preparation for that final ride? I was fully aware that I wouldn't be moving north of the surface and that my future path lay south. I knew that the devil would own my soul and I didn't care! Get it over with. Take my body. Take my soul. Just fucking do it already.

But death didn't ride up for me on some pale horse. He didn't float in on his creaking boat. I couldn't see his long and flowing black robe. All I could see was the wide lake.

And it was beautiful.

The trees along the banks were turning now, their deep greens already smoldering into brilliant yellows and reds. Soon, they would be a mixed duvet of vibrant hues. Absolutely beautiful, it would soon be fall in Tennessee. I once loved this time of year. The air would soon begin to chill, the oppressive heat of summer would finally be shed just before the angry cold of winter could be prepared.

It had been cold when I had gotten sick. Was that possible? I could remember thinking that the flu was horrible that year. The flu shot hadn't worked for me. It hadn't worked for anybody. Everybody was sick. Everybody sniffled. Everybody avoided everybody. Nobody wanted to share their diseases. Those who weren't sick avoided those who were—which was almost everybody. People hid in their houses and nobody spoke when they did come out.

Yes, it had been cold. No snow, but bitterly cold.

Bob was at the horizon now. The sky lightened and the clouds were cast in the pink, orange, and red that only the sunrise could blend. It reminded me of fishing and family. But there was no fishing for me here and my family was gone.

I was ready to die.

I only hoped that it would hurry up, because my patience was beginning to thin.

CHAPTER TWENTY

The boat's engine thrummed up slowly, the sound a million miles away. The mob of infected were gone now, their noses tracking another human they could chase. I could hear its reverberation, could feel the propellers spinning tentatively. I knew Zoe had come back to get me. I didn't want her to get me. I wanted to die. What did she not understand? I wasn't her puppy. I was *not* her damned toy. Just leave me here and let me claim the end that I deserved—a painful smoldering into a blackened raisin in Bob's hot light.

Zoe's voice called out over the side of the boat. I could see her scared face staring at me, wondering if I was still alive.

Leave me alone!

But she wouldn't. I knew she wouldn't. She couldn't. She needed me.

And I needed her.

Small hands pulled me up. She couldn't pull me into the boat; she *shouldn't* pull me into the boat. I was a monster. Didn't she know that? I was just like the mob who'd chased after her.

I was one of them.

I was not human.

I ate humans.

What part of that did she not understand? I was cursed and I could only curse her.

But Zoe pulled with all of her strength. It wasn't enough.

Bob edged above the trees, his full light shining on me now—hot and painful. It hurt. Not just a physical pain, either, I could feel it filling my head with light and boiling that little pea of a brain in its bright fluid.

My body helped her. I pushed while she pulled, though she was doing the lion's share. I didn't possess the strength to help much more than just kneeling and leaning into the side of the boat.

"Please hurry." Her words were hot with terror. She knew that I would soon die.

She cared.

Her love gave me strength. Why did she care so? I wasn't her father. I was a monster. I had chased her only nights before, bent on killing and eating her. Why did she care if I lived or died?

But the 'why' didn't matter when I could feel her hot tears on my face. My teeth were only inches from her tender throat as she pulled, but they didn't even consider biting into that soft flesh.

It was weakness.

No, it was love.

Was it possible that I could love this little girl? Was it possible that a monster, such as I, could cherish and worship this human? I didn't feel love. My heart had shrunk. It was two sizes too small. I didn't feel that emotion.

But I did.

My feet pushed off the bottom of the lake. Only a little, but it was enough to fall over the edge of the small boat and plop onto the floor like a caught fish. I could hear her voice as she thanked some god and turned back to the boat's controls.

I watched as she steered the boat. It amazed me that such a small being could know how to drive this boat.

Then we were out from the cover of the trees and Bob's brilliance raked across my body. His heat was agonizing. I could feel it caressing my body with its sandpaper and steel wool touch. It scraped and gouged at my skin.

I screamed out. A low, guttural scream that echoed like a whale's cry in my head.

Darkness, sweat darkness, enveloped me again.

CHAPTER TWENTY-ONE

The day passed as I baked beneath a large tarp stretched across the floor of the boat. The small craft rocked with the silent water and I continued to lose my mind. Sweat, blood, piss, and shit pooled around my weak body, but it was the heat that chased my sanity away.

Every second hurt. Every minute stretched to pain-filled days. Every hour was an eternity in the mouth of hell. I could not move; could not do anything to cool my body or to escape the soft lapping of the water in the silence. So I lay still beneath the oppressive tarp and waited for release like a trout torn from its stream.

Zoe waited as well. For what, I didn't know, but I could hear her beside me. She cried. She talked. She sang. She even laughed. But, for the most part, she simply sat silent.

I liked that silence. There was a nothingness in that quiet which just felt right. But I found myself enjoying the sounds even more. Her words somehow soothed the ache in my head; her voice relaxed my soul and her songs soaked up some of my pain.

How long had it been since the sickness had come? Flashes of thought interrupted the silence and filled my empty head with memories. It had been cold. I could clearly remember that now. It had been cold in Nashville, but the sickness hadn't started here. Hadn't even started in Tennessee. 'Worldwide pandemic' had been the news for months before the first case had been noticed in Nashville.

It was cooling now. Not yet cold, but still cooling. Could it have already been nearly a year? Could this disease have been spreading for three seasons already? It didn't seem possible, but nothing seemed *impossible* any more. It was possible. More than possible. It was almost a certainty, now that I put more thought to it.

Thought. That was a word I hadn't used much over the last months. I thought very little now, only reacted to the demands of this disease. It drove me to kill. It drove me to eat. It drove me to insanity.

"Hello?" Zoe peeked her head under the tarp before pulling it back out again. I could hear her fighting to choke back her revulsion.

A smile crossed my face, despite the pain in my body. I stunk. I knew the scent of my kind, it was a smell that hung heavy on the infected. It had been the first sign of the sickness in the earlier days, the cloud of odor clung to their clothes, their bodies, their very souls. It had gotten worse, though. The smell now started at my feet and just grew as it climbed my crooked body. Nearly a year of crapping on my bare feet had left them stained red and black with unwashed shit. The only thing resembling a bath had been my recent journeys into the lake after the young Zoe, but that had merely left the butt-scent and doubled up on the wet dog aroma.

"Are you still alive?" Fear cowered in the corners of her voice. I could hear it, though I couldn't understand the words. "I'm scared. I miss my mommy."

Tears dropped on the tarp near my head. I heard the sound. It was a heart-wrenching sound, silent tears falling from her unseen face. We sat there for some time; me listening to her cry into cupped hands, she pouring her soul into those hands.

"Please. I'm so scared."

She was pleading for me to be there.

I wasn't.

How could I be? I was a rotting flank of flesh, barely better than a half-dead deer crushed by a Peterbilt and left to disintegrate from time and exposure. I wasn't human. She couldn't depend upon me to protect her. Couldn't hope to trust me. I ate her kind. I suckled on their insides. She shouldn't trust me. I shouldn't be here.

But I was.

"I miss my daddy."

That word. 'Daddy'. I recognized it. It brought back memories. First words, first steps, tears of joy, tears of pain. They all flooded my mind; hot and painful, yet soft and freeing. Emotions filled my mind, puffed my chest. I didn't think it grew my heart, but I could recall the reference and I even thought the mean little green beast might have resembled what I had become.

If he'd been evil and ate the Who's.

"Please talk to me! Please!"

Her words meant nothing to me.

"I'm all alone. Please say something."

Her words were the quacks of ducks; the clucks of chickens. But I knew what she was saying. I didn't have to understand the language; she was scared and wanted someone to protect her.

I shifted slightly; just enough to make a sound, but not enough to actually move. My body had traitored alongside my mind. What would be next? What else did I have? The question hung in the air of my skull, but was quickly forgotten as I felt the girl's small body settle onto the tarp.

Gentle at first. Tentative movements. She settled her body in slowly, carefully. Each movement raked the heavy tarp against my thin skin, but I didn't notice. All I could feel was the tender little body moving above me, searching for the comfort of a paternal body.

It took minutes before she stopped moving. Her small body backed against mine, wrapped into the spoon of my body and pushed solidly against me. I didn't push away, didn't even move.

I felt her cry, the shudders wracked her tiny body and I could smell the warmth of her teared breath.

Or were they my own tears?

#

CHAPTER TWENTY-TWO

The remainder of the day passed quietly. My pain had subsided slightly, its edges softened by the slumbering angel only inches from me. Her breathing had slowed and evened until it wasn't much more than quiet whispers in the darkness of my tarped prison.

It was difficult to breathe beneath the hot and oppressive darkness. I couldn't open it for fear that even a sliver of light would intrude inside. I couldn't sleep and I didn't have the strength to move. So I lie still and waited for the dark refreshment of night.

I could feel the light as it began fading. Its pace was slow and torturous, but Bob finally slid behind the horizon and his heat began to fade. I could feel the temperature dropping inside my tomb, single digits slinking off the thermometer at a sloth's speed.

The cry of the infected sounded in the darkness outside. I hadn't moved for fear of waking the tiny Zoe, but I could feel her shift against me. She pushed even further into me and small whimpers escaped her sleeping body. She could hear the cries of my brethren in the well of her dreams and the sound turned those dreams to frightening nightmares which would only worsen once she awoke.

I fought the urge to join in the cry. It was difficult, but I didn't have the strength to cry out anyway. So I continued to lie beneath the blue tarp, knowing that I could escape it, but also knowing that my escape from this nightmare would only hasten her arrival into it.

It was hours before Zoe shifted. She probably would have slept through the night as well, but we could both hear the sounds of the infected on the nearby banks of the lake.

We were floating ever closer to that beach and the hungry monsters patrolling that sand could smell her blood and hear the heartbeat which pumped it.

Feet splashed at the water outside the boat, much closer than I would have thought. My brothers were coming. They were swimming towards us with the slow and uncoordinated movements of a fish pulled from the water.

Zoe was on her feet near my own. I pulled the tarp off, fighting its length and pushing it to the side. It wasn't until I was free that I realized how close we had actually drifted. The front line of creatures was only short meters from the edge of the boat now.

The motor turned as Zoe tried to start it, but it was the slow and painful churning of a battery that had nothing left to give. She'd left the key on through the day and the battery was just as dead as I was.

"What's wrong with it?" Zoe asked me, her terrified voice filled with childish ignorance of mechanical equipment.

I knew what was wrong with the boat, but I didn't know how to fix it. The knowledge of batteries and engines was instinctual to me, but my brain lacked the ability to extract that information from the pits of my being. It didn't matter, though, the boat was dead and she would soon be too.

The monsters pushed closer to the boat, their movements like epileptic seizures in the water. I knew how they felt; I had looked like that only days before when I'd chased after this very same boat with the very same intentions.

My eyes surveyed the world around us like a civil war general surveying the battlefield. We were just a short swim from the monster-covered coast, but a long one from the other bank. I searched that other bank. It was empty. That made sense; we hunted in packs and killed in mobs. The girl's scent had been closest to this beach and they had come quickly en masse.

"What do we..."

I didn't allow Zoe to finish her question as I grabbed her with my remaining hand and ran her to the bow of the boat. Swinging with every ounce of power I had left, I twisted and threw her little body as far as I could into the water.

Zoe flailed and screamed as she sailed through the air. Her tiny body hit the water with a heavy splash. I could hear her screaming at me from the lake's surface behind me, but I didn't wait to see if she went under or not. All that I could hope was that her booted father had taught her to swim and that she had learned his lessons well.

The boat rocked as the others started climbing on board. Their movements were still ungainly, but they were much more comfortable climbing than swimming. None seemed to notice the girl's screams in the water behind me, but I didn't let them gain their feet to find her gone. I swung and kicked; ripped and spat. The grated remains of my foot stomped on their hands as they tried to climb up and my single arm flew through the air as I used it as a club.

Splashes surrounded the boat as the battle for control raged on. I couldn't hear Zoe and couldn't tell if she were still swimming or if she had drowned beneath the dark surface. All that I could hear were the growls and screams from my own body and the water splashing around the boat.

They were persistent and I was weak. Once they had surrounded the boat and pulled themselves up, I lost control. My brothers had stormed our floating refuge, but they weren't interested in me any longer. I watched as they ripped the tarp apart, their delicate noses smelling the human's scent upon the blue plastic. When they'd pulled it apart and came up empty, they lifted their noses to the air again and found the trail of Zoe's scent leading into the water.

We could all see her out there, her small body kicking through the water with slow, but strong, strokes. She was already half-way to the other coast, but it would take her hours to get to the safety of that beach.

Swim, I urged her. Swim for your life!

And she was.

The others dove after her, but they wouldn't catch her. She was much faster than they were in the water and she had a head start that nearly guaranteed her arrival at the coast. Even so, I ripped at their legs as they dove off.

I watched the chase continue in the water as I drifted closer to the beach. Zoe's single wake was gaining distance from the thick and churning multitudes, but there was still a lot of lake for them all to cross.

Around me were the bodies of the infected. They floated thick and belly up like dead fish after an oil spill. There were dozens, maybe even hundreds, of them spreading out to either side. Moonlight gleamed off their pale bodies which looked like a worn trail across the water's surface.

But I was too weak to look much longer. My body collapsed in exhaustion and fell into the boat's padded seats. I didn't move for several hours as I stared into the night's sky and enjoyed the cool and dark air. The splashing continued in the distance, but it slowed as it grew further from me.

I was nearly asleep when the boat's belly rubbed against the soft sand beneath. The sand rubbed quietly, soothingly.

Shhh...

Shhh...

Shhh...

I wanted to stay still, wanted to sleep, wanted to die with the others, but the boat shook me awake as it turned broadside to the beach and rocked even harder. Soon, the boat was swinging from side to side with the tempo of the lake's swells. It pushed me around the small chair and then finally out of it.

I tried to continue lying there, minding my own business, but the boat continued to slosh from side to side and I soon found my head buried in the scraps of blue plastic. My nose twitched as I sniffed Zoe's scent from those scraps and I couldn't ignore it any longer.

Oh hell, I thought as I pushed my feeble body off the floor. I swayed and leaned as I tried to get to my feet, eventually falling over the side and smashing hard against the soft beach.

#
CHAPTER TWENTY-THREE

The daily ritual of my curse would soon send me scampering back into the shadows, but I didn't know if I still had the strength to make it. Part of me wanted to just stay right there, but I couldn't. I didn't know why I couldn't, but something pushed me back to my feet just as Bob was itching at the horizon.

I left the boat and the beach, my pathetic frame dragging and jerking across the asphalt parking lot. The steep incline of the boat ramp nearly rolled me back into the water, but something kept me upright and pushed my feet on. I wasn't the first of my kind to make this journey, I had seen several escape the grasp of the lake water and make their own way to safety. I followed their trails, knowing that their sense of survival was now much stronger than mine.

The march of my kind was obvious on the weed-infested parking lot. I followed the wet trails of a dozen infected—some tracks were wet with lake water, most with blood. The trail led to a small park restroom in the trees. This was their protection, a brick of a building so small that it would turn to an oven by midday? I had to question whether they truly wanted to survive the day's heat, but I knew there wasn't the time to argue now. It would be cramped, but it was the only shelter I could find before Bob peeked his bright, bald head over the eastern coast of the small lake.

Pulling harder, I looked like a failed attempt by Dr. Frankenstein as I heaved and dragged myself across the ground. The crust of blood and shit on my foot ground open again, leaving a trail of black blood behind like a sickened snail's trail.

I jerked open the door to the restroom just as the pure light spread across the lake. Screams echoed inside; dozens of angry voices cackling with fear and pain. For a quick moment, I considered holding the door open and letting the light cleanse the dark room.

But I didn't. I didn't know if it was fear or self-preservation, but I jumped inside and yanked the door closed behind.

The room was dark, hot, and full. The infected stood silently, their bodies waiting for the unseen hand to release them before sinking into a crouch.

I was home again, among my own kind.

Yet, I was alone.

Could they sense that? Did they know that I was one of them? Did they know that I wasn't? Were there thoughts running through their heads? Were the voices of their own minds screaming inside their skulls?

My mind shrieked out question so loudly that I couldn't hear the sounds of the others until they shifted as a group. Grunts and moans filled the room as they sunk low. Every creature in the small room moved as one and then went still again. Breathing quickened and shit spilled from their low asses.

I stood alone. I could feel the rush of their bowels cross my feet as I stood on the edge of the room. Fear enveloped my body. I was surrounded by monsters, yet I was still one of them. Was I one of them?

Yes.

No.

Yes, you're home.

NO!

But I was home. These were my people. This was my clan. Whether I cared for them or wanted to be among them didn't matter. They were all that was left for me now. Those dreams of some lost child were just that—dreams. My Zoe Jane was nothing but a memory and the pale little Zoe I had protected was nothing more than another small and sumptuous meal.

I settled to a crouch along with the others. My bowels were empty, but they pushed anyways as I hugged my arms around my knees and closed my eyes for sleep. Deep and rejuvenating sleep encapsulated me quickly as the day drifted lazily away.

I was home.

I was happy.

I was a hunter again.

CHAPTER TWENTY-FOUR

The cry of my kind rattled in my throat as I stood and waited for darkness to take the land again. It felt good, though my body was still too weak to truly embrace the sound as I once had.

We shifted and waited. Hurry up and wait—a strange mantra from another life filled my head. Why was my mind still working? Why was I cursed with the extra baggage of a brain? Was I not perfect without it? Was I not predatory precision with just my instincts and fellow hunters? I didn't need that small nugget that only seemed to question everything without ever providing any answers.

Was I the only one? I searched the dark eyes of the others for any sign of thought. There was none. Was I the only one who still possessed a grain of brain or were my eyes just as dead and dull? It didn't matter, we were family and I forgave them their ignorance just as they had forgiven my traitorous behavior.

I had protected a human from my own kind.

I had killed my own kind for that human.

I would not stray from my kind again. They were monsters, but they were *my* monsters and I would not fight against the will of the mob again. I needed them, needed their strength, their power. Without them, I was nothing more than the ridiculous pet of a privileged child—a dirty and demented Bubbles the chimp.

Night settled through the cracks of the restroom and the chase was on again. I pushed at the door, but hadn't made it a step out before my body was thrown into the woods.

I stumbled, fell, and rolled into a ball as the stronger creatures pushed their way out. Like the decrepit wolf too old and weak to hunt, I was cast aside and left to fend for myself or die. The mob moved through the night, their noses tracking the human scent too distilled for me to taste.

My body was too broken to pull together again. I lay against the tree and settled in for death. My left arm was gone, my shoulder drooped from the shattered framework within, and the stump of my foot had been worn clear through until I was dragging bone against ground.

Still, I couldn't die against the foot of a tree. Something controlled my body. It pulled me up and got me moving again. I followed the mob's trail until I lost it and then continued on without it.

The breeze off the lake to my right felt cool and comfortable as I fronted its water. Without a guide, I merely walked the beach until it led into a road. I walked the road until it turned into a dam. I walked the dam until it turned into a road again. The road left the lake's edge and I begrudgingly followed it. I would go until I stopped and then I would stop until I went again.

No thoughts filled my head, only the silence of the night and the rough asphalt below me. I was comfortable. Satisfied. It was peaceful within my skull for the first time in so long.

Hours and distance passed behind me—unmeasured and unseen. I basked in the golden silence from my manic mind and trusted that my instincts—or some unknown force—took me to my ultimate goal, though I didn't know what, where, or when my goal would be.

I nearly stumbled down the steep embankment as my feet left the small road and climbed onto a highway. Cars filled the asphalt's expanse, but I easily tracked around them. I didn't know what guided my feet, but they never stopped pushing on.

Step.

Drag...

Step.

Drag...

More distance fell beneath my feet. I was a mindless monster marching the Nashville highway system. Darkness was fading quickly as my instinctual being began looking for safety from Bob's brightness.

A tall building loomed above the highway to my right. Five stories of beige brick and blue glass, the building had once been used for medicine. I didn't know how I knew that, but something pulled me to that building.

I stumbled over the grass embankments and crossed the parking lot as the light of day brightened the top levels. My arm pushed through the door and I climbed over tall piles of the dead to get inside. I ignored them, their dead and decomposing flesh didn't matter to me any more than the insects and small creatures now feeding upon them.

I moved into the inner sanctums of the building where I could smell the stench of my fellow infected. The familiar disgust overwhelmed my sleep-walking mind as I moved slowly through the building and into the room that my kin had used in the long past.

The door closed and I was left in the total darkness of a long-sealed conference room. I was alone. Something within me clicked and I realized that I would *always* be alone now. Even when I was with my own kind, I would be alone for that was how we all died—alone. And I *was* dying. Or maybe I was dead. It didn't matter which because I was alone now, I would be alone when the night came again, and I would always be alone. A strange, solemn feeling washed across me as I sat in the human's meeting room, surrounded by the remnants of my kind, alone for ever more.

I settled to my tired haunches and awaited the comforting sleep to overcome by body. My arms were about to clench my knees when I smelled something different.

Something human.

Something fresh.

94

I sat silent in the dark crypt and sniffed. Had I smelled it before?

I had.

I'd been following that scent all night. Without thought or awareness, I'd been following the human's footprints all night. Flashes of memories were just beginning to warm my dark soul when I heard the footsteps. They were quiet and gentle, but they were just outside my room.

I nearly sprang to my feet as I raced to the door. My shattered nose sucked in large gulps as the human crossed just outside. But the light outside my tomb was too bright to open the door. I could feel it on the knob, like the heat of a fire warming the metal and warning me not to open it. I was forced to leave the door closed; forced to let my prey escape.

Yet a familiar thrill ran through me again. It was a thrill that men had searched the world for. The thrill of the chase, so pure and delicate. It was so abundant, yet so easily spoiled. Animals let their prey dangle at the edge of their paws, just to enrich the enjoyment. Men chased animals that could easily kill them just to heighten their sense of ecstasy at the kill.

Both man and animal were often left disappointed and sorrowful when the chase ended.

Would this chase end in emptiness?

I didn't know. I wasn't even sure what my prey was. I could only allow it to toy with freedom before wrapping it into my arms and squeezing the life out of it.

I sat back down, my arms wrapped around my legs and my bowels pushing at only air. I was weak, I was starved, but I had purpose again. My eyes closed and I escaped into the darkness of dreams, a smile splitting my ragged face.

CHAPTER TWENTY-FIVE

The cry of the infected was merely imagined as the night fell. I could feel the urge to cry out, but I couldn't hear another voice joining in. Was I too far away? Had the rest all died?

There were no answers, nor did I care to find any. My path had been laid out for me and the voices of the infected were behind me now. I could feel the urge to kill welling within me; it strengthened me with its cold hand.

I was a monster again.

I had haunted the forest and made men avoid *my* woods.

I had perched upon the door and called out 'nevermore'.

I had hidden in the closet for little children to crack open my cage.

I was *the* monster again.

My feet couldn't be captive any longer. I stepped and dragged still, but there was an urgency in my movement again. I had to eat or I would die. I had mere days remaining before I must face that ultimate punishment—feast or death.

That was my challenge. That was the thrill of my chase. My enemy did not worry me, it would die—or I would die. It didn't matter to me now. I would either relish in the feast of my success or die upon the sword of my failure.

I escaped from my dark tomb thinking that I wasn't the first to see that room behind them with glee. That room had served the humans as a boardroom, I had smelled the torture in the walls and overturned chairs, and I had dreamed of the boredom, anger, and apathy which had filled the room when this world had belonged to the humans.

Outside the cell, my nose picked up the human's scent again. I recognized it. The scent was as familiar as that of my own ass, yet as distant and forgotten as that of my own family. I could taste the familial connection, though it took me several moments to recall the relation.

The girl.

Zoe.

The name and the face were slow, but they eventually flashed through my wooden brain.

The girl had climbed the bodies. I could smell her on the dusty shells of their souls. She had walked out and continued walking.

Why I had chosen her, I no longer knew. The mysteries of my mind were lost to me again. But she was the mouse in my cage and I would only allow her enough string to reach the edge of it.

Out in the freedom of the night again, I could smell her scent carrying us further from the town. It was an easy trail to follow, despite my weakness.

Step.

Drag...

Step.

Drag...

I chased her scent. The thin string I had allowed her was shortening with each hour. The tiny crumbs of her body were dropped in even steps; she didn't run or move erratically as she rejoined the highway and moved along its edge. Did she think that she would be safe on that interstate? Did she not know that I was behind her; tracking her every step with a doctor's precision?

Whatever she was thinking, it didn't concern me. She didn't try to cover her scent or to jump in one of the cars to drive it away. The girl didn't run, but she would have if she'd known what was behind her. She would have ran if she'd known that the devil himself were on her trail.

She should have.

I was reeling her string in quickly as I pushed forward. Even as the night was beginning to brighten, I knew that I would find her before darkness closed on the two of us—prey and predator.

Step.

Drag...

Step.

Drag...

The muted light of the night was giving way slowly. Bob was already touching the sky with gentle streaks of reds and oranges. Not many, but I knew he was there. My arch enemy, Bob. He waited for me every morning, his bright light holding stealthily just below the horizon for me to step into the open, then he'd pop out to blind me with his damned glow.

But my prey had been limited by time as well. She had been forced to escape the coming of darkness just as I was forced to escape the light. I could smell her fear as her steps left the highway and moved quickly into a large mass of red and yellow fronted stores. The trees, meticulously trimmed in the time of humanity, were hanging heavy over the parking lot that was cracking from nature's weedy assault. Dozens of stores lined the parking lot, a human shopping center already beginning to melt back into the forests behind it.

Bob was on the brink of the horizon now, but I knew that I was close to my prey. Maybe even close enough to find her in this maze of cars and stores. I had only minutes, but I was close. I could smell her now. I could almost hear her.

We would pass. She on the way to continue her escape by the light of day and me trying to escape from that light. She was in those stores. She was waiting for the light to move high enough to ensure her safety.

Another smell crossed my nose. I stopped, unsure of the smell. Unsure if I'd even smelled it.

Sniff.

Human.

Yes, I had smelled another.

He was close. I couldn't see him, but I knew he was close.

"Hey!" A man's voice called out near the entrance of the stores. I didn't think he'd be stupid enough to yell out to me, but I couldn't see any others in the nearly empty lot. He hadn't been calling to me. There were others. There was more meat for me to eat. I moved faster, trying to pick my foot up as I moved. I didn't want to spook my prey.

"Girl!"

His voice called out again. I could smell him now. He stunk of liquor and tomatoes. What a strange combination, my mind thought as my body continued to edge closer.

"Stop."

She didn't, though. I could see her now, moving away from the stores as he turned to cut her off. They were at the far side of the parking lot, moving further from me even as I cut through the maze of empty cars.

"I'll shoot'chu if you don' stop."

"Leave me alone!" Her voice was filled with fear. I could hear it; could feel it. What an odd reaction. My mind questioned the rationality of her fear, though it feared the question of its own rationality. I moved faster.

Step.

Step.

Step.

Drag...

My body wouldn't move any faster, though I could feel Bob's warmth as his light tinged the sky brighter. The girl was running from the man now. Why would she run from him? It made no sense.

"Get o'er here!" The man waved the gun towards her, but she only ran faster. "Stop, you lil' bitch."

Anger? I recognized the sound. I knew the sound of anger just as I knew my own blackened heartbeat. He was mad that she was trying to run away? I could hear something else in that voice, something primeval and dangerous—just as dangerous as me. The man was crazed. He was sick, though his sickness was different than mine.

I moved faster, my lungs sucking in large mouthfuls of air. The two humans were racing away from me, their string getting longer with each second.

A gun blasted in the distance. I nearly tripped as I tried to stop, but the man wasn't aiming at me.

"Tol' you to stop."

The man had shot into the air, but I could see the girl on the ground now. She was terrified, I could smell it. Anger welled in my gut. I didn't know where it came from or why, but it was there—as hot and deadly as Bob's rays already popping above the horizon behind me.

"You don' listen, do you?" The man stood over the girl and peered around the lot to ensure they were still alone. Satisfied, he grabbed her by the hair and pulled her up until her tiny feet were nearly off the ground.

"Please!" There was pain in her voice now.

Pain and terror.

I could hear the emotions in her screams as he yanked her across the lot and into the building. Bob was blearing my vision, but I knew he would soon do worse. It wasn't Bob that I was scared of now, though. I couldn't understand the human words, but I knew what was happening.

And it scared me.

I didn't know why it scared me. My tin heart was empty and didn't feel the emotions of humans any longer. Those sentiments were for the weak.

But I felt something.

The humans disappeared back into the shopping center, the man holding the girl by her waist as she bucked and kicked against him.

My feet were suddenly moving as the door closed behind the humans. They never stopped their motion as my body pulled them forward and my mind struggled to make sense of what was happening inside the building. Every step took me closer, but I wasn't sure what I was getting closer for. Surely the escape from Bob's wrath was one thing, but something else was driving me on now.

What?

I didn't know. Did I care whether the little girl was scared? Did I care that she was in pain?

I think I did.

But why? I was there to kill her, after all. I had tracked her for only one reason—to eat her entrails. So what would it matter if I did the killing or the man did? In my weakened state, his success would only make mine easier. But that wasn't it. I didn't *want* him to kill her.

Why?

Questions bounced through my skull as if my mind and psyche were playing a killer tournament of racquetball with the small fragments of my heart. My feet never stopped, though.

Step.

Step.

Step.

Drag...

I was close, only a few steps from the door when I heard the scream. It was the girl's voice, terrified and shrieking with the struggle.

It was Zoe's voice.

Zoe.

The name meant something to me. The racquets were set down inside my head and the silence inside was suddenly deafening.

Zoe.

My little Zoe.

My pale little Zoe.

Another scream.

A breath of air, hot and bright filled my lungs as I reached for the handle. Something filled my chest, ballooning it out. It wasn't air. It had form. It had function.

My heart?

Yes, my heart.

I still had a heart?

But the question didn't require an answer. Yes, it was my heart. It filled up and begged my body to respond. My little Zoe was scared. She was in danger. She was screaming.

I was suddenly a flurry of motion.

And emotion.

The door nearly flew off its hinges as my heart willed the strength in my body to return. I ran through the expensive clothes on the circular racks. The clothes barely even moved as I moved past—Emmitt Smith with the ball turning, spinning, and eyeing the end zone.

I could smell the human's path, but it was Zoe's pain that guided me deeper into the store. I never slowed as I ran silently, angrily.

There.

At the back of the store.

He was trying to mount her.

Rage filled me.

Hot.

Steely.

Deadly.

I was a bullet shot from the barrel as my feet left the carpet. My single hand led out in front of me. It contacted soft flesh—fatty and bare. It sunk into the flesh even as my body slammed into the man's shoulders. The talons of my fingers dug deeper and we rolled off the girl's kicking body together.

Rolling over top of the man, I pulled him close. Close enough that we shared each other's breath. I could see the shock in his eyes, but it was the pain in them that pushed away any shred of emotions I had felt only seconds before.

I was the predator again.

He was my prey.

Spinning, I threw him against the wall. I didn't want to kill him so quickly. I was an animal; a monster. I wanted to play with him, to tear him apart one tiny piece of flesh at a time.

The man bounced against the back wall, toppling a bank of sunglasses on top of him as his breath exited his lungs. His pants were wrapped around his ankles and they tripped him as he fought to get to his feet. He barked out something, part animal-part human.

I was on my feet again, running for him with the sudden speed of a cheetah on the hunt. My hand led out again, this time reaching low as if I was preparing to throw the winning strike in a bowling competition. And bowl I did. My palm struck the small and naked orbs hanging loosely between his legs. Fingers tore into the tender flesh and yanked.

The man shrieked. His voice filled the store in high-pitched and pained tones as I dove back into the man's gut and began digging for his intestines. I could have gone straight for the heart, but his final moments would have been shorter and less painful.

I should have gone straight for his heart.

A bullet ripped through my shoulder, sending me back onto my ass. I hadn't seen the pistol in the man's hand; hadn't cared for or feared anything the man could do.

It had been a mistake. A pain-filled, nearly deadly mistake.

But the man was already dying. I still held his intestines tightly in my lone hand. One bloody end had been pulled loose, but the other had held firm. It unraveled from his gut like a spaghetti noodle pulled from the middle of the bowl.

He raised the pistol again, weakly trying to point it towards my head.

I yanked on his intestines, reeling the noodle in until it reached the end. Blood sprayed from the man's belly and he looked down as the bottom of his intestine was pulled against its mooring. His face drooped in shock.

My face lit with humor. I tugged again as the pistol sagged downwards.

I could remember fishing, the small tug of the fish on the line and the satisfaction I'd felt when I set the hook. Not too softly, but not too rough either.

I set the hook. Using my wrist, I pulled back on the intestine and felt it jerk the man's whole body forward. I would have toyed with him until he passed out, but I saw the pistol rising up again.

Yanking myself up by the man's intestines, I drove my arm through the small hole in his gut. My hand passed his emptied belly and his lungs. My fingers, sharp and bony, collapsed around his beating heart as we toppled into the darkness of the store's back rooms.

The man didn't fight me. He was already dead; his body just waiting to sign the surrender papers. My teeth bit into his throat and I used my head to hold his body still as I yanked the beating muscle down and through his fleshy belly.

We were alone in the back room and I felt the warmth of his blood coating my throat and filling my belly. My hand nearly shoved the man's heart down my gullet as I continued to rip his body apart.

I could see the death in my meal's eyes.

I could taste the fear and pain in his blood.

I could feel the strength in my body returning.

I could hear her crying.

CHAPTER TWENTY-SIX

I squatted in the dark of the store's back room as the day slowly bled away. My feet filled the big man's chest cavity as I squatted in his dead body like a vulture perched upon a dead carcass. My arms were wrapped tightly around my body and I moved only enough for my hand to dip down and tear away another chunk of flesh.

Outside the room, only feet from where I feasted, I could hear the girl crying. She lay against the wall, tears of fear or pain spraying forth. She never said a word. She barely even made a sound. But she was there. Crying.

I didn't know why she didn't leave. She should have. Her tiny body still had fight left in it and the day still had light in it.

Why did she not fight for her life? She should have. She had seen what I'd done. She had witnessed every second of my killing.

Surely she was frightened of me. She should have been. I was a monster. I was a murderer.

Surely she knew that. She had to see she wasn't safe near me.

I was dead.

No, I was undead.

You're a zombie.

The strange voice filling my head had changed. It had always been my voice before. It had spoken to me in my tone and used words like *I* and *we*. Yet it now spoke as some other voice, some voice that wasn't mine and used the word *you*. It was a small thing to notice, so small that I didn't know if I'd heard it correctly, but I had.

That voice—that ethereal alien voice—was not mine. It was the narrator of the play now—my play. It spoke from behind the curtain, stage left, as I stood upon the thrust stage to bare my soul to all.

But its words didn't make sense. It had made an outrageous claim, one that I hadn't thought of before. It had said that I was a zombie.

A zombie!

A zombie?

I could recall the word. A punch line for jokes. A bad theme for bad movies. A subject for shitty novels.

But was *I* a zombie? The thought hadn't occurred to me before. In fact, no thought on the matter had occurred to me before. I had never really tried to boil down my new existence to get a name, a moniker, for what I now was.

But a zombie? Surely there was something else. Surely there was a better description for what I now was.

Infected.

Infected with what?

The disease.

What disease?

The strange voice resounding within my head was right. Surely I should be able to name my illness. If I was just sick, I could name my sickness. Right?

Captain Trips?

Gray Death?

Red Death?

Solanum?

Cooties?

Oh God, what did I have?

My body shivered as my mind fought for some fragment of the truth, some self-realization. I felt my ass evacuate the man's innards; replacing them right back where they had begun. The smell was overwhelming, but the long strings of semi-digested intestines clung to me before another ass-belch blew them out.

A zombie? There must be another explanation, another title to give my disease. I struggled against the fog inside my skull to find the small chocolate chips of my mind. It was too thick, my mind was too small and too far gone.

I absently tugged another chunk of brain from the man's skull. Chewing it like a piece of taffy as I tried to envision what I had become.

Not a zombie, I knew that much at least.

Then what?

Something else, I argued. I was just sick. I just had the flu.

The flu? Since when did the flu cause a human to eat another human?

Yeah, but...

Uh huh? Yeah, but? That's your best argument?

Zombies don't think! That's my best argument. Take that, zombies *don't think!*

And you think this is thinking? You're arguing with yourself as you hide from the sun in the...

Bob! His name is Bob!! The words bounced angrily through the emptiness of my skull. I could almost hear the echoes resonating inside. I lowered my voice—the remnants of my voice that never exited the cranial box I carried around on my shoulders—until it was nothing more than a soft whisper. There is no more sun, just that *damned Bob* and his hellish heat.

Uh huh? Tell me again why you think you're not a zombie.

I don't fit the description. My voice was confident again, though my soul didn't carry that same opinion.

Reeeeally? Let's just say that a zombie was once a human. Now inflicted by a strange disease, the zombie roams the earth in packs or mobs searching for human brains to eat. Little is known of the internal workings of a zombie's mind because they are mostly mute, animalistic, and violent. They are often pictured in some advanced stage of decay, with dead eyes and dragging a limp leg behind. Though they are extremely dangerous, zombies exist only in fictional tales and movies.

I was human once.

Yep.

I was inflicted by a strange disease.

Uh huh?

I roamed with others when I could.

A mob?

Another chunk of brains came loose and I shoved it down my throat.

Mmmm, brains.

Mute?

Sorry, couldn't hear you.

Animalistic.

Grrrr.

Violent.

You're really starting to get pissed off, aren't you?

Limp leg.

What would you call that hunk of flesh following behind you?

Fictional?

If only.

Oh shit.

I'm a zombie.

CHAPTER TWENTY-SEVEN

Night was closing on our shopping center. I hadn't moved since my painful realization. I couldn't move. The world, my world, had just crashed at the edges of my mind. My reality had been stretched, folded, cut, and burnt. I no longer wanted to move. I didn't want to breathe. I didn't want to exist.

Why would I want to exist? Why would I want to survive? I was a *zombie*! Why would I want to continue another inch, another second? I was a *fucking zombie*! I canvassed the earth and searched for humans. I ate people and crapped them out as I stood upon their shells. I was a speechless, mindless, heartless, and soulless monster suited only for survival at the expense of the remnants of humanity.

I had caused the downfall.

I was guilty of the worst genocidal massacre in history.

I was a zombie.

There was no hope for me. Nobody would lower the life jacket to hoist me out of the shark-infested waters. There would be no rescue for I *was* the shark. There were no magic shots that would clear this nameless disease. No penicillin to stop my drip. No super glue to hold me to the girders. I was lost and there was nobody to find me now.

I'd watched zombie movies before. I wasn't a fan of them, though the brainless killing and thoughtless acting did have its own appeal. I'd thought, once or twice, about what I would do if the zombies had attacked. I'd given it more than a moment, but less than a full thought. I'd never thought about actually *being* the zombie, though. Nobody ever thought about what it was to be *the* zombie. Sure, everybody wondered at one time or another how they would survive a zombie attack, but nobody ever wondered what they would do if they *were* the zombie. To look out the window of your own eyes and see yourself eating people; munching on their muscles; nibbling at their brains. What kind of sick bastard would ever think of that? What kind of demented dick could write that story or film that movie? Who could sleep at night after they'd dreamed such a disturbing dream?

My mind fought against the reality, still trying to latch onto the thought that zombies weren't merely fictional creatures found only in strange voodoo cultures and big screen productions. It struggled to find a more rational explanation. I couldn't be a zombie, it screamed within the emptiness of my head. Zombies didn't think. Zombies didn't question their existences. Zombies didn't know that they were zombies. Zombies weren't self-aware. Zombies didn't...

But you are a zombie.

That voice, not my own, yet just as familiar as my own, whispered back.

And you do think. You do question. You do know.

I sagged lower, the torn and stained seat of my pants touching the remains of my latest kill. I give up. I surrender. I was a zombie. I was a murderer. I was a monster. There was nothing left to question. There were no more reasons to question. I was guilty of every accusation being leveled against me. I was my own attorney and I had no more witnesses to call. The gavel had fallen and I was convicted. Tell me my sentence and send me back to my cell, there were no more motions to file, no requests for retrial.

So, what did I do now? I was a zombie and I wasn't proud of what I'd become. There were no twelve-step program for zombies. No 'Zombies Anonymous' meetings to attend. I couldn't confess my sins by starting 'hello, my name is ZEd and...'

What did I do?
You finish it.

That damned voice. It echoed in my head and enraged my body. I was tired of hearing from it. Tired of hearing *it*.

Finish what?

It.

What the?!? Shut up! Go away! Leave me alone you sanctimonious bastard. Take your megaphone voice and pack it back in the suitcase you brought it in.

Then finish it.

What? What was I supposed to finish? My mind searched for the answer, but we both knew what 'it' was. 'It' was me or, more precisely, my life. Yes, that was what 'it' was. To finish it would be to end my life. Was I ready for that? It was already finished, I supposed. It had already ended, hadn't it? It had ended for me the day I had become this; the day I voided my humanity with the first taste of another human's flesh. Yes, it was done and all that remained was for the tiny muscle in my chest to stop pumping its black oil.

Was I supposed to kill myself? Was I supposed to end the only life I'd ever known? Questions swirled within my head so fast that I was getting dizzy. I could feel the nausea building in my gut. It was only a touch stronger than the anger that always lived there now. Should I finish it? I half-expected the voice to answer. It didn't. I knew the answer. Yes, I should finish it. Dahmer should have finished it the moment he ate his first boyfriend. Yates should have finished it before he hired his first working girl.

They were me. I was them.

We were the devil together. We were the end.

Yes, I should finish it.

But how?

Even as I asked myself the question, I knew the answer. The man's pistol sat only inches from my feet. I'd handled pistols before. Surely it wouldn't be too difficult for a knuckle-dragging zombie to pick up the human tool and use it to smash my skull.

I reached out for the pistol. I was ready to finish it. Surely that was the least I owed the world; to rid it of one more cockroach. It hurt me to think of the end, but it was the only way out. I needed to finish it. I wanted to finish it.

The pistol, so heavy and solid in my hand, was barely more than a wizard's wand to me now. I had once owned several weapons, but I no longer understood the tools of man. I looked at the angled metal, felt the smooth sides, massaged the rough handle, but, in the end, it made little sense to me.

The man's hand was only inches from my feet. I picked the limp hand up and pulled at it until I could hold it between my knees. Flipping the pistol around in my sole hand, I pushed the metal tool into the man's dead hand and rotated it until everything made sense. Give the chimp a round peg, I thought as I turned my own round peg in search of the round hole.

And then it made sense. Yes, I could see how it worked. Of course! But my victory lasted only a moment, just long enough for me to reclaim the human tool and remember why I was trying to unlock its mysteries.

To finish it. That was my purpose. To finish my life.

My hand shook. My muscles weakened. My ass belched.

But I knew what I needed to do. Never mind the pain. Never mind the eternal blackness. Never mind the end. I had to do it. It was the penance which must be paid. I owed it to the world. I owed it to my little Zoe Jane. Hell, I even owed it to myself. I was Dahmer. I was Yates. I was the cockroach. Better that I finish it than let the monster within roam for even one more night.

The pistol fit into my palm nicely. The heft felt good. It felt right. I could feel my hand moving up beside me. It was another hand, not mine. It rose until the pistol was level with my temple.

Cool, smooth metal touched my hot skin. The ring of the barrel seemed magnetic as it jammed itself home at my temple. My finger slipped into the trigger guard. The bony, blood-crusted tip of my finger touched the round metal trigger.

Nothing shook. This was right. Yes, I had to finish it.

My hand tightened around the grip. My finger pulled against the trigger. My heart beat at my temples.

I was ready to finish it.

I was ready for the blackness.

But I was not alone.

Two small eyes watched me in the darkness. I hadn't heard her come in, but she was there. She'd been there for some time, her back was against the wall and her eyes watched my every move. She saw my hand holding the pistol, but didn't react. There was fear in her eyes. There was pain in those orbs. And there was curiosity.

Neither of us spoke. We sat in the near complete blackness and stared at each other. Time passed, how much I couldn't tell, but it passed still and silent. Eventually, I pulled the pistol from my head and set it down by my feet. My hand wrapped itself around my legs again, as if it were embarrassed that she'd seen what it was about to do.

Her head tipped and her eyes tracked back to the pistol, silently questioning why I would have held that small chunk of deadly metal. Still, no words escaped her lips. She just sat there and stared at me.

Was she waiting for me to finish it? To finish her? She had seen me attack the man. She knew what I was capable of, was that what she wanted? For me to kill her? I stared into her sad eyes and wondered if that was why she was here.

It wasn't. She didn't want to die. I didn't know if her young mind could even grasp that deep thought. No, she was too young to think of ways to 'finish it'. She wasn't here to watch me finish it for myself either, though.

Then what?

I didn't know.

Finally, her lips cracked open just enough to allow two words to pass between them. "Thank you."

I didn't understand the words, but I could sense the sentiment.

She was grateful? For what? I had tracked her across half of Nashville. My kin had killed and eaten her parents while I had watched. I had killed the only human she'd seen since losing her own family. What could she possibly be grateful for?

And then I understood what 'it' really was. 'It' was this girl's punishment, her pain. I was supposed to finish her torture. I was supposed to save her from that torture.

She was my mission.

She was my savior.

And I needed to be hers.

CHAPTER TWENTY-EIGHT

The cry of the zombies seemed stronger than ever as Bob began melting into the horizon. It was as if the cry were calling me out; declaring *me* as the traitor that I was. Did they know?

I fought against the grunts and cackles rising in my throat. The sounds went on and on until I finally realized that the cry wasn't strong in the world of reality—only in the twisted drive-in movie playing within my skull. Despite the violence of my struggle against the cry, deep and guttural sounds eventually found their way out. I clenched my teeth, refused to breathe, even tried to choke the sound with my own hand. Nothing worked. I was still the animal; still the zombie.

But she was still there, still staring at me curiously.

I could smell the man's blood below me.

Anger clenched my body. It ripped at my consciousness and shook my entire frame. My feet shifted and my hand trembled. Every inch of my tall frame seemed to quake with the struggle—mind versus body.

It was all so confusing.

Rage shook my body.

The smell of blood swilled within the remains of my nose again—metallic and primal. I was the animal again. I could feel the urges grinding through my body.

I wanted to kill again.

I wanted to eat again.

I was strong once more. Free to roam the world again, ready to track the humans and feast upon their flesh. The man's body had made me whole again—strong again.

But you're weak.

I was not weak. I was strong again.

Then fight the urge.

I didn't want to.

You can't.

I could.

No, I couldn't. It was true, I was weak. My body had been renewed, pulled together once more by the man's flesh, but my mind was not. It was weak. It had abandoned the resolve I had discovered during the hours of light.

Then fight against the weakness.

I knew that was the answer, but I didn't want to. I was a punch-drunk boxer who couldn't step out of the ring; a closet masturbator without the strength to pull my hand from my own junk. I knew what the right answer was, but I didn't want to do it. I wanted to do wrong. I wanted to allow my mind to ride shotgun while my instincts drove my body to commit horrendous acts.

The hard right...

Who was that?

The easy wrong...

Where was that booming voice coming from? Leave me alone. Leave me to my business. Let me kill in peace.

You said that. You said 'the hard right over the easy wrong'.

I didn't say that. I wouldn't say that. I'm a fucking zombie! I didn't think about the hard decisions. I didn't have to make any hard decisions.

I sniffed out the humans.

I chased them.

I killed them.

I ate them.

I crapped them back out.

Rinse, repeat.

Nothing difficult about that. Now, go away!

But the voice wouldn't go away. Life, even as a zombie, wasn't that simple. The voice was silent, but my eyes strayed back over the girl's face again. She hadn't moved, hadn't averted her eyes even as I'd evacuated the last of the man's innards.

Why?

Why would this little girl sit and watch with no fear of me. Did she not understand that she was a zombie's favorite donut? A puerile, brain-filled human donut? Soft and sweet flesh stuffed with a brain/blood crème filling.

I was getting hungry just asking myself the question. Who was she to sit there and watch me? Who did she think she was? Why did she not fear me? Why did she think I wouldn't kill her? Why didn't she know that she was holding the donut at the window of my police cruiser?

Just one nibble.

No.

One?

But I knew the answer. Not one nibble. Not a lick or even a deep sniff. She was not to be touched. She was protected. She was *familia*.

Despite my many arguments, the discussion was already over. I wanted to scream. I wanted to run. I couldn't do either. I was trapped. A lion in the circus, this little girl had tamed me by her presence. I was nothing more than a part of her act now—her act of survival. She had done it without whip or gun, using the chair of my memories merely to distract me. I was tamed; trained. I couldn't kill her any more than the well-trained lion could bite down upon his trainer's skull—no matter how much the lion may have wanted to.

And I did want to. I wanted to crush her little body. I wanted to suck those judgmental eyes from her skull. I wanted to stand in the remains of her body and shit her innards back into them.

But I couldn't.

I wouldn't.

Enough said.

How could I think so clearly? I could. Think clearly, that was. For the first time in so long, my mind seemed to be working again. What had changed? Why did I notice the floral painting on the wall of our cramped space or the blood-soaked carpet under our bodies? I hadn't noticed those things before. I wouldn't have noticed them. They were merely noise in the background; an untuned frequency blanching out in static. But I saw them now. I smelled them now. I felt them now.

Why? Nothing had changed, I was still a zombie. I still stunk of my kill and still stood in his remains.

"You need new clothes." The girl said as she stood.

I grunted out my response, neither of us understanding the other. She turned her back on me as she stepped over the crooked door. I didn't jump at her. I didn't even bare my teeth and consider chomping through her thin spine.

I was tamed.

I was domesticated.

I was her pet.

Her obedient and docile puppy.

#

Seriously?

I was a zombie, not a damned Suzy dress up doll.

No!

I growled out my anger, low and dangerous like a momma pit bull. She growled out her own irritation, though her growl came in quick-fired words that were high-pitched and insistent.

There was no way she would get me to change my clothes. I was a zombie, damn it! Zombies didn't change outfits to suit our moods. We didn't dress up to go to dinner or out on a date. Hell, we didn't even change for the seasons.

I wouldn't do it. I shook my head and growled even louder. I loomed over the tiny girl; staring hungrily down at her.

She pushed the clothes into my good hand and turned around. Problem solved, she must have been thinking, decision made.

Staring at her incredulously, I wondered—and not for the first time tonight—why I wasn't eating her. It would be so easy, I wouldn't even have to chase her. I only needed to reach out my claw and pull her closer. Ten seconds, maybe just five, and she would be half-digested already.

So why was my gut not working at her heart?

I knew the answer, though. *She* was working at *my* heart. I wasn't in charge of this situation any longer. I hadn't been in charge since the moment she'd flashed her sad and scared eyes at me. There wasn't anything I could do about it and there was no way I could hurt her.

But this was taking my obedience to an all-new level. Was she testing me? Was she trying to see if I would break? Was she trying to get eaten?

I watched her moving through the still and dark store. Her body moved quickly as she searched out another outfit for her pet monkey. She was humming and smiling, completely oblivious of my attention. I stood and watched, untouched clothes still hanging in my hand as if I were their hanger.

Finally, she turned and stared back at me. I could see her eyeing me across the long racks of once expensive suits. Her impatience was evident as her voice carried across her demands. She tapped her foot in a grand display of her displeasure and threw both hands up in mock disgust.

Zombie! I wanted to cry out.

"Hurry up!" She cried out.

Zombie! Not dress up doll! My throat rattled out grunts and sighs, none of them sounding anything like 'zombie' or 'doll'.

"Put them on."

No! I'm a ZOMBIE! This game was beginning to make me angry.

"On!" She pointed at me, pursed mouth nearly hidden behind one single finger.

I babbled out a long string of zombified-expletives, none of them making sense to either of us.

"Do I need to come over there?" Her hands hit her hips. She was imitating her mother now; imitating that angry stance of every mother through every generation in every country. Her foot tapped impatiently and her head tilted to the side. But her smile couldn't stay hidden for long.

Her pretty little smile.

Her soft and innocent smile.

So full of life.

So full of faith and forgiveness.

So full of love.

I had to look away. I couldn't stare into her eyes any longer. They were filled with too much innocence, too much love. She was looking at me like a loving daughter looked at her perfect father.

But I wasn't her father.

I wasn't perfect.

I was...

A zombie.

Tears welled in my eyes. The soft flush of hotness crossed my eyes and filled them with hard tears.

I was once something more.

I was once human.

I was once a father.

I was once perfect in a little girl's eyes.

I was once everything for my little Zoe Jane.

My Zoe Jane had loved me despite my flaws—and I'd been flawed, even as a human. Maybe I'd even been more flawed then. I'd worked long hours; cared too much about money and my job. I'd had a temper. I had yelled and pouted, storming through our expensive apartment like a furious monster. I'd watched TV and ignored the one being who forgave me all my failures, all my faults.

I was a good father! I tried to argue in defense of my old self, but even the crazed zombie that now controlled my body could hear the tin of my argument. I wasn't a *bad* father. I had loved my little Zoe Jane, loved her more than anything. I just hadn't always shown it. I never beat her or did anything awful to her, but I let *my* life come first. I hadn't put her needs first—not once, not ever. Even when I played with her, I did it on my own terms and on my own timeline. I never let her set up tea sets and pull me away from the demands of my life. I never stepped beyond my own humanity to be the father that my perfect little angel deserved. She only wanted to be loved and cherished. She offered everything in return for my time and attention. She would have given me her whole heart; all of her love, her time, her attention. Everything.

And that was all this little Zoe wanted. She wanted my love, attention, and protection. That was all she wanted. She wanted to pull out her tea sets and sit down with me. That was all.

Could I step beyond myself now? I couldn't do it before. I couldn't set aside my job, my friends, my life. But I didn't have a job now. I had no friends now. I had no life. All of the things that made me human were now gone.

Could I do it?

Yes. I thought I could. I could play dress up if she wanted me to. I could protect her. I could cherish her as if she were my own little Zoe Jane. I could correct the mistakes I had made with my own princess. I could lose my humanity and still grow beyond it.

Then do it.

CHAPTER THIRTY

Playing dress up was more difficult than I'd imagined. It stressed my limits, both physically and emotionally. I tried to remain patient, tried to stave off my temper with images of my own Princess ZJ, but I quickly grew tired of the outfits being thrust into my hands. I was doing better than I had as a human, though, and I could take solace in the knowledge that *no* zombie would have lasted this long.

No *real* zombie, at least.

Did that mean I wasn't trying before? The question was sparked deep in my body, but it wasn't the mindless megaphone which asked it now. I had asked it. I had wanted the answer. Did I try with my little chocolate chip or was I the impatient and uncaring father that many had accused me of?

You were.

Damn it, I wasn't asking you! The thoughts in my head were so loud now that some even escaped in angry grunts that filled the dressing room in the low and guttural growls of my kind. I didn't care what the voice said—no matter how correct it was. His opinion didn't matter; his opinion didn't count. He hadn't been there; he didn't know me then. The excuses pounded against my empty skull like a flood building upon a dyke.

But I was there.

No! No you weren't! You weren't there when we lived hand-to-mouth like pot-licking beggars. You weren't there when I prostituted my soul for promotions. You weren't there when I drove to work in the dark and drove back home in the next dark. You weren't there when I was tired and only wanted a few moments to myself. You don't understand the pressure I was under just to feed my family. You don't understand the pressure I felt. You couldn't. You weren't there.

>*I was.*
>
>Shut up.
>
>*No.*
>
>Shut up.
>
>Shut up!
>
>SHUT UP!
>
>*Seriously?*
>
>Yes.
>
>*You're arguing with me now?*
>
>SHUT UP!

I'm a simple voice in your head. Right? Nothing more than the voice of some long lost being. And you're going to argue with me? Hell, you might as well argue with yourself.

Just shut up. I was tired of arguing with the voice. I didn't want to hear the booming sound of his words any longer. I just wanted to be left alone. I didn't want to argue with him, or try on outfits, or play house, or anything else any longer. I just wanted to be left alone.

You could still run.

Shut up.

You could make it if you go now.

I didn't want to hear him, but I knew he was right. There was just enough darkness left outside our little shopping center for me to make my escape. If I ran now, I could make a few miles before Bob crested the horizon and beat me back into the darkness of another hideout. The little demon imprisoning me with her blonde curls and soft smiles couldn't follow after me in the dark—humans were more terrified of the darkness than we were of the light. She couldn't follow me and she couldn't find me once I'd made it across the parking lot. The humans were weak and defenseless, we were strong and capable. I could make it. I could be alone again.

The small dressing room was surrounded by the shadows, almost no light filtered into the corner I was in. I peeked out from the gloom and searched the dark store for the little Zoe. It took me several long moments before I captured the brief wisp of her hair moving from one rack of shirts to a wall filled with slacks. She was on the far side of the store and, even with the limping gate of my zombie-march, I could make it out the front and into the freedom of the night before she could catch me. I looked to the wall of windows between me and the cool night outside. That was all that separated me now—a dozen steps and a row of paned glass.

Do it.

Shut up.

Make me. Do it.

Damn it. The voice was taunting me, its rasp light and joking as if he thought I couldn't do it. Like he thought I was scared to do it.

You are scared.

Shut up! I wasn't scared. I could do it. I could make it. I could be free. I could be alone—again.

The dressing room door opened in front of me. I knew it was my own hand pushing it open. I knew it was my own body sneaking through the opening. Yet it wasn't. I could feel the rough movements, but they were as distant as the stars—seen and felt, but not within my grasp. My body was an unguided missile sneaking through the store. Its target—freedom. My body would prove the voice wrong, even if the pebble of my mind could not. I could make it away from the grips of the tiny girl, I could escape her clutches.

But even as my body drug my gimp leg slowly and quietly through the store, it drug my soul with it as well. I could feel the remnants of my very essence—maybe even the final strings attaching me to my sanity—screaming for my body to stop. Somewhere in the damaged core of my body, something didn't want to escape.

Something didn't want to be alone.

Something didn't want *her* to be alone.

See.

The gleefulness in the voice would have angered me had I cared what it thought at that very moment. But it was right. I couldn't escape. I didn't want to escape. I was scared. No, I was terrified.

Of the girl?

I didn't really think that I was scared of this pale mirror of my baby.

Of being alone?

No, it wasn't loneliness that scared me either. I was a zombie, we liked to work alone. That was our thing, after all. Lone hunters. Group hunters. Mob hunters. It didn't matter to us whether we were hunting alone or in packs as long as we were hunting humans.

So you are a zombie?

Yes. I was a zombie. I nearly screamed the words at the voice, but I knew that I wasn't being completely honest.

Yes, I was a zombie, but no, I wasn't. Only days before, I hadn't even been aware of my new state of being. Only weeks before, I hadn't been aware of anything. Only years before, I hadn't been aware that there were things such as I now was. Was it evolution? Was it devolution? All around me were signs that humanity had grown strong and successful, but within me were the signs that humanity was weak and ready for death.

I had been human.

Humanity had created this disease.

This disease had eaten my humanity.

I had eaten humans.

I had changed.

I was becoming something different.

Was it the natural order of this disease? Was it a long and deadly flu that, if survived, would weaken and transform into something different—taking the carrier with it and making it into something wholly dissimiliar? Or was it the girl that was changing me? Was she having some effect on the disease; weakening and fighting it like a penicillin?

Either way, I was changing. I was not human, there was no doubting that, but I was also not the zombie that I'd been only weeks before. I could feel myself changing, though I knew it was solely an internal alteration. My physical being was faltering with each step, but my mind was no longer the sunken ship in the cracked fishbowl of my skull. It was stronger now. It was alive again. I could feel it growing. I could feel my brain puffing up and swimming around as if it were the sole fish within that fishbowl and not the decoration any longer. There still wasn't much water in the bowl and my mind seemed willing to belly up at any moment, but it *was* swimming again.

So, was I different? Was I the only human-turned-zombie-turned... something? Was I the sole survivor of this disease or were there others like me? Was I evolving? Had this disease made me into something further right along the Darwinian tale of human evolution? Was Carl Sagan out there somewhere clasping his hands and explaining the process?

Amoeba.

Fish.

Reptile.

Monkey.

Man.

Me?

Or, more likely, was I the devolution of man. Maybe I was the missing link that had been sought after for decades. This disease that I had contracted might have turned me into the baser shells of my former self, devolving me into 'primitive human' as I combated Jocko Homo and asked myself 'Are we not men?'

Did any of it matter, though? Left or right of man was still not man. Was I something other than man? Or was I just sick? Was I suffering from a disease that cast me out from the light and made me hide in the shadows? This disease thinned my skin until it was barely more than a thick and slimy coating of clear saran wrap. It cooled my body, but left me afraid of the heat. It made me hunger for the blood and flesh of what I had once been, yet those morsels seemed to run through my body even before I could wipe the taste off my bloated tongue.

So the true answer was no. No, I was not a zombie. I was just a human—diseased and dying—but still human.

The sniffle pinged through the silence like a submarine's sonar. It wasn't more than a single sniff, but it penetrated my thoughts and ripped my eyes off the glass door only feet from me now.

Zoe stood near the dressing room door, silently staring at me through the darkness. I turned to face her, but couldn't look into her eyes. I didn't have to look into them. I could feel them on me, filled with fear. It was more than the simple fear of loneliness, though. It was the terror of being abandoned. She knew where I was going; knew what I was going to do.

I couldn't continue out the door, not because I couldn't make it, but because I couldn't abandon her. I had already abandoned my own Zoe Jane and I couldn't do that to this Zoe as well. I had already abandoned my own humanity and I could see a small refraction of my former self in this little girl. I could not recover it, I knew that. The disease had taken me too far to ever be the man I had once been. But this girl, small and scared, was the one pill that could keep me from completely killing that man that had once been me. She was the only thing that kept me centered on humanity; she was the only thing keeping me from taking my seat to either the left or the right of humanity as some strange and awful offshoot.

Nodding to her, I shuffled back towards the dressing room and reached out my hand to take the large pile of clothes from her hands.

I would play dress-up.

I would play house.
I would play human.

 CHAPTER THIRTY-ONE

Daylight began streaming through the wide windows of the store as Bob once again began ruling over the day. He was a dangerous foe, clever and deadly, but he was too predictable. I only had to wait him out to claim my victory.

Though the tendrils of Bob's arms reached into my hiding spot, they were weakened by the overcast skies outside. My eyes still burned from the brightness, but I never left Zoe to scamper into the darkness of the back rooms.

"Here!" Zoe thrust out another outfit.

I merely nodded towards the ever-growing pile beside my dressing room as I modeled a powder-blue turtleneck and beige cargo pants. It pained me to walk the runway for her, but that was my penance and I paid it willingly—well, semi-willingly.

After receiving the expected wavering of her hands and a shake of her head, I grunted out my own discontent and then drug my limp leg back to the shade of my room. I grabbed another outfit from the top of the pile and looked at it with disgust. Pink pinstripes on a white dress shirt with a white business collar.

Really?

Zombies didn't wear pink. Didn't she know that? Wasn't that the rule?

Didn't we need to follow at least *one* rule? I'd broken the first rule—zombies don't think. I'd even broken the second rule—zombies eat all human brains they could find. Did I have to break the third as well?

I tried to cast the shirt aside, but Zoe pounced on me like a zombie on fresh meat. "Put it on."

I didn't have to understand her words to know what she was ordering me to do. I grunted back at her. No.

"Put it on." Her words were insistent, but patient.

Grrrr. Rule number three. No.

"On." The one word was accompanied by her wagging finger.

Rules! Don't you understand? There are rules here. Refer to them at your leisure, but, until you do, the answer will remain 'no'. A loud and resounding, NO!

"On."

No. Who made you the boss, anyway? We bantered back and forth, neither understanding the other, but both knowing what was being said. We were parent and toddler, one crying out and the other reasoning their point. It just wasn't obvious who was the parent and who was the child.

"You put that on or you'll be in big trouble, Mister."

No. Zombies don't wear pink.

Zoe stomped her foot and pushed me towards the dressing room. There was a small twinkle in her eyes that betrayed the anger in her words. She was having fun, maybe the first fun she'd had in a long time. I let her push me for a moment before nodding my head and babbling out a long stream of grunting curses that sounded more angry than I felt. I was having fun, too. Despite the pain in my eyes and the pink on the shirt, I was having fun.

The turtleneck finally came off after a lengthy wrestling match. It was nice to get the hot and tight shirt off. I was about to drop trou when I caught sight of my bare chest in the long mirror. The tall and muscular frame that I could almost remember was long gone now. Replacing the tight stomach and thick arms was the body of a poorly-preserved pharaoh. One arm, my left, was nothing more than a short stump that looked like a hairless bird's wing. The elbow was still there, but the bone leading to it had been broken in enough places that the path from shoulder to elbow looked more like a thin and crooked creek. Flesh hung off the ends in dead clumps and muscle peeked out through several different tears. The rest of my chest wasn't much better, but it was the small hole in my side that held my attention the longest. It was a bullet hole—or rather, the scar from a bullet hole. I couldn't remember being shot. How could I not remember being shot? But the more I stared at it and the more I played with the gnarled flesh, the more I was convinced that this scar was not new. In fact, I could see faint stitch marks at the edges and somehow knew that this pre-dated the disease, pre-dated my fall from humanity.

I searched the rest of my body slowly in the dim light illuminating the dressing room mirror. My leg was twisted at the knee, which was crushed and now useless. It ended in a stump which had worn a size twelve boot at some time in the forgotten past. There wasn't enough flesh and bone left on the foot to fill a child's boot, but it didn't hurt. In fact, none of my wounds seemed to hurt. Strange, but completely true, none of the individual wounds which would have debilitated me as a human hurt. Yet, they all seemed to hurt. My whole body hurt in such an orchestra of pain that a single pain couldn't be selected any more than a single horn could be picked out of a great ensemble. Despite the unending pain, I could still move and think past it all. It was there. I was aware of the pain. The pain was aware of me. We ignored each other. No more than that had to be said between us.

Pulling the pink and white dress shirt past the stump of my arm, I had to admit the cloth felt good. Not the heavy and oppressive cloth of Zoe's earlier choices, this shirt was airy and smooth. It slipped over my shoulders and hung long enough to tuck into the business slacks that I pulled up next. After fiddling with the tiny buttons with the nubs of my numb fingers, I finally got the outfit together.

Looking at the mirror, I tried to tell myself one last time that zombies didn't wear pink.

Regretting what was about to happen, I pushed myself out into the brightness of the quiet store and back into the view of the little girl's glare. Her face changed almost immediately as her hands clapped together. She liked what she saw, the shriek of approval was evidence enough that she didn't understand rule number three. She walked around me, jumping with excitement as she pulled and played with my new outfit. Zoe was the very epitome of a loving mom as she complimented and straightened. I, playing my part as the dutiful child, only stood silently and allowed her to act out her part. She reveled in the game and I enjoyed watching her growing excitement, even as she left me in search of accessories to my new outfit.

I was left alone before a wall of three angled mirrors. I fiddled with the shirt and told myself again that zombies didn't wear pink. Even as I listened to Zoe's excited voice running through the store, though, I knew that *other* zombies didn't wear pink. I was, whether I liked it or not, going to ignore that rule—along with the first two.

Zoe popped back to my side and held up several ties, all disgustingly bright and striped. Like a doting wife, she held each one to my shirt and tossed them aside until she picked out the one she liked most, a smooth silk number with angled pink and black thick stripes separated by thin silver lines. It looked good and felt even better. The whole outfit felt good. The shirt and pants were loose, but clung tightly where they needed to. The outfit probably cost more than I had spent on my entire human wardrobe, but I could feel the quality in the smooth cloth. Zoe definitely had a talent for picking out clothing, a talent that would be wasted by the reality we now lived in. But, for the moment, I let her pick out my clothes as she enjoyed some semblance of normalcy.

I stared at myself in the mirror as Zoe stood proudly behind me. The reflection wasn't half-bad. I had to admit that the dark pants and tapered pink shirt fit well.

Hell, this zombie made pink look good. I tugged the collar together and modeled myself in the mirror.

This zombie rocked the pink, I grunted with approval.

Yep, other zombies didn't wear pink.
But I did.

 CHAPTER THIRTY-TWO

"Wake up."

Her voice was barely more than a whisper, but it shook me awake like a thunderclap. She was so close and I was so hungry. My mind whirled as my tainted instincts gaped my mouth in preparation for the next bloody meal.

It wasn't right. I knew it wasn't right, even as I leaned towards her. My salivating mouth was only inches from her unprotected neck. Yet she had no fear. No fear of me, at least. This small and innocent little girl trusted me. It was that trust that steadied my mind again and closed my mouth—empty and hungry, just like my soul.

I grunted my anger at being awoken and tried to settle back to my haunches. The daylight outside filtered through dirty windows in misty waves that seemed to hang above us. Pushing her away, I tried to explain my irritation in short grunts. She was too close; I was too hungry; it was too bright. But she didn't leave me alone, in fact, she pushed even closer. I grunted again, this time louder. Leave me alone. What part of that didn't she understand?

I sat without moving, my ass hanging low between my feet. I tried to ignore the girl and drift back to sleep, but she wouldn't be ignored as she continued shushing me. I tried to remember why my ass was bare, but the memory was as far lost as my sanity. She had demanded me to change out of my pink executive outfit, that I could remember, but I couldn't recall how I had understood her orders or even how I'd gotten it off. But there it lay, only an arm's reach from my missing arm and folded neatly into a short stack of black and pink.

Zombies didn't wear pink.

You do.

I had tempted the voice to speak. I'd almost asked it to infiltrate through the empty holes in my head. It had complied. Yeah, I wear pink. I even liked the pink. It made me look like the Liberace of the zombie business world. And, so what? So I wore pink. What was I worried about? Would my pals at Zombies R Us pick on me for my pink? Would they ban me from the annual zombie cookout? Did I really care what they thought? If they even thought? Did I care about that damned voice in my head? Or even my own voice in my own head? Wasn't that the wonderful thing about being a zombie? I was free of the 'appearances' of humanity. I was free of the superficial disguises I'd put on to live as a human. I was free to do as I wished. And I only wished now to love and protect the little human clinging to the gnarled end of my arm. She didn't reel in disgust; didn't plug her nose from the smell; didn't run in fear of my withering face. What did she ask from me in return? To be loved and protected. Oh, and for me to play dress-up. I could do that. I could love her and protect her. I could wear pink. I could do all of those things. I could do it because I hadn't done it as a human. I could do it because I was no longer human.

"Did you hear that?"

I could almost understand her words. It was strange, as if I'd awoken in a southern Irish pub. The words danced through my head and I struggled to understand them. I was almost desperate to grasp their meaning as if I were trying to order a pint from an attractive Irish barmaid who wouldn't serve me if I couldn't decipher her strange sing-song Corkonian English. I could touch the words' meanings, but I couldn't quite get my hand around them and it was frustrating.

"That? Did you hear that?"

I didn't have to understand her words to know her meaning. I didn't have to ask her why she was tucked up so close that she was sharing the space my missing arm would have used. I knew what she was saying and I knew what was making her so scared. I could smell them outside the store. I could hear their tentative movements in the parking lot. I could taste their blood on my tongue.

Humans.

She was afraid of the humans.

Afraid of her own kind.

Zoe was more afraid of the humans lingering outside than she was of the monster inside. How perverse was that? This little human would shake with terror from her own kind, yet cling to a zombie and pray for it to protect her? I ate her kind. I could barely control myself from eating her. Every time her heart beat, I wanted to soak my lips with the fluid running through it. And she though *I* would protect her? *I* knew that I had to protect her, but why did she believe so strongly that I would?

They were getting closer. I could smell the perspiration on their clothes and the blood in their veins. Three men. Their smells stirred my gut and reminded me of my hunger. My heart beat faster and my senses cleared. My whole body seemed to vibrate like a plucked string and I was ready to pounce on them; ready to rip their soft bodies into small and tasty morsels.

I could hear their footsteps outside clearly. They were moving towards our little store with more confidence now. They knew that they owned the daylight, but they didn't know what darkness was hidden within the shadows inside this little store.

Zoe released my arm and threw my new clothes at me. She was terrified. I could see it in her eyes, there was something in those footsteps outside that was shaking the very foundation of her soul.

Though the terror filling her only angered me, I obeyed her silent order and pulled the pants over my legs. It irritated me that I was being rushed to get dressed; it irritated me that she had insisted that I stripped off my good clothes in the first place. I wasn't a damned child that would mess my Sunday best.

But I was. I would mess anything that I wore. I knew it. She knew it. And I was having a hard time trying to figure out why I really cared. Wasn't that part of being what I now was, too? I was a freak. A monster. A zombie. Not a human. Humans dressed in clean clothes and worried about their appearances. We did not.

The men moved across the front of the store. Their shadows hit the front windows and moved smoothly from the left edge towards the doors near the middle. They stepped carefully, hunched slightly with weapons high. Their footsteps reeked of military training and I suddenly shared a bit of Zoe's terror.

I didn't bother buttoning the shirt or grabbing for the noosed tie as Zoe pulled me through the back room door. The men were almost at the front doors when she pulled up short and turned back. I didn't stop as quickly and her hand yanked me back with a strength I hadn't credited her with before. We both felt the rubber of my shoulder muscles give way and she immediately dropped the arm. As it bounced lifelessly against my side, Zoe stared at the arm with a mixture of disgust, fear, and sympathy. I could see that she must have forgotten what I was, that somewhere in her childish mind she might have convinced herself that I was just a filthy and smelly image of her own father. She had forgotten that I was not her kind; that I ate her kind. Zoe stared at me for several long moments as the men got closer. Maybe she was remembering that I was the monster. Maybe she was remembering what I was and how we had chased her down and killed her parents. Maybe she was reeling from the agony of loneliness and hoping that these men might take her away from all of that—from all of me.

Whatever thoughts were running through her mind, I couldn't understand any of them. I could understand the terror I'd seen in her eyes, that was an easy concept to grasp.

But the tears welling in the thick underlining of her tired eyes and the quick movements of her steps weren't as easy to comprehend. I didn't have the time to wipe those tears away, though, nor would I have given those moments if the men weren't at the door. I didn't understand the young Zoe's feelings any more than I understood the hunger dwelling within my belly every time she moved close. I was no longer human and my only thoughts of humans were that their blood quenched my thirst and that their skin filled my belly.

But Zoe wasn't human to me either. She was something different to me now. Something to be protected. Something to be cherished. She was not to be fought over for scraps or chewed on for nourishment. This little Zoe was above all of that to me and my only thoughts were that I needed to protect her until we found a place where she would be safe from monsters—whether they be of the human or zombie varieties.

CHAPTER THIRTY-THREE

The men flanked the doors leading into our store—a shadow on either side and one in the middle. I watched their movements with interest as Zoe turned away from me. Everything slowed as I stood in total shock. I could feel the blood moving through my veins and the air filling my lungs. Zoe's feet beat against the thin-carpeted floor as she ran away from me.

Do something!

It almost pleased me to hear the desperation in the ever-arrogant voice. But what was I supposed to do?

I wanted to fight.

I wanted to feed.

I wanted to hide.

I wanted to run.

I didn't want to do anything.

My body pulled low, instinctually hiding and waiting, but I didn't know why. I could feel Zoe moving farther away with every heartbeat. She was running towards her own kind and, though I knew she needed to be with them, I felt the pain of abandonment and loneliness flow through my veins like a bleach-filled IV.

Leave her. Run.

I knew the voice was right. I couldn't beat these men. They would kill me. I hadn't ever thought of that before. I had never stopped to think of my own mortality before attacking. That was part of my strength—the belief that I was immortal—and, without that belief, I suddenly felt weak and inconsequential. Even worse than that, though, was the knowledge that they might also kill Zoe if I attacked them.

Some stray bullet might find its way into her thin body if I didn't run.

Run!

I could only nod my agreement. I needed to run. I needed to escape. We would both be better off if I disappeared and she was left to her own kind. I finally found the strength to move. My feet turned slowly as I watched Zoe running towards the front of the store. The movement felt so slow and stretched that I could watch her small arms pumping away at her sides as her blonde hair flowed behind her. I was nearly turned when I saw Zoe's feet skid to a halt and her body crumple to the ground. I stopped my turn and watched in fear as she fell. I felt like the scared mother of the playground as I watched my child falling from the swing. I wanted to rush after her, but I could only watch as she grabbed at the pile of brown cloth that had sat under my ass as I'd slept.

She picked at the pile for only a moment before grabbing hold of my forgotten tie just as the men got into their final positions. They would burst through that door in only seconds and I was getting angrier as I watched Zoe yanking at the tie. I wanted her to continue running towards them; wanted her to run back to me; wanted her to do something other than foolishly play with my damned pink tie.

Her hand pulled away with a flash of silk as she stood and did the unthinkable—she ran back to me. Still half-turned, I watched as she sprinted the few feet between us and felt her hand yank at my limp arm again. She never stopped as she passed me, my body twisting and following mindlessly like a leaf behind a speeding car. We passed through the door and into the back room just as the men burst through the front.

Our door flipped silently closed as human voices shouted behind me. I was as scared as Zoe had been only moments before. Fear was such a human emotion and I couldn't imagine having to endure it, but it was there—cold and clammy as it clutched my heart and tried to crush it.

My feet followed behind Zoe's, not as swift or nimble, but scared enough to move quickly. We slipped through the darkness and tried not to stumble. An odd couple, human girl and zombie dad, but we moved in unison as if we'd been a team our whole lives.

Leave the girl.

Even as the voice filtered through my skull, I could hear the lack of enthusiasm in its tone. It knew that I wouldn't leave her, it knew I couldn't. Though the voice might try to sound cold and calloused, it knew my heart and knew that I would protect my precious little princess with my life—no matter how broken and useless that weak offering might now be. She was scared, she was in trouble, and I couldn't do anything but protect her.

"Over there."

Zoe's voice was barely more than a whisper as she pulled me towards the back corner. It took me several steps to see where she was guiding me, but it wasn't the escape I'd hoped for. She was planning to hide me like a nut concealing itself from the squirrel. It wouldn't work. How I knew it wouldn't work, I couldn't say, but I knew it wouldn't. I would have to fight to protect her from these men.

We ran through the back room as the men searched the front. I could just barely hear them moving, but their scent carried nicely across the distance and through the door. They were dirty and sweaty men, but it was the death on their skin that disgusted me. I had killed many humans since my becoming, but these were not those sorts. These were not the typical humans who fell before my kind, begging for their lives and dying with the name of their gods on their lips. No, these were not the defenseless humans who fearfully fought us off.

These were hunters.

Like me.

They were hunters who hunted things like me.

These men were my equals and they deserved my respect. But not her fear. Zoe had nothing to fear from these men. I didn't know how I knew that, but I did. It was on their scent, it was in their steps. These men didn't care to rape or murder their own kind, they were here for me.

Go to them. I tried to grunt out to Zoe. I pulled hard on her arm and tried to push her back towards the men. She never stopped, though. Zoe pulled even harder and I couldn't dig my heels in fast enough to keep her from throwing me towards the stack of clothing. She was small, but her strength was stronger than the fear she was feeling. I fought against her tiny hand, but found myself obeying as the men approached the lone door separating us now.

"Hide!"

Her voice was a mere wisp of wind in the darkness, but I heard her and I knew what she was saying. Again, I obeyed. Falling into the stacks of clothing, I felt her hands stacking the others against me as I tried to lean even deeper into the pile. It was an uncomfortable feeling, being hidden from these men, and it made me feel human again.

Human.

Weak.

The two words were nearly synonymous to me now. I had watched dozens, maybe even hundreds of humans, hide from me. It had never helped them, nor did I believe it would help me. These humans, these hunters, would sniff me out just as I had sniffed out the weak of their race. They would find me and they would kill me.

Death. So long forgotten; so long ignored. I had been strong when I hadn't thought of death. I had been powerful when my only concern was avoiding the painfully hot rays of Bob's brilliance. But I didn't fear Bob right then. I didn't worry about what I would do if I were exposed to the light of day or even if I were shot by the powerful cannons in these men's hands. My only thoughts at that moment weren't about what would happen to me if I were caught.

My only thoughts were of Zoe. What would happen to her if she were found hiding a zombie? Would these men of power and death understand? Would they forgive her for hiding from them to protect one of my kind? Would these men look at her with pity for her loneliness or would they convict her as a shepherd of the Underground Railroad? I could smell the men closing on me, I knew they were here to kill *me*, and yet my thoughts didn't dwell upon my own risk. The recently barren lands between my ears were now ringing with the multitude of thoughts banging against the inner walls with chisels and hammers. My head screamed out in pain and I tried to fight against Zoe's hand.

It was no use, though. As strong as I might have been as a zombie, this tiny girl was much stronger as my charge. I knew I had to protect her, yet she was the one tucking me behind the curtain and guarding me with her own hand. How could she be the one to protect me?

I was strong.

I was a zombie.

But she was stronger. I struggled for only a moment more before settling into the thickness of the assorted outfits. The clothes were dusty from long storage in the ignored store, but they surrounded me like the thick cotton batting of an expensive comforter. I sat there, my knees high around my neck and my back against the wall. I was swaddled in the forgotten rags of a race that had abandoned the luxuries of fancy clothing. Though I was ready to pounce upon the men if they came after Zoe, I was beginning to understand the truth of her fears.

She was not in fear for herself.

She was not hiding herself from these men.

She was hiding me.

She was protecting *me*!

I watched her as she stacked the final bits of clothing around my head. Yes, I could see in her eyes that she wasn't afraid for herself. She knew these men wouldn't hurt her. Something inside her; something just as plain as the nose on my sagging face had once been, told her that she was safe.

Yet she risked her life for me.

She had to know that they would kill her for her treason. Even her childish mind had to understand the dangers that she was piling upon herself as she piled the clothes upon my head.

Why?

I had no answer. I couldn't understand why she would hide me. I couldn't understand why she would protect me any more than I understood why I would protect her. We were of two different worlds, two different races even—she was still human while I was...

Not.

Yet I felt human at that moment. I felt every bit human. I feared like a human. I raged like a human. I loved like a human.

But Zoe was the human. And she acted like a human while I could only fear like one.

"Keep quiet." She piled the last outfits over my head as I dissolved into the darkness of my fold. I listened to her feet scamper away, leaving me in the quiet black of loneliness.

This was what it was to be human. This was what it was to be afraid. I could feel the terror tingling at my back and reaching over my shoulders. Yet I couldn't act. I couldn't respond to the terror other than to sit silently in the small womb she had packed me in.

My ears searched the darkness, listening to Zoe's movements as she hid herself. I could hear the fear in her breathing, but there was something else there as well. It was something so subtle that I would have ignored it if I couldn't smell it too.

Courage.

This little girl, not much taller than my hip, was filled with ten feet of courage. The smell followed her like stink follows a skunk, but it wasn't pride that glued the scent to her skin—it was fear. She wasn't being courageous just to protect her own; she was spitting her valor into the face of her own fear because she was built that way. I didn't know if she had been born courageous—an inherited trait from the man I'd watched die—or if it was just the result of this damned disease and her pained circumstances. Whichever the case, I knew that she was worth fighting for and that her life was more valuable now than mine had ever been.

#
CHAPTER THIRTY-FOUR

The door slammed open with venomous force. The man's heavy boot hit the door so hard that the top two hinges burst inwards and the bottom could only struggle to hold on for mere seconds before twisting and snapping. The frame splintered and the door fell to the side with a loud crash.

I shook, only slightly, but enough to drop a shirt from the pile I was hidden beneath. The small crack in my protective layer allowed me to see the men in the dark doorway. A single beam of concentrated light split the oppressive darkness, catching stirred dust in its beam as it swirled across the silent room.

One beam became two as the first human moved confidently into the room. Two beams quickly became three. I could make out parts of their bodies, all swathed in black, but their features were hidden by the blinding beams poking out before them. I watched as the powerful flashlights moved out of the empty doorway. They moved quickly as the men cleared the room of all immediate dangers.

They didn't see me, I wasn't an immediate target as I hid like a frightened child. It pained me to stay hidden while these humans cockily walked the room. *I* was the alpha here. Not them, I was the king of the night, the ruler of the darkness. Anger and frustration shook through my body. The animal within me began taking over again as the three men searched for me.

It would have taken over if I hadn't heard the smallest sniffle from the lump of clothing beside me. The sound was more imagined than heard, but I knew Zoe was fighting back her own demons next to me, though hers were more allergies than anger.

My mind slowly took over again as my predatory instincts were quelled. I still wanted to attack the humans, still wanted to rip through their bodies as I feasted on each of them. But I couldn't. I knew that I couldn't. I had to hide, had to behave, no matter how much it hurt my zombie ego.

I was amazed by their efficiency. They looked like a SWAT team moving in for the kill. It was barely even seconds since the door had burst open and the three men were already taking the corners and preparing to clear the center of the room. The powerful lights bounced only slightly with their smooth steps, but I could imagine the deadly shotguns that they were mounted beneath.

These men were hunters.

They were killers.

They had hunted my kind and they were here to kill me. Anger, pure red and white fury, welled deep in my gut and I felt it stirring as my muscles tensed. The anger began taking over my mind again, filling me with the courage of the stupid. I was ready to fight to satisfy my rage.

The lights swept the room, their beams moving with perfect synchronization across the darkness. They were long, thin beams of white that reached out into the black like angry arms. I could feel the light pass my small pile and then return again.

"Here, zombie, zombie."

The man's voice was light and filled with humor. He was taunting me, I couldn't understand his words, but I could feel the laughter in them. They made me even angrier as I sat squatting in my small pile. Darkness overwhelmed me again as the light moved past, but it was a darkness even deeper than the lack of light had created. It was the darkness of my zombie instincts. I had almost forgotten how deep my mental crevice was until I was standing at its edge again. I could see the pit of my mind before me and I knew that I was about to leap back in. I would jump in with both knees curled to my chest and the stump of an arm wrapped around them. I would fall and be lost to the darkness again, no longer aware of my new being. No longer aware of my lost humanity or of the shreds of humanity I had regained. No longer aware of the little girl who was trying to protect me or of the fatherly love I now felt for her.

The scent of these men, sweaty and powerful, reminded me of my hunger. It reawakened the thirst that could only be quenched by their blood. I could feel the emptiness in my gut building and twisting my innards in pain. I wanted to kill these men. I wanted to drink their life-blood.

My legs tightened and my mind loosened. I could feel the mental knot within my skull slipping loose and it would take only seconds for it to completely untie itself. When it did give way, there would be nothing that would stop me from pouncing upon these men. Except, of course, the large shotguns they were wielding. I didn't fear those guns, though. They were the protection of the weak, the last defense of the defenseless. I didn't think of these men as powerful trackers any longer. They were humans, just like all the other humans I had killed, and they would die just like the rest.

I could taste their blood, hot and salty, across my lips as they moved deeper into the wide room. It would take them only a few more moments for them to get close enough to ambush. Maybe this was my evolution. Maybe I *was* becoming something more than a thoughtless and diseased zombie. I could feel my body trying to jump out, but my mind was holding it still and waiting for the right moment. Maybe this was my progression beyond the mindlessness.

"C'mon zombies! Show yo'selves so's we can put'chu down."

There was no fear in this man's voice. It wasn't dripping with terror as it should have been. I wanted to show him fear, wanted to remind him of why he should be wetting himself when the dark enveloped the land.

My body hummed with power again. Every bit of my humanity was gone and I was steadying my mind for the last great leap back into the mental pit of zombiehood. I would never return from that immense hole in my head, I wasn't strong enough to climb back out again. That didn't bother me, though. I was ready to give up my sanity, to free myself of the heavy chains of humanity. I didn't want to be human any longer, I didn't need to be. I was so much more than these humans who hunted me. *I* was the one who hunted *them*. They might have thought that they were the most powerful beings walking the light, but they didn't control the darkness. They might have moved through the dark with relative impunity, but they hadn't met me yet. They might have laughed as they taunted my kind and killed them by the dozens, but they hadn't hunted one like me before. They had never found a zombie as powerful and evolved as me and they didn't respect the darkness that would soon devour them.

"Ain't no zombies in here, Frankie."

The man was only feet from me now as he moved along the wall with his light wavering through the darkness. I couldn't see him, but I knew each step that he took. His back rubbed the wall and his feet padded the floor, but it was his scent that lit his position. Only a few more seconds and I would have him. Only a few more steps and he would know fear, he would know death.

My body clenched even tighter and my feet turned slightly in the short pile. I would explode from the clothes and rip the man's head free before he even knew that I was there.

Step...

Rub...

Step...

His back rubbed the empty wall of the large storage room and I knew he only had a few more steps of life left in him.

Rub...

Only two more steps of life left for him.

Step...

Rub...

One more. My body quivered with excitement. I was the hunter again. How I loved this feeling, the feeling of power and might. It was so much better than the weakness and fear that came with being human.

"Check the corners and look for anymore signs."

The voice came from across the room. It was a powerful voice, filled with strength and authority. That was the leader of this group and I would thrill even more at the taste of his flesh.

"Tha' things long gone. We's too late."

I had to kill the man near me first, though. He would be a small treat as I licked his blood from my hand while crossing the room to kill the other two. Just out of reach now, only one more step and he would be my first victim.

"Just shut up and check that pile."

Take the step, damn it! I was anxious to kill him. My body was completely coiled and ready to spring forward to devour him. Take the step!

A hand fell on my foot. It was a small and gentle hand. I nearly jumped in surprise as it pushed through the pile and silently surrounded the stump of my foot. That tiny hand tore me away from the ambush and grabbed at my mind even as it leaned into the pit of mental blackness. It was Zoe's hand, I recognized the small fingers as they moved up to my ankle and held on even tighter. She knew what I was about to do and she was silently trying to stop me.

What did I care? I was a zombie. I should pull away and kill these three before returning back to devour her.

Step...

The man was in range now. He was right where I wanted him, only feet from my little pile and just above me. I could erupt out like Mt. St. Helens and cover him with the ash of death before he could even turn his shotgun towards me.

Do it.

The voice pushed my mind out over the pit. I could feel the first foot of my mind stepping out into the void, but the second was held tightly by the tiny girl's hand. She was trying to hold me back, to keep me from disappearing into zombiness again.

Do it!

The voice was angry now. It boomed in my head and demanded me to ignore the girl's hand.

Do it. Do it NOW!

I tried to move. I tried to pounce. I couldn't. Zoe's hand was wrapped around my foot, but her fingers had dug into my soul and wouldn't allow me to move.

The light turned towards me and I knew I was about to lose my greatest advantage—surprise.

Ignore the girl!

But I couldn't. I would die right here, hidden in the small pile of clothes, before I could ignore the stranglehold she had upon my heart.

The shotgun's barrel pushed into my pile. I could feel the jagged edges of the sharp muzzle brake poking at my skin. It was only inches from my head and could take my face off if the man only tightened his finger around the trigger. I had lost my advantage and I would die for that moment of weakness.

My mind stepped back from the edge and seemed to collapse at the precipice. I felt the fear and weakness of humanity overwhelm me as I waited for the shotgun blast to take me away.

"Ya think he's hidin'?"

The man laughed and pulled the shotgun away from my pile. I could feel the tension dripping from my body as the man took a step away.

"I think you're getting careless, Larry."

"Ya know they don' hide. Ain't careless, Frankie, jus' know they don' hide."

I watched in rapt fascination as the men moved towards the center of the room. There wasn't any tension left in their steps, they were sure that they were alone and safe now. Two lights focused on my last meal while the third continued to move across the room.

"They might not hide, but he ain't far away."

The men moved closer to the remnants and I could see them bend over the stripped ribs.

"This guy's a fresh kill. He hasn't been dead more than a few days, if that."

They panned the room with their lights one last time before moving towards the door. They didn't seem so efficient or deadly any longer, but I was still afraid of them. My humanity had returned and, with it, the weakness I hated so desperately.

"Let's move, our zombie can't be too far now."

CHAPTER THIRTY-FIVE

Bob was taking his final limping steps towards the horizon and the sky was a bruised orange and purple before either of us moved. Sometime after the men had left, Zoe had fallen asleep. Her small hand had released its grip and her body had twitched with dream. I could hear the soft rustling of her skin against the clothes we both hid beneath, but it was her uneven breathing and fearful sobs that signaled her pass from the nightmare of her reality to the nightmare of her dreams.

Anger and hatred gripped me just as the fear gripped her. Those men had come for me. They had tracked me here and they hadn't come to discuss politics or to explain that zombies simply didn't wear pink. They had come to rid their world of me, to keep their families safe from me and mine. This was survival now. It was war. Human versus zombie, round two. Zombies had kicked ass in round one as the disease had turned a large majority of humanity to the dark side. But there was a reason humans had ruled Earth before this disease, their God was in their corner and He was a pretty damned good cutman. Humans were down ten to eight going into the second, but the fight hadn't been beaten out of them yet. We had to get a knockout in the second because humans had proven their resilience too many times before. If this fight went long, humanity would take the fight purely because they could out produce us. The disease was gone now and, with it, the only means to bolster our corner. Humans didn't have that problem, though. They were a bunch of fucking bunnies that would quickly outgrow their warrens and push us into extinction if we didn't shut them down quickly.

Only hours before, I'd been convinced that we were the foxes to humanity's rabbit infestation. I didn't believe that any longer. Those three men hunted zombie foxes like me. They probably counted their kills and posted bets to who would collect more of our pelts. If there were even a hundred more of those men strewn around the world, the fight would never get out of the second round and humanity would hold their arms high while zombinity would be carted from the ring with big cartoon Xs across our eyes.

I didn't hate the humans, I hadn't even hated them when I was a true zombie. I had been emotionally indifferent to them then—they were nothing more than a dangerous, but delectable food source then. Now that I was something else, something not human and not zombie, I respected their strengths and feared their weapons—though I still hungered for their blood.

My anger and hatred was not for them, they were merely acting their parts. I was angry at myself. I hated myself. It was a low and desperate loathing that moved in waves across the remaining shreds of my soul. The anger churned in my gut and erupted with each sleeping cry that escaped Zoe's throat.

I had done that to her.

I had taken her family from her.

I had imprisoned her and made her a pariah from her own kind.

I was guilty for all of it because it was my kind that had done this to her and I had once been a mindless tool in the deadly zombie toolbox.

What should I do, though? I would leave her if I believed she could survive on her own. I would madly rush the armed men if they would allow her safe passage behind their own lines. I would do whatever was needed to secure her safety, but I couldn't see any answers to the hundreds of questions and problems whirling through my head in a tornadic twirl that seemed to unhinge that little pebble of my mind and send it spinning with the other trash collected inside my skull. Maybe that would be good, though. Maybe a thorough sweeping of the dark pit of my head would be for the best. It might clean out the darkness and allow some fresh air and ideas in.

But my skull wouldn't be cleaned out and it would never allow the light in again. This was my new existence, this was my new reality. I was condemned by it just as I was blessed with it. I couldn't change myself any more than I could deny that I didn't want to.

I wasn't human, I would never be human again, but my humanity had risen from the watery depths where my sickness had deposited it with lead boots. It couldn't swim, but it did bob at the surface and nag at my mind as it harshly reminded me of my many failures.

Enough!

I stood, easily shedding the swirl of activity in my head just as I shed the pile that had protected me during the day. I stood to my full length, enjoying the feeling of power still trapped in my body. My mind might shake from the mere hint of those men, but my body was still just as strong as theirs. I ran my lone hand across my powerful chest, still meaty with muscle, then along my rounded shoulders. I was disfigured and different, but I still carried the muscle I had carefully crafted as a human. My arms, one full and the other halfed, were still thickly bound with muscle and my neck was still stretched wide. I hadn't ever been a bodybuilder, but I had been slender in the right places and thick in the others. My new construction wasn't human any longer, my back was too bent and my skin was too sagged now to be mistaken as human, but I must have looked all the more powerful for the change. I could feel the way my face drooped; the openness at the bottom lids of my eyes and the puppy jowls taking over the edges of my scruffy face. I could feel the new slope of my shoulders, the hollowness of my stomach, and the limping strut. Like a new model year of a car, my human lineage was obvious, but my lines and options were changed.

Yes, I was something more than human; something more than zombie. I stood even taller and felt my strip of spine stretching to its full length. It felt good. I flexed my muscles and growled as my neck popped and snapped. I was a monster; a thinking, raging, and killing monster that would never hide from another mere human. I did not need to and I couldn't do it again.

My charge, the beautiful princess now stirring at my feet, wouldn't like my vow to always fight, but she needed my protection and needed me to be the man—or thing—that I truly was.

CHAPTER THIRTY-SIX

We had to leave.

I didn't know where we needed to go or how we'd get there. I had no plan. I had no ideas, but I knew we needed to get moving before we had more visitors.

Edging to the glass front doors, I could still smell the scent of the men. They were long gone now, probably holed up somewhere to wait for my kind. They wouldn't be gone for long, though. This was their home, I could smell their stink on the area. They had families nearby. Houses, kids, things to protect, things to kill for. That was why they'd come for me; why they were hunting my kind.

I respected that, even if I feared it.

They were surviving.

And we were surviving, too. Zoe and I. Two unlikely traveling companions, just trying to find someplace safe where we could survive. I knew this was a good place for her, but I also knew she wouldn't stay here. She wouldn't stay with her kind because *I* couldn't survive here. I couldn't blame them for their prejudices. We were at war and, in war, only one force could be the victor. Any sway from total annihilation of the enemy would crown the king on the other side of the line. Political correctness and kindness had no place in this war—if it had any place in *any* war—and those men knew that.

No, they wouldn't allow us to live. They would kill me and then make a mockery of the girl who I loved as my own. They would let her live among them, but she would forever be known as a traitor to her kind, a moniker that might carry more punishment than being actually infected. I couldn't allow her to suffer—either at their hands or at the hands of my own.

So we needed to go.

Where and how were two questions that I didn't know the answers to, though. I could only protect my pale little Zoe if I could find a place where she wouldn't be at risk from those who would do her harm—both human and infected. I knew that I wasn't her best steward, but my kind would feast on her bones and her kind would feast on her innocence. I gave her more opportunity than either of the other sides would, but where I could take her to give her those opportunities was more than a little difficult to determine.

Where?

How?

Why?

Shut up! I screamed at the voice, though I didn't know why I even bothered. It would speak its piece when it decided I wanted to hear it and there would be no peace until it decided I'd had enough.

Rather than continue the irrational argument with the voice, I decided to focus on the problem itself. Where? Where would I take her? Where would she be safe?

Is arguing with me truly irrational?

Where could she hope to survive? Where could she build a life. Where would she be safe from the enemies closing in on her from both sides?

Ignoring me now?

Where?

Stop it.

North?

Stop.

South?

Stop ignoring me!

The coast?

Stop it!

West?

West. Just stop it. Just stop ignoring me! Go west!

Why west?

Oh, so now you're speaking to me?

The thought occurred to me that it was my own voice speaking from some dark and dusty hallway in my mind, but the thought seemed both ridiculous and insane.

Why west? I demanded now, I was tired of asking.

Bob.

What about Bob?

Bob cleans all. Bob kills all. Bob is the great equalizer.

Bob cleans... Yes, the voice was right. Bob *was* the great equalizer. My kind couldn't stand the mere touch of his fiery hand and the humans couldn't stand the heat that dried everything he touched. There were places to the west where Bob would burn every inch of the terrain. Surely, my kind couldn't live there for long and the humans who did had to be more worried about dying from water loss than blood loss.

But, if my kind couldn't survive there, how would I?

Does it matter?

And, again, I agreed with the voice. I was dead already, lost the moment that this sickness took hold inside me. Survival wasn't what I was interested in, at least not long-term survival. I wanted to survive long enough to protect Zoe and get her somewhere safe. I wouldn't survive to see the next comet cross the sky or even the next summer. And I was okay with that. I didn't need to live that long. I only needed to live long enough to protect her; long enough to make amends for my failures as a father to my own Zoe Jane.

CHAPTER THIRTY-SEVEN

The 'where' decided, the 'how' worked itself out quickly as we stepped into the darkness and let our feet answer the question. The shoes fit well enough, though one looked like it belonged to a child and the other to a clown. Zoe had pushed the shoes on my feet, the first slipping on easily, the second covering my stump only after some turning, pushing, and crying. The pain had been vibrantly delicious in its excess, like a loose tooth that aches across the entire skull but can't be left alone.

The night surrounded us, dark and chilled. It felt like we were the only living creatures in the universe as we crossed the parking lot and stepped onto the grass embankment leading down to the highway. Deer and rabbits scurried in the silence around us, but they weren't a threat and I ignored their scents as I struggled to find any sign of the true hunters—man.

A change had been digging its bony fingers into the hard, round shell atop my neck, but the fingers now dug even deeper. I could feel them starting to pull and twist against my skull like a young child with an unwieldy doll. Change was going to happen whether I agreed to it or not and I knew this change wouldn't be all fun and fortune. Some of the changes had already occurred. I knew things that I hadn't known since punching out of humanity and stamping my zombie card. I knew we were going west, though I didn't know how I knew what west was. I knew that I'd chased this little girl along this very same path only days before.

Zoe pulled at the stump of my arm excitedly. She looked like a child at the front gates to Disney World as she tugged and pushed me on. I'd be tugging at her before the night was through, but I followed behind her, my feet shuffling as fast as they could manage. I wanted to tell her that this was a marathon, not a sprint, but I kept up with her as she ran forward with the enthusiasm reserved only for youth.

My mind drifted as we walked between the thin string of cars parked along the highway. How beautiful it was, that childish passion. To have just a taste of it now. To have had just a bit of it when I'd been human would have quelled some of my regret. I might have been a good father if I'd had a small bottle of that passion. I hadn't been a good father, I knew that now. I hadn't known that then, though. I had *thought* I'd been a good father. I'd thought that I'd given my little brown bear what she'd wanted.

I hadn't.

I'd provided for my family, given them a home, food, and comforts. I had given them everything I could afford to give, but I hadn't given them the one thing that didn't cost anything and, in truth, gave back more than it ever took. I had never given them my love—truly given every bit of it, freely and unbidden. There was always something keeping my love from flowing between us. Like some disgustingly emotional example of Ohm's law, my expressions of love always suffered from eighteen-gauge line loss. I didn't know how I failed so dramatically without ever realizing it, but I could see clearly now—perhaps more clearly than ever before—that I hadn't been the man I should have been, the father I could have been.

You were a zombie.

I laughed, a burbling and angry sound barking through the quiet night, I had been more zombie as a human than I was now *as a zombie.* It was true, I couldn't argue with the voice. I *had* been a void then, a constant physical figure in my daughter's life without ever being an emotional presence. I had cloaked her with presents of cloth and cord, but never of the heart. She had held my hand—just as her stunt double was doing now—and she had always poured her heart through that touch. No Ohm's law; no line loss. She had been my biggest fan, my biggest supporter, and I had half-heartedly played my part as her Superman. There had always been something to keep me from returning her love; work, calls, drinks, buddies. I had never given her my everything; had never just opened myself to her.

Was it fear?

Ignorance?

Life?

What could cause a man to ignore the most important thing in his life? How could I have not held her hand and been happy? How could I have not wanted to spend every moment at her side, to drink imaginary tea or dress in pink shirts?

There was nothing I wanted more *now*, but *now* was too late. Now, she was gone. Now, she wouldn't recognize me. Now, she wouldn't look at me with love. Would she look at me in horror? Would she even know it was me? Would I know it was her and would I know how to tell her that I had finally realized that she was my everything? How could I tell her that she was my winning lottery ticket, my brick of gold, my oasis in the desert?

None of that mattered, though, for my Zoe Jane was gone now.

"Sun's coming up."

I followed her finger as she pointed behind us. Bob was about to peek over the horizon. We had walked the night and crossed countless miles, but I hadn't noticed any of it. I'd just followed Zoe's steps in the mindless trance of memories. We'd already passed Nashville and were deep into the hilly countryside southwest of the town. I didn't know how I knew where we were, but I did know that there were humans in the hills around us. Their scent littered the fields and I was suddenly scared again. We had walked past countless homes, some of them probably housing humans who would gladly have disposed of my body in their fires and made an example of the traitorous daughter I was following.

I pulled her now, my steps falling faster as I sniffed at the air for a house that didn't stink of humanity. Each rushed step seemed to pull Bob up faster and I could feel the desperation tightening in my throat. I turned off the main road onto a dirt road that hadn't been touched by human scent in some time. The woods thickened on both sides and I was beginning to think I'd have to hide from Bob's touch beneath the stand of trees.

Finally, the square framing of an old house peeked through the woods in front of us. I was nearly running as we approached the steps. Trees grew tight to the house, their gangly limbs ignored long before humanity had disappeared from this area. An ancient push reel mower sat rusting on the front stoop, a strange sign that maybe the previous tenants had also disappeared from humanity long before the disease had taken the others.

CHAPTER THIRTY-EIGHT

The heat of the day passed quickly and quietly. The house had sat vacant since the first days of the disease, I was nearly sure of that and I had to wonder if this might be the place for us to settle. Maybe we'd come far enough already. What did the Bob-bleached terrain of Texas have that this couldn't provide? In fact, these hills probably provided so much that Texas didn't.

Like company.

Hadn't been a human here since before the days of the plague.

A human, but...

The voice was right, we hadn't come far enough yet. We might never see another human along this empty stretch of forgotten driveway, but that didn't mean we were safe.

I walked the creaking wooden floors of the small house, my dragging foot kicking up small puffs of dust behind me. Several nails stuck up from loose boards on the floor and I was suddenly happy for the new shoes. If I was to become something more than I was, I needed to preserve what little I still had—which included the leprous-looking foot that had been drug through sand and water, across cement and rocks.

The entire home wasn't much bigger than Vick's dog house. The walls were bowed and bent, giving the appearance that the builder's hands weren't quite steady, but there was love in the construction. I couldn't shake the feeling that two pairs of loving hands had built this home together; their pockets light, but their hearts full for each other. It made me sad to think of the loving couple who had made this their home and I tried to avoid looking at the pictures spread across the walls. I didn't need to see the photographs to see my own grandparents in them. This wasn't their home, but I could feel them here. My grandparents had been like this couple; more will than riches, asking for nothing that they hadn't earned. It made me sad to think that this couple had disappeared from earth.

I must have been an amusing sight as I scoped out the house, a teary-eyed zombie wearing pink. I could be the new poster boy for *ZQ*. I could even see the cover lines—*ZOMBIES-We just want to be loved!*

Zoe had already gone through the kitchen; I could smell the stench of the food she had eaten. It didn't smell appetizing, though I wasn't sure if that was the food or the fact that I didn't eat human food any longer. Either way, it didn't much matter, I wouldn't be fighting Zoe for her scraps and I was pretty sure she wouldn't be fighting for mine either.

The kitchen wasn't much more than a break between the living room and the table, but it suited the house well. I moved through it without pausing and found myself in the small living room, surrounded by a room that was clean and stark. The two reclining chairs looked well-worn, but comfortable. I suddenly wanted to spread myself across their leather and lean back human-style. I couldn't, though, my body wasn't suited to reclining now and the comfort would just be another reminder of the weaknesses of humanity. Still, the chairs clutched at my imagination.

Better to just imagine, I thought as I rubbed my clawed fingers across the dusty pillows. Something else was vying for my attention now.

Something human.

Something dead.

I could smell it. The scent was as subtle as a wisp of erotic perfume, but it hung lightly on the still air outside the bedroom door. I followed it, my nose leading me onwards and my brain completely disengaged. My body was nothing more than a sleep-walking mechanism to carry the guided tracker onwards.

I stopped outside the door, not wanting to open it. I knew what I would find behind the door, I had smelled that ancient death many times before, but this time felt different. Before, I had lived in the fog; my mind a silent rider on the back of my violent body. That smell—the smell of death left unattended—had just been a lost opportunity to feast then. But now, I recognized the smell as much more. It was the scent of lost lives, lost loves, lost dreams. I could smell that sorrow in the scent now. It hung heavier than the actual odor and I couldn't turn the handle without wishing I didn't have to.

I had to see, though. I didn't want to. But I had to.

I spun the handle carefully, surprised that I remembered how to operate such a human tool. Things were getting easier for me now. I could think more clearly and grasp concepts much faster. I didn't know what was changing, but I could feel the heavy mist being gently blown from my skull.

I would have preferred thinking about the fog and my new talents, but they were mere distractions from pushing the door inwards. There was death behind the door. I should have been accustomed to death by now, but this was different. *I* was different.

The door pushed open and my eyes searched the walls, not wanting to turn to the large bed that dominated the room. Everything inside was perfect, not a paper or piece of clothing out of place. It wasn't much to look at, but the owners had certainly taken good care of it.

I felt dirty as I stood at the door and peered into the bedroom. This was more than the room the owners slept in; more than the room where they loved each other. This was their sanctuary and their crypt. The pair lay together on the bed as if they'd been positioned there after death. Their bodies no longer stretched the wedding outfits they'd died in—decay and disintegration had shrunk them until the seventies tux and dress had collapsed. They were held together in a final loving embrace, his arm propped around her neck and her head turned towards him. They had died in each other's arms as if they were characters in some Sparks' novel.

I moved closer, somehow unable to resist the strange romance of the scene. They had held each other at the end, their love holding them together as they passed from this world to the next. There was no struggle, no sign of obvious cause of death, which meant that they must have drugged each other after dressing in the reminders of their union. I could feel the pull on my heart as it grew another two sizes. They had chosen to die together rather than die apart—torn by either disease or the diseased. Was it courage that had made them choose death? Or was it fear? I didn't know, but I knew that I was staring at the very essence of human love; the epitome of devotion and union. These two humans, tied together by life and death, were the flame of the human soul that no longer burned in my chest. They were what I had never possessed—true self-sacrifice for another.

A hand filled mine. It was soft and respectful as the small fingers wrapped into mine. She understood their love. Even at her young age, she could see that these two deserved her reverence.

We stood there, silently worshiping the two bodies. If my eyes had been capable of producing true tears, they would have fallen unabated. I didn't know if Zoe's eyes showered outwards, nor did I look. It didn't matter, we shared the moment in silence without judgment or reservation.

CHAPTER THIRTY-NINE

We left the crypt at dusk. I didn't want to leave the house, I knew it would have been a perfect place to hole up. But this house was the end of two lives and couldn't sustain the start of two others.

The road stretched out before us, just as it had so many times before. But today was different. Today, I could see the road; I could see the cracks in the asphalt and the lines upon its surface. The trees whistled out to me, the grass waved us on. The night's gentle breezes were cold and dry, the colors brilliant in their depth. The sky was filled with a million pin-points of light, just as it had been when I was human, but now they twinkled to catch my eye and turn my face skyward. I was alive again. I could feel the life flowing through me. Everything seemed more vivid now.

I had changed.

I had become something more.

Again.

Did the caterpillar feel this way? Did it know that it was changing? Did it feel its innards rearranging and its skin molting into the new being?

Did the butterfly know when it was no longer the caterpillar?

Would I know?

I was changing. I did not know what I would become or even what I had been, but I knew that I was changing. Every molecule within me was unstable; every muscle; every tendon. Even as I walked the hills, I knew that I would emerge something different.

The road passed beneath my feet.

Step...

Drag...

Step...

Drag...

I could feel it now, though. Every crack in the pavement nipped at my new soles and every dead body upon it grabbed for my new soul. Nothing escaped my sight. I felt like I was reborn, like I was seeing it all for the first time.

Maybe I was seeing it all for the first time; maybe my pre-diseased mind had always been sightless to the life around me. I didn't know where the truth might lie, but I did know that it was the first time I noticed the true silence of the night; the true darkness of it all.

There were no sounds—not human, not zombie, not animal, not nature.

There were no lights.

There was nothing.

It was as if the world held its breath through the night and awaited the light again. No house hummed of life. No light burned in their windows. No life existed beyond the four feet moving along the centerline of the road.

Step...

Step...

Step...

Drag...

We were alone in the world. Totally, utterly, completely alone.

We could walk the earth this night without meeting another human or zombie. It felt like there was nothing that moved through this night now but us.

Alone.

Lone.

One.

We were alone now. Every memory of humanity was gone. The hills hummed with no remembrance of man or beast as we walked through the silence. It was eerie, almost frightening.

I tried to push the thoughts of loneliness away. I tried to ignore the complete silence that surrounded us. I couldn't do either. I was aware of it all as we marched along, our hands locked together in support. We were the only beings still alive on earth.

The feeling of oneness was so thick in my mind that it couldn't have been shaken even if the whole universe had come out to greet us.

"I'm scared." A small voice sounded near my remaining elbow, the tiny words understood but lost in the immensity of the night.

I'm scared, too.

My constant companions, both Zoe and the ethereal voice, were announcing their fears to me. I understood them both. I didn't know how or why, but I knew they were both searching for my guidance; for my strength. I could only nod and tighten my grip on their hands—physical and emotional.

But I was scared, too. I wanted to be brave, wanted to ignore the loneliness that gripped us all, but I couldn't. We were walking the ruins of humanity and there wasn't anything in the world besides us and Mother Nature.

I knew that wasn't true. I knew there were thousands—millions—billions—of others surrounding us, but the night showed no signs of them. There were no smells, no sights, no sounds beyond our small party as if every star besides our own had flipped their switches and we'd been left alone in the universe.

The night passed in silence as we marched along, our steps the only sounds of the lonely night. We passed cars. We passed houses; businesses; towns. Everything passed in the blur of the night; nothing moving, nothing alive.

I held Zoe's hand, though I didn't know if I held it to lend her my strength or to absorb hers. We traveled the night together and waited for Bob to excuse us from our journey. Every step hurt and every mile seemed to be hard fought.

I had been alone before. Hell, I'd spent much of my life without anybody. But this was different. I was all alone with somebody right beside me. It was like we were the last thinking creatures to inhabit Earth. It even seemed like we were *the* last creatures.

Nothing moved.

Nothing breathed.

We were alone.

Alone.

It was a cold and painful feeling—loneliness. I thought that I'd known what being alone was like, but this was something different. It was like we had been tossed down the well and forgotten; left to escape or die. The darkness seemed to taunt us and the trees whispered their encouragement, though I couldn't tell if they wanted us to live or die. Every moment that passed seemed to stretch into a lifetime and each lifetime seemed to stretch into an eternity. We walked, we listened, and we waited.

At the end of the night, as Bob finally decided to push above the horizon, I was exhausted and pleading for some stoppage to our journey. I wasn't sure why the night had been so difficult or what had made it so different from the others, but I was ecstatic as we moved into the safety of another small house.

CHAPTER FORTY

The remains of Earth's greatest race—the human race—were collapsing around us as we walked. Nights turned into days and days into nights as the miles moved from before to beyond. As we walked the back roads and slept in the emptiness of once-beloved homes, I began to realize how empty the Earth had become. There was still life surrounding us, but it was empty of the 'life' it had once contained. Birds still passed on the wing, dogs still barked out at our passing, deer still flitted through the underbrush, and coyotes still cried out in the night. But their lives went on without some crucial puzzle piece, as if someone had stolen a wing or a leg from them all. It took me several nights to realize what that piece was, but, once the truth was uncovered, I couldn't understand how it had taken me so long to unearth.

Humans.

Earth was bereft of the greatest animal that God had put on it.

But it wasn't just the current humans, it was their offspring as well that was missing. I couldn't smell humans. I couldn't smell the infected. I couldn't smell any of them now. Their remnants were strewn across the landscape—cars parked or crashed; empty houses gaping open and empty; bodies dead and bloated. But nowhere was there any life.

It made me sad.

It made me lonely.

I couldn't imagine how Zoe must have felt. That made me even more sorrowful. Surely she saw the emptiness. Surely she could feel that hers were the first human feet to have hit these roads in weeks. Months? Years? I didn't know. How long had it been? How long had the houses begged for someone to walk their halls? How long had the cars sat silent, their engines thirsting to be revved? How long had the other animals ruled over the forests and towns, their numbers growing too quickly for their food sources?

I didn't know. I couldn't know. The humans had disappeared and they hadn't left a calendar of the days since they'd left. Their creations were rusting and disintegrating. Their jobs were left unperformed, their chores left undone. Their songs didn't fill the winds, their smiles didn't light up the days, and their fears didn't weigh down the nights. The world was empty now. The humans had been removed, amputated from their earthly body. It was barren. It was cold. I wasn't even part of the race any longer and I could feel the loss. We marched through the nights alone, possibly the only two-legged human—ish creatures left on the surface of Earth.

Was I just being melodramatic? Was this just lonely straights of a road that climbed and descended through even lonelier hills and valleys?

I couldn't tell any longer. I would have asked Zoe, but my words were still as unintelligible as the babblings of a baby. I would have even asked the voice, but he had disappeared with the others.

So we were alone. Everything around belonged to us. Every house; every car; every morsel of food and drink of water. Yet there was no satisfaction in those belongings. There was no desire to move in or turn the keys. Zoe ate what she could find and I suffered without through the hungry miles. I even started eyeing the deer and squirrels as they chanced the occasional sniff, but the thought of their meat and blood only churned my twisted pipes and made me want to eat the pink shirt that still covered my steadily-decaying body.

Something kept pushing us on, though. We walked through the nights, blindly keeping the setting sun before us and to the right as the moon seemed to stop in only long enough to occasion a quick greeting.

I didn't know why we kept moving. The riches of humanity surrounded us like Khufu's pyramid; but it was an empty, dry, and dusty wealth that didn't interest either of us. I saw cars that my heart had thumped for when it had pumped human blood—brightly-painted Italian wedges with exotic names ending in I's or rounded American steel that pre-dated my parents. They didn't excite me now. They didn't send my heart to flutter or my mind to dreaming any longer. I didn't care about them and neither did Zoe. They were just dented and rusting obstacles that we had to avoid now. The houses were just as easily disregarded. Expansive mansions only posed more difficulties to defend during the light—not that there was anybody to protect against.

There were some advantages to the emptiness of Earth, though. Zoe didn't have to fight for food—she ate well each day and packed enough to picnic an army during the night. She also seemed to change her travel arrangements with each night—one day peddling a bright pink bicycle and the next she was foot-pumping a stylish Razor scooter.

I missed all of the distractions of reality, yet I didn't really miss any of them either. I missed my tender human meals and my fellow zombiphiles, but didn't miss the dangers that either posed to us. It was the noise that I missed the least, though. Everything was quiet now—the winds still blew, the birds still chirped, but there was a silence I had never heard before. And it was beautiful in its quiet elegance. No cars hummed in the distance; no airplanes buzzed overhead; not even a generator or air-conditioner dared disturb the peaceful slumber of Earth.

Lonely? Yes.

Peaceful? Yes.

Spectacular? More than anything I'd ever known before.

There was something in the silence that I loved. It was something I didn't want to disturb; something I couldn't dare touch. Peace. Stillness. Tranquility. A thousand synonyms for the simplicity of quiet that just couldn't explain the intoxication of it. It gave me strength. It gave me hope. I didn't want it to end.

But it always does.

And it did.

#

CHAPTER FORTY-ONE

The hills were long gone and the flats of mid-America now stretched before us. I didn't know where we were, I only knew that the days were getting hotter and the reminders of humanity were getting smaller. We could see the road before and behind us as it stretched into the horizons and few cars or houses corrupted the simple beauty of the dusty landscape any longer.

I was hungry.

I was angry.

Maybe I was angry because I was hungry. I hadn't eaten in weeks—or maybe it was months—and I could feel the hot air escaping my ass as my stomach clenched and croaked out its anger. I felt the weakness in my very soul as my body slouched and collapsed upon itself. Zoe offered me her own shares, but I couldn't stomach the human food and getting close to her only brought the ribbon of her scent deeper into my nostrils, tempting me even further.

I didn't want to eat her.

I didn't want to kill her.

But I knew the hunger would soon overwhelm the tiny bits of humanity I had regained. I knew that I only had a few more days before I would be suckling on the juices of her tiny heart.

I didn't want that, but I knew it wouldn't be up to me for much longer. We were walking through the desolation of the middle of nowhere. In fact, this 'middle of nowhere' had been the 'middle of the middle of nowhere' even when there had been 'somewheres' left on Earth. Now, we were just two satellites circling the dead planet—alone in the nothingness.

Tonight would be the time to leave her, I thought with a sadness that nearly broke my heart. As soon as darkness came, I would have to run. I would run with everything I had left within me and, hopefully, die trying to leave Zoe's gravity. I didn't want to do it. I didn't want to leave her alone and defenseless, but I also knew that it wasn't up to me—or, at least, it wouldn't be up to me for much longer. I had to make my escape soon or...

I could see my escape. I would leave even before the sky was dark. I would leave as Zoe searched our next house and packed her bag for the day. My feet would push me on, my lungs would burn, and my arm would twist me in that strange running/churning motion I had nearly perfected.

I couldn't make it far, I knew that, but I could make it far enough to hide and let Zoe pass me.

I settled in and we slept through the day as always, her on the master's bed as I crouched at its foot. She was the sheep and I was the shepherd, ready to defend my flock from the wolves—human or otherwise.

Her breathing was slow and steady, comfortable and unafraid. She knew that I was there; knew that I would protect her with my life. Yet I had to leave her alone to protect her now.

What kind of shepherd did that make me?

What kind of parent?

What kind of human?

But I wasn't human anymore. I answered the voice's question without questioning where it had been for so long. It was a girlfriend returned from a tryst across the beaches of Europe—I was glad to have it back and was afraid to scare it away again by asking where it had gone.

You are human, though.

I had been human, but I wasn't any longer. Any thoughts of my humanity had disappeared the moment I'd eaten human flesh before Zoe's innocent eyes—swept away by the disgust in those tender orbs. No, I wasn't human now. I would never be human again.

You're more human than the human you last ate.

I fought to recall my last meal. Had it been the man who'd attacked my snow-colored Zoe? It took some time to remember and my stomach kicked even harder with that memory.

Yes, he wasn't human. He didn't deserve to hang that moniker around his neck. But that didn't make *me* human. I didn't eat like humans. I didn't talk like humans. I didn't move like humans. I didn't even think like humans.

I was a zombie—whatever that meant. I didn't even know if that was the correct term for what I was. I was infected. I had died. I was undead.

Did that make me a zombie? Was I just sick? Was I just infected? I tried to remember it all. I struggled with the mental gymnastics required to step back into the past.

The sickness had swept every continent quickly. It had started in Africa, I could remember that only because they'd likened the disease to AIDS and tried to isolate it before it surrounded the globe. They hadn't succeeded. The disease was too easily transmitted. It had been airborne even before the doctors had realized it was contagious. The world had quickly been lit on fire, the flames of disease climbing steadily higher as the coals of humanity had dimmed and broken apart. It had only taken months before the civilized rules of 'civilization' had shattered. I had guarded my family—especially my tender little Zoe Jane—just as I now guarded her replacement, but I'd had a job to do. Just because the world was collapsing around me didn't mean that bills were paid if jobs weren't completed.

Many around us had closed their doors and isolated themselves from the world. They had protected themselves from the illness which I succumbed to, but they didn't succeed in defending themselves from what the illness did to the sick. I had changed. I had become something different, just as the other 'infected' had, and we had feasted on the ones who thought themselves smarter and safer. Would it have been better to be uninfected? Would it have been better to be the small minority fighting against the overwhelming majority? Would it have been better to retain my humanity only to fight for it against those vile creatures who would strip my bones clean?

It didn't matter which was better—human or otherwise—because I had become infected and I'd killed every human I had found. Every human, that was, except for the tiny one snoring on the bed behind me. I had tracked, fought, and eaten any human I could find. There was no prejudice to it, I happily ate them all—white, black, yellow, red, it didn't matter. The fats ones fed me longer, the skinny ones were more entertaining to catch, and the ones in wheelchairs only filled my gut with no satisfaction to the kill.

Humanity had disappeared steadily. At first, we had become sick and they had hidden from us. As we became stronger and more numerous, they fought back, moved, or died. The illness burnt out quickly, but the ill walked the earth and killed the healthy. They killed us, too. It wasn't a one-sided genocide, they probably killed ten for each one we could, but our numbers were so vast that even a twenty-to-one rate couldn't sustain them for long.

Sometime back—I can't even remember it happening now—both sides had disappeared. It felt as if I had been asleep when it had happened, as if I'd been in a coma when the bomb had been dropped on both sides of humanity. There wasn't anything left of either now except the diminishing swirl of flies over the long-dead bodies.

I didn't miss them, though. Either side. I had no love for what I'd been and even less for what I'd become. The silence of their absence was my own lullaby and I would have whistled its tune if I'd had that much control over my body now.

But Zoe didn't feel the same. I could see it in her eyes as she searched the houses—half-hoping that she'd find another human, half-fearing it. I searched the houses behind her, wholly hoping to find a human armed and ready to defend her from me. If I had still prayed, my lone prayer would be that we could stumble across a band of humans who would take her in and put me down.

I was tired.

I was ready.

And that brought me back to the reality of the moment. We hadn't found any humans. We wouldn't find any humans. We'd crossed great expanses of land and we were alone. We were alone now and, left alone, only one of us could survive. It wasn't some overly-dramatic Hollywood moment, but there truly could be only one now. We couldn't live together—human and zombie. One of us had to rule Earth's final breaths, only one of us could hold the flag of victory.

I stood and walked over to the bed. The house was about the size of the Cowboys' stadium and stocked with enough cans to feed the full compliment of their fans who'd actually been considered human before the disease had hit. I hoped she would stay here after I was gone, the house just felt right. I knew she wouldn't, though. My little pale Zoe needed somebody—whether it be human or zombie—and she wouldn't just fill the halls with a few puppies and be happy.

The light outside was beginning to dim and I knew I wouldn't have much longer before I couldn't make my escape. I didn't want to go, I'd known that for days, but the closer I got to this decision, the deeper that pain in my chest became.

It was my heart breaking. I could actually feel the shrunken and blackened muscle ripping apart inside my chest as I stared down over Zoe's sleeping body.

It hurt. More than the loss of my arm or the laming of my leg. It hurt.

I watched her small body growing and shrinking under the covers as the life moved in and out of her.

And my body only shrunk.

I couldn't take in air.

I couldn't take in life.

I could barely even stand as I readied myself for leaving. My chest burned and tightened, each breath falling short of filling my lungs. My eyes burned and I felt the tears falling down my warped face and onto the sheets beside her.

She wouldn't know how much it hurt me to leave her. She would never understand that I left her *because* I loved her. It didn't matter, though. I had to leave her. Now. I needed to leave her now. I needed to leave before the emptiness of my stomach—and of my soul—devoured her sweet and innocent life. I knew it wasn't a matter of days any longer, only a matter of moments, and I needed to leave before those tender moments were replaced by the mindless and depraved moments of feasting.

Good bye, sweet Zoe.

I turned to leave. I was still in control of my hunger; still in control of my body. I was almost to the door when the world around me changed and I was no longer in control of my hunger.

CHAPTER FORTY-TWO

Human.

Flesh.

Blood.

Heart.

Brains.

I could smell it all. The smells which drove my kind crazy. The smells which turned us into blood-crazed animals, capable of ripping through walls and tearing apart bone and flesh.

My gnarled fingers, tipped with dagger-like nails, flexed and readied for the kill. It was unconscious, I couldn't hope to control the impulses any more than I could hope to control Bob's movements through the sky. I was a murderous beast set on auto-pilot and ready to rip apart the human flesh that I could now smell.

"No."

I heard Zoe's word, but I couldn't understand it. No, that wasn't true. I did understand it, I just didn't care. I wasn't myself any longer; I wasn't in control. Her word was mere fodder before the angry circus lion—heard, but unheeded.

My heart ached still, but my body twitched in anticipation. I would eat soon. I *had* to eat soon. The smell of human flesh wafted through my nose like the scent of popcorn through a crowded movie theatre. I wanted it. I needed it. I would kill for it.

"No!"

Yes.

"Stop!"

The word cracked through the room. I didn't care. I would not be controlled like a dog on a leash.

I could smell the fear in my meal's breath. It knew I was here. It knew I was coming for it.

"Don't!"

Zoe's words were infuriating. The shrill tone of fear in her voice dug into my skull just as the claws of my fingers drew blood from the palm of my remaining hand. I wanted her to be quiet. I wanted her to return to her peaceful slumber while I did what I had to do.

What had once been my fingers and nails were now stiff, curled, and deadly. The fingers themselves had tightened until they were as hard as metal rods, but the nails had taken the more horrifying changes. They were long and pointed, their edges as sharp as a Spartan's sword. I stretched out my claws, reveling in the dangerous cup they now formed. In minutes, that cup would be filled with flesh and blood—fresh, human flesh and blood.

"Please!" Zoe pleaded with me. "Please calm down."

I didn't care. Her words meant nothing to me now.

I was a zombie again.

I was powerful again.

I was not her pet.

I was not her servant or her protector.

I *was a zombie.*

She couldn't control me anymore than I could control myself. I had to eat. I had to feast. She couldn't understand it, I knew that. She wouldn't understand it. I didn't care.

My claws tore at the door. I couldn't work the knob, nor did I even think to try it. My mind was blank beyond the thought that I must eat.

The nub of my missing arm reached through the holes and pulled the door open even as my claws continued to rip at the thin wood. My head followed and the scent of flesh—human flesh—filled my senses and sent my head swirling again.

Human.

Downstairs.

Fearful.

It heard me.

It knows I'm here.

It's running.

My body was clear of the door and racing downstairs. I watched from inside the globe of my skull as my body tracked the scent down the stairs and into the fading light. I could see it all happening—the stairs, the doors, the human's screams, Zoe's screams—but I was just a passenger along for the thrill ride. My mind was buckled into the seat, my body was the coaster clicking up the steep incline. It chased the human into the open and towards a truck that hadn't been there when we'd found the house.

I could feel the rush of excitement as my body reached the apex of the first drop and we prepared for the true beginning of the coaster ride.

I could see the edge coming closer as the human's gun cracked out at me. I felt the bullets whizzing by my body, so close that I could feel their breeze rustling my pink business shirt.

My body leapt out and my mind followed with it. We hung at the very precipice of the first drop—hung there for several breaths as time paused and the realization that we were on the edge of falling finally occurred to me. The thrill drove my heart now; squeezing and releasing so quickly that it felt as if it would burst. The thrill wrapped a strong arm around my lungs and held them tight; they couldn't breathe in or out.

I saw it all.

I waited.

I was pissing my mental pants as my physical ones flew towards the truck.

And then we fell.

The coaster's tracks seemed to disappear before me as we raced downwards. I felt it all—the rush, the fear, the *thrill*.

But it was over in a short breath. The thrill, the excitement—it all ended in a final crack of the pistol. I saw the human's gun spit out its last bullet. I felt it speeding at me. I almost thought that I could see it as it snaked towards me.

And then it passed me. I felt it pass me. I heard it pass me. Shit, I nearly tasted it pass me.

But it struck flesh. I heard it strike soft tissue. I smelt the blood of the strike.

I knew that blood.

I knew that scream.

I knew the sound of that body collapsing.

CHAPTER FORTY-THREE

I was myself again. It was the scream that had stopped the maniacal zombie coaster and unbuckled my mind. I felt the sudden jerk as my body hit the truck's door, but it was my brain's exit from the ride that dropped my body back to the ground.

Looking over my shoulder, I saw what I had feared.

There, only steps from the front door of the house, was Zoe's body. She was crumpled in the high weeds like some spoiled giant had thrown out their ragdoll.

I could smell her blood.

I could hear her breath.

I could feel her fear.

No.

No!

NO!

Those bullets were meant for me! That human had meant to stop me!

Zoe had meant to stop me!

I pushed myself up and away from the truck's crumpled door. I crawled at first, then stood, then ran.

Zoe?

Nothing. Only the sounds of her cries.

Zoe! I grunted out something that sounded close. *"Grrrrrooooooeeeeeeeee!"*

No answer.

I ran faster.

I couldn't ever remember running so fast before. I couldn't remember getting so far from the house either, though. It seemed like the entire Grand Canyon stood between me and my weak little Zoe now.

I didn't hear the human's truck motor start or the tires spitting gravel. I didn't care about that any longer. I only cared about my little Zoe.

My feet hit the paved walkway to the broad house and sent me flying towards Zoe's curled body. My hunger was forgotten. My thirst for blood was gone. My zombie card had been checked in and probably revoked for life. My only thought was to stop the flow of blood as it spread into a bright red stream that stained her clothes and soaked into the earth beneath.

The bullet had hit her high in the right shoulder, a tiny hole just below her clavicle in the front and a fist-sized churned-meat hole in the back. Zoe was curled into a tight ball of pain and I could hear her screams of shock, even above my own grunts of terror.

Don't die!

Please don't die!

I cupped her body into my arm, gently picking her off the ground before holding her tightly into my chest. Her blood coated my hand and shirt, but I had no stomach for the taste now. It was Zoe's blood. My baby's blood!

She looked up at me, her eyes veiled in pain as she stared into mine. Words—none understood—babbled from her lips, but it was her eyes that spoke to me. She was dying. Her eyes told me it all. She was near death already and I could do nothing more than watch as the light dimmed around us just as it dimmed in those tender globes.

You can't save her.

I had to.

You can't.

The voice spoke now? After so much silence, it spoke now? Shut up!

She's going to die.

No! I argued, as if the sheer vehemence of my word could stem the tide of her blood.

She will.

NO!

Just like your Zoe Jane.

No.

No!

No! No! NO! NO!!!

You can't save her.

Shut up! Shut up! SHUT UP!

You can't.

I twisted my head in hopes of spinning the voice into silence. I spit in hopes of coughing up the voice. I cried in hopes that it would leave me alone.

But it was right. I couldn't save her. I hadn't saved my Zoe Jane. I remembered it all now. The sickness. The pain. The change. My little chocolate chip. My baby girl. She had caught it at school. Her mom, my wife, had argued that we needed to pull her out, but I'd been stubborn. I had to work. I had to do my job. And so did she. Even as the world had closed its doors to stop the spread of that damned disease, I had insisted that our little Zoe Jane go to school while we kept working. By the time we'd found out that the disease was fatal—or as near fatal as my current life would be considered—it was too late. It wasn't supposed to happen to her; to us. We were above that. *We* didn't get sick. *We* were stronger than that. But she did. She caught the disease and it had shrunk her quickly. It had only taken days before my baby girl had gone from a diesel power plant to a withering rose. There were no cures for the disease and the sickness only got more painful the longer it progressed. It never really killed its host, but the infected prayed for the ease of death.

The doctors were no use. They didn't know how to cure the disease. They declared it uncontrollable and issued the one chickenshit piece of advice they could come up with—don't get infected.

My Zoe Jane had cried for death. She'd looked at me with the devil's pain burning in her soul and begged me for death.

I had put her down on her tenth birthday.

That day had been the last of my life. I'd died that day—my body still pumping the required fluids, but my mind had been dead and gone. My own hands had done the duty and I'd have cut them off if I hadn't been infected myself. I was half-crazed from the fever, but I'd known what I was doing. Sympathy had driven me to kill my baby; sympathy for her pain; sympathy for what she was already turning into.

I couldn't save my Zoe Jane.

I hadn't saved her.

And I couldn't save this Zoe, either.

I couldn't.

But...

#

My feet were moving even before the voice finished the thought. Zoe was tucked tightly into my arm and I ran even faster than before. The stub of my missing arm pumped quickly beside me and my limp leg barely drug the ground.

The smell trailed behind the truck, but I didn't need the smell to lead my way. The truck's tires had been the first to move across the road in months and they left unmistakable tracks behind them.

I ran for hours, the moon lighting my steps as I crossed hills and valleys. Zoe's breath came in small gulps and blood no longer poured from her limp body. She was dying, maybe she was even dead, but I never stopped more than a moment as I pushed my body far beyond anything I'd ever done before.

Step...

Wheeze...

Step...

Stumble...

I cried as I ran.

Step...

Wheeze...

Step...

Drag...

I screamed as I ran.

I died as I ran.

I could feel my feet getting heavier and my body giving up. I wasn't getting any closer to the human who had shot my Zoe. I wasn't getting any closer to saving her.

I had killed her.

Just as you killed Zoe Jane.

Just as I'd killed my Zoe Jane, I didn't even bother to argue. The voice was right. I'd killed my baby. I had killed her even before I'd put the pistol to her head. I'd killed her when I'd gone to work and sent her to school. I'd gambled with her life.

I had lost.

I had killed my Zoe Jane because I'd chosen to go to work instead of buttoning my family into our apartment. I'd killed her with my drive; with my ethics; with my ego.

And I'd killed Zoe just as I'd killed my Zoe Jane. I'd killed her with my temper and with my hunger.

I wanted to die.

I wanted to give Zoe my last breaths; my last heartbeats.

But I couldn't. She would die in my arms, just as my Zoe Jane had. She would die and I would live. Her blood would be on my hands and her eyes would torture my mind until I was finally allowed to succumb to death.

I would have stopped if I'd known that I was still moving. My body followed the scent without any interference from the pebble of a brain rattling inside its carrier. My feet drug along without any real guidance and my body sucked the air in without any real desire.

Drag...

Drag...

Drag...

Step...

I was dead. My lungs breathed and my heart pumped, but I was dead nonetheless. I couldn't go any further and I couldn't stop. I couldn't save Zoe and I hadn't saved Zoe Jane. I was worse than a zombie, I had always been worse than a zombie. I was human and there wasn't anything weaker or more fallible than humanity.

So I kept moving forward.

Drag...

Drag...

Stumble...

Drag...

Nothing mattered, nothing could change the fact that I'd killed my Zoe Jane; killed my own child. Nothing could change the fact that I'd killed my Zoe; killed this strange substitute for my own child. I'd failed. I deserved to die. I deserved to die in failure. Even worse, I knew my punishment would not be death. I would survive, despite my desires, and I would roam the earth alone—suffering the true punishment of failure.

Drag...

Drag...

Stumble...

Fall...

I heard her quiet cry as my heavy body fell on her. The cup of my claw, once tight with deadly intent, cupped and protected her head, but it couldn't keep her safe from my weight.

Her cry was weak and barely more than a moan. I had to struggle to even hear it over the sound of my collapse. But it was there, feeble and delicate. Turning carefully, I rolled Zoe onto my chest and then lay there on my back. I could feel her frail heart beating the last bits of blood through starving veins. She was close to death's grasp now, maybe even within it already.

I lay there, staring into the sky and listening to her lungs chugging out. The darkness would lift soon, the sky was already beginning to go grey. Above me, the sky was filled with a million pin-pricks of light. Gorgeous. I had never seen so many stars twinkling above before. It was the total darkness, unencumbered by man's creations, that made the stars sizzle so brightly above me.

I was one with the sky, somehow floating in the brightness of space without leaving my back. The stars seemed so close that I could sweep them into my arms and pick them between my fingers to examine like small diamonds.

Free.

That was what I felt. Free. I was free of everything. Free from my humanity. Free from my job. Free from my pressures. Free from my disease. Free from my inhumanity. I felt free from everything as I floated through the sky and tried not to disturb the delicate pebbles of light. Most of all, though, I was free from regret; free from pain; free from failure.

My eyes closed.

I welcomed death.

CHAPTER FORTY-FIVE

But death didn't come.

Pain did, though.

It woke me, bright and hot.

No, it was the sound that woke me. The pain only reminded me that I was still alive. The truck's engine had woken me. It was only twenty feet from me, the exhaust chugging out clouds of steam in the cold morning air. The clouds weaved and bobbed behind the idling truck.

Bobbed.

Bob.

Bob!

I tried to shield Bob's light with the stub of my arm, but the stump barely even covered my chin. I often forgot that the arm was gone and I was left with little more than a crooked stump.

I could feel Bob's heat as it sizzled me like bacon in a pan. But the pain didn't matter. Zoe mattered. I could feel her heart beating against my chest.

Thump...

Wait...

Wait...

Thump...

She wasn't dead and neither was I.

The woman who'd shot Zoe stepped from the truck. I could see the fear in her eyes. I could even smell it, though I was too weak to pull in the scent. She was walking cautiously towards me with her pistol in one hand.

I was on the driver's side of the truck, not more than ten feet from the door. Pushing myself up with the crooked stump, I felt the semi-healed broken bone grind and then snap again. Pain shot through my arm and into my skull, as bright and hot as the sky above, but just as distant.

I rolled onto my side and then used the stump and my good elbow to push me up to my knees. Every inch of my body burned, ached, and rejoiced. I had found her. I had found the only hope for Zoe. The pain didn't matter, I would gladly die from it if this woman could just take Zoe's pain away.

I didn't even try to stand as the woman stepped closer. There was a moment of confusion and fear as the woman tried to decide what I was.

I used that moment.

My good arm thrust forward. Zoe's tender head still lay in my claws and her body drooped limply over my arm. I stuck her as far out as I could and cried out softly.

"Groey... Dyyyyyyiinggh..."

The woman's pistol rose even as she backpedaled quickly, but her feet tangled and her ass hit the ground just as the first shot echoed through the quiet morning.

It missed me. Not by more than a cat hair, but the bullet missed me. The woman scrambled at the ground and tried to line up her next shot. I didn't move. I knew the woman was terrified and fighting for her life, but I could only pray that she hit me in the head with the next shot.

"Ppprrreeeezzz. Zrroeeeeeeyy. Dyinnngh."

I understood my words. I knew they were right. I also knew she couldn't.

"No." Zoe's word was so faint that I barely heard it. I stuck her even further out, nearly tipping over as I offered Zoe's body to the woman.

The next bullet was high, but I felt the third tear off the bottom of my stump. It twisted me around, but I managed to stay on my knees with Zoe stretched out towards the woman.

"No." Zoe's voice was louder now, almost loud enough to be heard above the truck's idling engine. "Please don' shoot."

The woman was still trying to scramble to her feet, but she'd heard Zoe's soft plea. I could see her fear and I could smell it in the puddle of piss trailing her. She would kill me, I knew that, but I had to make her see Zoe and make her understand that Zoe was not infected.

"Pleezh Zroey dyhing." The words hurt. They burnt in my lungs hotter than Bob's touch, but I babbled on as I set Zoe's limp body down before me.

The woman was on her feet and backing up carefully. Her pistol never left my head and I could feel the canon-like chamber locked on now. The next bullet would be my last; I had no doubt about that.

I was gentle as Zoe's body touched the soft dirt at my knees. Her wilted body seemed so light and empty as it settled into itself. Tears, hot and painful, hit my eyes. My sobs were not the gentle weep of a baby for her bottle, but the wailing tears of a woman burying her child. I watched Zoe's chest rise. I waited for it to fall. I waited even longer for it to rise again. Raindrops of tears burst out of my burning face as my hand found my mouth. I kissed my fingers and then lowered them to Zoe's forehead.

The woman looked at me. She stared at me. She waved the gun at me and waited for me to attack her.

I ignored her.

Slowly, almost imperceptibly, I turned from Zoe. I prayed that the woman could save her, but I knew there was nothing more that I could do.

I crawled on my hand and knees away from the truck. I was the only thing moving on Earth at that moment. Nothing else broke the silence of that moment beyond the dragging of my knees along the powdery dust road. No breeze blew. No birds flew. No dogs barked and no humans breathed.

Just me.

And nothing else felt pain. It was all mine. A world's worth of pain pushed down on my back. Bob flogged at me with the flagrum used on Jesus' back; the earth ripped at my clothes and tore apart the soft flesh underneath; and black blood dripped from the new hole in my arm stump. But those pains—those earthly pains—were forgotten as I crawled, fell, and crawled some more. Those were pains of the flesh, easily ignored. The true pain, the pain of the entire universe, lay silently behind me.

Zoe was my pain.

Zoe was my failure.

Zoe was my love.

I would suffer a thousand painful deaths just to save the single life slipping away behind me.

Anything. My mind cried out that single word.

I would have given anything at that very moment to see Zoe open her eyes again. I would have given everything to hear her breath fill her lungs and to feel her heart beat again with the strength and power it once had.

CHAPTER FORTY-SIX

Bob was high in the sky before I finally made it into the house. The long shadow of the house had thinned until it hid at the foot of the brick house. I barely had the strength to pull myself through the broken patio window after the sizzling I'd just received.

Well done.

Not now.

I'm just saying... Well done.

My body hurt too much to argue. I had thought I'd been close to death before; thought I'd known what true pain and desperation felt like.

I hadn't.

I was a crisped slice of bacon now; my burnt and blackened body sizzled like I'd just pulled it out of the pan. Maybe I had. Maybe that was exactly what I'd just done—pulled my crispy body out of the frying pan. But, if I was out of the frying pan where did that leave me?

In the fire.

Exactly.

Yup, exactly. Well done.

My feet pushed weakly against the wall. I could feel the burnt and loose skin peeling from my back as the pink shirt stuck to the oozing flesh. Despite the pain of the ripping and burning flesh, I had to laugh. Yes, well done, indeed. I was more than well done, though. Bob had seared me on both sides and every inch of my abused body was pinker than the damned pink shirt Zoe had picked for me.

Terror gripped my heart again. All thoughts of my own pain were gone as I remembered my little Zoe, the crescent of her blood slowly staining the rough ground outside. I could remember those small ribbons of red as they refused to soak into the loose dirt; they looked like the Colorado River as it fought against earth and rock to create the Grand Canyon.

You're better off without her.

No. I wasn't better off. I needed her. I depended upon her. She was the light that burned softly in the darkness of my life now. She was the only light that burned in my life now. I ignored Bob's brilliance as he shone through the broken window. I could remember breaking the glass and pulling myself through, but I didn't know where the strength had come from.

No, that wasn't true. I did know.

Self-preservation. Probably one of the basest reactions of any organism, the desire to continue on. It wasn't so unusual, at least it wouldn't have been before the disease. But zombies didn't care about self-preservation. We weren't wired that way. I knew I hadn't cared about my own survival weeks before. I hadn't cared whether I died or not. I hadn't cared about anything then. I hadn't had a thought bouncing through the blackness of my skull beyond the chase for 'braaaaiiinnnnsssss'.

But now?

Exactly! But now I did.

Now I cared.

Now I loved.

Now I wanted to survive.

And she didn't?

Of course she did. I didn't even have to ask the voice which 'she' it was referring to. I knew what it was getting at and I knew why it was asking. Yes, she wanted to live. Yes, she wanted to survive the moment; the day; the year. Yes, she had a better chance to live with them.

But...

But nothing!

But, I...

Exactly! I... I... I... That's all that you care about! The 'I', the 'me'. That's all that matters to you now.

No!

Yes! If you cared about her, you wouldn't have attacked that human. If you'd cared about Zoe, you would have sent her down to escape with that woman without going for the woman's blood..

But...

Shut up. You killed Zoe Jane because you just had to go to work and you killed Zoe because you'd just had to eat. Just shut up already.

The voice was right. I tried to feign disgust. I tried to hide the truth, but there it was. I cared only for me now. It didn't matter that I would have died for the tiny human. It didn't matter that I'd killed my own kind for her. It didn't matter that I would have left her; that I had been leaving her. I was the pitiful widower standing at the burial hole and asking 'what do I do now?' Did I care about her? Or did I only care that she was my light?

And if she was still alive?

Alive? The thought hadn't even come to me. I had seen the hole in her tender body. I had seen her blood pouring out and the death in her eyes. She had died.

But...

Did the insane know that the other voices weren't their own? I didn't know that the voice was mine. I couldn't have stopped the voice; couldn't have silenced it short of silencing my own. But the voice wasn't completely my own. At least, I didn't think it was completely my own. I couldn't control it. I couldn't tell it what to say or how to say it. But I did know that the voice fed off my own and that it obeyed my wishes to some extent.

That's what it was doing now. It was trying to fulfill the monstrous wishes buried deep within me now. It was teasing me with the possibility that my little Zoe might still be breathing. *I* knew she was dead. I had smelled the death upon her breath. I had seen it in her blood. I had *felt* the death in her eyes.

No.

But...

But... I nodded my head, the weight of that empty globe pulled and yanked at my thin neck. I couldn't control my body any more than I could feel it now. But, if she was still alive, I had to get to her. I had to protect her.

My body regained some small fraction of strength as I fretted over my little Zoe. It wasn't enough to stand, but it was enough to pull my body back towards the window and into the light again.

Bob's touch burned and sizzled as my lone arm pulled me towards the window. The claws of my fingers dug into the thin carpeting. The nails bent and snapped as they gained purchase, but I only pulled my hand back up and stuck it out further. The slivers of nails caught and tugged at the carpet, but I shook them off as I tried to continue forward.

At the window, I used the broken stump of my arm to leverage myself up as I threw my good arm over the inner ledge. Glass shards tore through my thin, burning skin and blood—as black as the night I once owned—covered the ledge and greased my climb. I pulled with every last ounce of strength and propped my wallowing head up on the ledge.

Glass bit into my face like razor-sharp teeth, but they were also ignored as I squinted into the brightness outside. The truck was gone now. Everything was gone now. The woman. The girl. All that was left was the snail trail of my bloody escape.

Gone?

Yes, damn it. You can see it as well as I can. Gone!

Gone where?

The last strings of my strength snapped and my arm released its purchase. My body slipped down and I felt my head drag across the shattered glass before bouncing off the thin carpet. It struck hard; hard enough to dim the light around me.

My stump tried to push against the carpet and my hand tried to gain purchase. Neither worked as I tried to push myself away from the deadly light streaming through the window. My body arched up like a baby seal and then I collapsed again.

It burns.

Did it matter?

We're dying.

Did it matter?

Please! It hurts!

It didn't matter. Self-preservation was an emotion I no longer possessed. I was ready for death again. She was gone. I had done the damage. I had killed her.

It was the human's gun. Please, get us out of the light!

I might as well have pulled the trigger, though. I'd killed her. She was gone and it was my fault.

But the woman had taken Zoe.

Yes, that was true.

Maybe she was still alive. Please?

Maybe, but that was only one more reason to allow Bob's cleansing light to rid the earth of my kind. Maybe that was the best reason of all.

I could see the smoke tendrils rising from my arm as I lay face down at the window's edge. Everything was so vivid and bright. I felt like every nerve and every breath was buzzing with their own life now. The lights surrounding me were dazzling in their clarity. I watched the smoke rising as Bob sizzled me silently like bacon in a giant microwave. I could feel my body clutching inwards, the muscles clenching in pain and my body shrinking in the heat.

Good, let me die.

No.

Yes, it was time. Zoe was gone now. I was gone. Everything was right, or as right as it would ever be now.

What if they were mean to your Zoe.

They wouldn't be. Maybe the woman could even save her.

But, what if they were?

They couldn't be.

But?

They wouldn't be. How could they be? No, they couldn't!

What if they beat her?

Shut up!

What if they raped her?

Shut up!

What if they killed her?

No! Why would they? Why would the woman save her, just to have her raped and killed? How could anybody do such things to such an innocent girl?

You would have killed her.

No! No, I wouldn't have.

But I knew that was a lie, even as I spit it back at the voice. I would have killed her. I would have eaten her, even as I ignored her booted father. I would have pulled that young heart from her chest and eaten it without pausing to...

NO! This was a trick. The voice was trying to trick me.

And if I'm not?

My arm twitched and then moved. I watched it plop onto the carpet beside me before grabbing hold.

#
CHAPTER FORTY-SEVEN

My body was nothing more than a dark pirate's ship floating upon the still and windless ocean. I could see my broken and burnt body just lying on the carpeted floor as day turned into night and back into day again. I was an abandoned ship, left to die with the sails as empty as my bulwark. The black ocean which I floated upon was a nearly unbroken sheet of dark water. No voices called out; no birds stirred the air. I was the lone ship floating no where with no one to take to my next destination.

The days passed uncounted. I saw them move, but took no notice of them. The endless stretching of shadows and light marked nothing for me except the slow death that I deserved.

Yes, I was finally dying. There was no disputing that final spiral down the toilet bowl towards the constrictions of the dead pipes beneath.

Yes, I welcomed it. I was ready for it. I had been ready for death longer than I could remember fearing it. I wanted to die; wanted to slip away in silence.

Is your family waiting?

The voice had taken a more tender tone as I had begun ignoring it. No, my family wouldn't be waiting. At least, I prayed they wouldn't be. As much as I wanted to see them again, I could only hope that they wouldn't be waiting in the hell that surely awaited me. I was tainted. I was evil. I would not be saved. I could only hope that they had been.

So I just sunk lower on my beam with each stretch of light. The stillness of the world around me never moved the ocean beneath. I was a dark ship taking on more water as the ocean continued to welcome me. I could see the whole scene as my waterless eyes were frozen on the ceiling. The ship—me—was dead in the water, my mast collapsed, and my crew mutinied. The water was so dark that it absorbed the reflections of the stars, but seemed to give off a thin veil of steam that couldn't hide the splinters of my soul floating slowly away. I listed to one side; the angle creeping steeper with each passing day, but never enough to just fall in. My deck was empty besides the abandoned memories of my life. I could feel those memories, feel their importance, but couldn't see them clearly enough to make out what they were.

Light stretched longer as the day shortened. This was my night to sink beneath the still water. It was my night to finally join the blackness that surrounded me. Bob's rays pulled their way across the carpet before climbing the wall. The light dimmed as Bob finally sat on the wall of the horizon before stepping over and down. With each downward step, the air around me cooled and my sinking ship took on more water. It listed to port, but never moved fast enough to disturb the oily black water beneath.

Darkness finally enveloped my world. It was a black, silent darkness that smelled of rot and death. I was that smell, it wafted off me and filled the house. I welcomed the scent as a man sniffed at the smell of his own flatulence. There was no breeze, no sound, no motion. I was alone; completely, totally, and eternally isolated from everything. Nothing existed outside the unseen fog surrounding my death ship.

I wanted to be alone. I wanted my ship to finally surrender to the dark waters.

It would surrender.

Eventually.

Wouldn't it?

Not until you raise the flag of defeat.

I have.

No.

But I have. I've surrendered. I give up. I capitulate. I am defeated.

Then raise the white flag.

I tried. Really, I tried to raise the white flag of surrender upon the remainders of my mast. I could feel the soft texture of the white cloth. The task, more mental than physical, began overtaking my body. Every muscle, including my mind, pushed and pulled to raise that imaginary white flag. Even in my missing hand, I could feel the weight of the flag as I tried to lift it. My mind told me that it was all a hallucination—the ship, the flag, my hand—but it was so real to me that I pushed aside my mind and pulled at the flag in my hands.

Raise it.

But I couldn't. I couldn't put the flag up. I couldn't surrender to death, even as the deck swayed closer to the void beneath. I could only stare at the cloth and the two faces imprinted upon it. The Zoe twins, separated by so many features, but so similar to me now that they were both my daughters.

I couldn't raise the flag; couldn't surrender them to save myself. Death could take me. Hell could punish me. But I could *not* protect my own soul by forfeiting theirs.

Raise the flag. Save yourself.

No.

Suit yourself.

With that, I felt the ship of my soul list until the deck was half-covered. The black water beneath parted only enough to allow the wooden fragments of my mind in, but they never rippled or waved. Slowly, painfully, my ship listed even further towards the beam's ends; sinking deeper into the murky depths. My hands clutched the flag to my chest as the blackness covered me.

Deeper into the darkness I sank. It covered my body. It covered my head. It covered my mind and my soul. I fell into the black; weightless and bodiless as the dim lights above me began to disappear.

Deeper.

Deeper.

I clutched the flag to my chest. It was all that I had left and I would take it with me into the next life, my one reminder that I hadn't abandoned my children.

Surrounded by black, I breathed in deeply and hoped that would be my last breath.

It was not.

CHAPTER FORTY-EIGHT

Night was coming earlier now, a reminder that the winter of man's existence was fast approaching. Though the extinction of man was still too large a concept for the frailty of my brain, I knew what the early nights and cold mornings meant for my human ancestors—death. Death at the hand of my kind; death at the hand of nature; death at the hand of God Himself.

The house was still now, it was just me—me and my many thoughts.

Something pulled my limp body off the carpeted floor.

Loneliness?

That felt right, but I couldn't understand why. I was different now. I didn't fit in, no matter what side of the disease I wanted to think fit me. Why was I different? How was I different? I didn't know those answers, but I knew that I was different.

Different and alone.

But that didn't matter any longer as my feet touched the gravel road. My dying body had already decided where I was going. I didn't argue with it, though, as everything within me simply swayed down the road. So my mind just nodded to the autopilot light and sat back to watch the stumbling, bumbling course pass beneath.

My body felt stretched, as if some evil child had pulled it long like an old Hulk Hogan super stretch toy. Every bone seemed flimsy and the muscles no longer felt attached. Yet my body moved. It was not a fast movement, or even a straight one, but it still moved. Tree limbs tore at my stump on one side and then, only moments later, I was in the trees on the other side of the road.

Though my body and mind wavered, their guidance did not. Diseased bodies had passed down this road recently. The scent of my kind pulled my body down the road like a sci-fi tractor beam, but my mind followed another scent. My mind, which was carted along like cheap Samsonite, took several hours to decide what *it* was following.

The many footprints of my kind spread out before me, some were clear shoe or barefoot prints in the road that had become more dirt than gravel, but most were alternating trails of feet drug along by bodies which would not wait. Without looking back, I knew that I left one of each print.

Step...

Drag...

Step...

Drag...

That was my trail and it made me wonder what trail this horde was following.

But my mind knew what trail the others were following. It was the same one that I was following. Below the stink of rotting bodies, was a faint reminder of another distant smell. That smell clung to the only tire tracks left on this road, soft and sweet. Like a lone cigar sparked in another room, the scent was unmistakable despite its distance.

I sucked in the scent, breathing it deep into my lungs just as I'd once enjoyed puffing in the tobacco smoke of expensive Havanas. It filled my lungs with hot openness as my chest rose and fell with the new freedom. I felt the smell relax me, just as I felt it begin to wake me. No salesman would try to sell me as a new model, but I could feel the sticker tag rising as I became slightly less used.

My body continued on a little faster, though my steps were still interspersed with just as many drags. I still weaved and banked across the dirt road which soon became dusty concrete, but I was able to remain within falling distance of the centerline now.

The road began opening as the miles passed behind me. The trees and houses moved farther off the road as they became less crowded. Where a thousand trees and a hundred houses had once loomed around the road, now only a few hundred trees and maybe only a dozen houses sat. In the new openness, I could actually see that I was gaining ground on the creatures ahead of me. I hadn't thought I could keep up with them, let alone catch up, but there was a new spark of strength beginning to fill me. It was a small spark, too weak to ever spread into a fire, but the spark kept pushing me on.

By the time the bright moon hit its apex, I could make out individual creatures in the armada ahead of me. There were hundreds of them now, a zombie army marching onwards and I finally realized what was pulling me forward. It wasn't loneliness or even a desire to belong. Those creatures weren't my family any longer. They were nothing more than a gang I'd finally outgrown.

No, I didn't miss them. I didn't feel lonely without them or feel any need to be with them now. It was duty that drove me on. A strange, but overwhelming, feeling of duty not yet fulfilled. I felt a duty to that weak scent we were all following. That trail of blood that dripped from my adopted human was the only thing now tying me to these violent lambs before me. They followed the scent to smash that small trickle of life from her and to eat any who might protect her. I followed the scent to protect her, though I knew the zombie army would trample me before they devoured their prey. I couldn't stop them, but that didn't matter. I had a duty. I couldn't just give up because I was too weak to accomplish it.

The road peeked over a tall ridge bordered by rocks bigger than the houses we'd left far behind. Nothing green had grown on this ridge for centuries, but tall white trees cut the night on either side—man-made trees, wind-powered plants for the lost civilization of man. I stopped to watch the few blades that still turned. It was hard not to marvel at the power of man and it made me miss my humanity just a bit. I had once belonged to mankind; I had once been one of them. But mankind was being extinguished and replaced. In man's place, a new breed would thrive. But that new two-legged terror—zombies—depended upon man's blood to survive. So what would replace the zombies? Would there be a replacement for man after they disappeared and zombies starved? Would there be another 'new breed'? Would it resemble me?

Probably not.

Those questions didn't matter, though. They weren't important to my duties, only brief interludes between the semi-conscious daze that drug me on. My feet began moving forward again, but stopped after only a few more steps. I was looking over the wide valley beyond the ridgeline and the view froze my feet to the cracked pavement below.

The dusty valley spread out below me, a brown swath of land stretching into the expanses of the silence. An artist's brush couldn't have captured the beauty of the valley as the morning's first light painted the wide brown valley in brilliant hues of reds and oranges. The far side of the valley stretched higher into the sky and some of the taller peaks reflected Bob's rays with white caps of snow. The lower valley was a brown mat that seemed to fill the floor uncut except for one small patch of grays and blacks where humans had once thrived. Beyond that patch of human history and the white windmills, there were no other reminders that man had ever existed here.

Nothing moved in the valley; nothing disturbed the painting as I stood and admired the serenity. Bob continued to climb behind me and the valley became even more beautiful with each additional degree of light. Streaks of Bob's brilliance began painting the basin of the valley, leaving only the backsides of the huge boulders in the darkness. The dark sky became smudged with pink clouds drawn long over the mountains before turning orange, then yellow, and finally the bright and brilliant white of pure innocence.

It was almost perfect.

Get out of the light.

The voice was right. I knew it was right. Yet my body couldn't make my mind release its hold on the position. The painting was too miraculous to leave before Bob had finished it—even if that meant I would die right where I stood and waited.

CHAPTER FORTY-NINE

Bob's touch was hot and painful, but it wasn't the blistering sting of a torch's flame any longer. Even as Bob rose over the horizon behind me, I didn't shrink from the light.

I felt the heat rising on my neck, but I ignored it as I waited for the picture to perfect itself. It took me some time to realize what had perfected Bob's creation, but then I saw it and couldn't believe I hadn't seen it before.

Every inch of the valley was now lit. The reds and oranges were gone now, replaced by the bright blues and whites of the sky towering over the snowy mountains in the distance. The valley had become a subtle beige littered with browns and blacks, but the gray of humanity had finally been streaked out. As if Bob had taken an eraser to his own painting, the basin of the valley was covered with a light coat of fog that hid the humanity beneath. One small tower of black rose out of the smudge, a sole reminder that man had once thought himself above nature.

Perfect, I grunted out. But it wasn't just a simple *grwwct* which escaped my lips, there was more to it. Even to my own curled and burnt ears, I could hear the humanity in the word. It was a human word and I had spoken it. Somehow that seemed to be less of a shock than I would have imagined. It was right that I was beginning to speak in human tones again. I was becoming human again. Not quite human, but something close enough that I would at least be able to die as one.

I was walking down the road before I realized that Bob's touch no longer burned me. It hurt, I couldn't suppress the pain that much, but it wasn't reducing me to a blubbering idiot any longer.

My back straightened as I walked down from the ridge. The shadow that stretched long before me was not the hunchbacked monster that I had been before, but of a man. A damaged man, but a man nonetheless.

Step...

Step...

Step...

Drag...

I watched my shadow as each step took me further down into the valley. My body fought to drag me to one side or the other, but my mind was too strong now to allow the gangly black outline of my body to waver from the road's centerline.

Morning quickly turned to noon and, as much as I might try, I could no longer ignore the stinging touch of Bob's brilliance. Feet that had been pushed with new vigor soon drug with the same zombiesque pattern.

Step...

Drag...

Step...

Drag...

Every step would be dragging within the hour and the hours would be dragging me soon after that.

I had to find shelter from Bob. Panic clenched at my lungs as I realized that I had to hide and then it nearly pulled my feet out from beneath me when I saw that there was nowhere left to hide. The road, arrow straight from the edge of the ridge to the basin of the valley, hadn't had any shelter from Bob even in the age of man. Now, in the time of zombies, the road was little more than an impossibly long ribbon of pain.

My back burnt as if Bob were actually rubbing the hot coals down the crooked edge of my spine. I could feel my teeth gnash with pain, but it was the sweat beading on my forehead which foretold the growing pain I would soon endure.

Car!

Of course! My feet stumbled even faster as I searched for an open car that might offer even a shadow from Bob's wrath. Miles ago, this would've been an easy search and the difficulty would had only been in choosing which car. Now, however, the search wasn't so simple. Few cars littered the edges of the road and those seemed to either flaunt large, open windows or were little more than burnt hulks.

I hurried past one and then another, neither offering enough shade to protect my lanky body. Ahead, less than a mile down the hill, were two cars. Both offered hope and I pushed my body as fast as I could.

As I approached them, however, I saw neither car had roofs. The pain was immense and I was grunting in fury as I stepped around the cars and searched the road beyond.

There were more cars, but I knew I couldn't make them. I would be a baked Zed soufflé before I made another dozen steps. As if my body knew the danger, my lame foot grabbed at a sharp edge in the pavement and sent me flying.

I bounced. I didn't fall or tumble, but bounced. An ungainly and pained bounce that dropped me to the ground, lifted me up, and then dropped me down again. My already decimated stump of an arm crackled and snapped as it was jammed into the pavement below my body. Gravel bit into my cheek and peeled back the loose skin all the way through to the weakened cheekbone beneath. I tasted the tainted blood fill my mouth as I bit through my tongue.

A stream of curses—some human, but most unintelligible rants of a language foreign even to me—erupted from my skull as I used my good arm to roll me onto my back.

Pain!

Bob's flames scratched at my face the moment I got to my back. My face had gone unburnt through the many encounters with Bob, but that only made the pain that much more intense.

I tried to flip back over; tried to shield my face. Nothing worked. I writhed in pain and felt the pan fall from beneath me as I fell head-first into the flames.

The remains of my fingernails, already rough and fractured from my last encounter with Bob, dug into the pavement as I fought to pull my body into the shade of the car. As my shoes dug for purchase in the dusty road, I rolled and fought to get into the limited darkness offered.

The expensive, but already tattered pink business shirt tore as my side wore against the pavement. The few remaining bits of my nails were left in the road and I felt them tear into my side as my arm pulled my body towards the shade. None of that hurt, though, at least none more than Bob's sizzling. I could feel the skin of my face tightening into leather as the heat rapidly aged me. My lips dried, pulled tight, and then split. My eyes bugged from their sockets and I had to fight just to blink the scratchy lids across them again.

CHAPTER FIFTY

Darkness finally came, though I could barely feel its coolness any longer. Night was nearly half done before I could convince my body that it was safe to move on.

I didn't want to move. I didn't want to do anything but lie there and die. But I had to move. I had to keep moving or I would simply lie there and wait for death. As much as I wanted to do just that, I knew I couldn't. I couldn't let myself die until my duty was completed.

So I found the strength to sit.

Then I found the strength to stand.

Then I found the strength to walk.

It wasn't a fast walk, but I was moving again. Step after step, the tightness of my burnt flesh loosened—some bending, but most just cracking and then tearing. Black, diseased blood beaded across my face like a heavy sweat.

I was nearly halfway down the valley road when the dragging of my gimp foot finally wore through the expensive shoe Zoe had covered it with. The black leather popped with exhaustion as the last of its strength gave way. My foot dug into pavement and the pussed-over scabs ripped open again. The pain nearly sent me ass over teacup, but I managed to stop and reset myself.

Pulling my limp leg up and in front of me, the rotted flesh of my foot peeked out of the split shoe. The smell wafted up to the remains of my nose and I gagged at the scent. Funny that I hungered for the dead flesh of humans, but the scent of my own dead flesh was enough to nearly drop me to one knee.

I pushed on, tenderly dragging the inside of my limp foot behind me. It was nearly another mile before the last of the scabs had been peeled off and left behind. It was another mile before I was able to partially ignore the screaming ache of my foot.

Despite the pain, a sense of excitement was beginning to build within me. Below me, the smell of humanity seemed to rise like a river fog. Though the scent was little more than a gentle hint of perfume on a cool breeze, I could smell a familiar tint of Zoe on it. That small taste of familiarity drove me on and helped me ignore the other sensation which seemed to be my constant companion now—pain.

Behind me, the rim of the ridge was crusted with yellow—warning of Bob's speedy approach. He was coming. He would not let me live again. I drug my foot faster, my body easily reverting back to that strange, almost epileptic, twisting that might have resembled running, but didn't.

Ahead, a single roadside service station beckoned me closer. I twisted and drug even faster as the beams of Bob started topping the ridge behind. Desperation turned to terror as I slowly closed the gap between death and safety. Like a terrible nightmare, though, my feet felt like they were mired in quicksand and the distance seemed too vast. I could see the shadows inside the single white building. The darkness taunted me like an oasis must have taunted thirsty desert travelers.

I twisted and pulled.

Step...

Step...

Step...

Drag...

But the gap didn't seem to ever close.

The building was now basking in Bob's light. I could see how the rays washed over the pumps and brightened even the far corners with the deadly sea of light. Still, my foot drug behind me and tried to grab each crack like a heavy sea anchor.

Bob's light hit my neck. It didn't hurt yet, but my mind was too gone to recognize that I still had some time before Bob dropped me to the ground again. Panic flooded my mind, filling the empty spaces of my skull with the thick mud of terror.

I nearly tripped again as I rounded the station's pumps. My gimp foot caught and pulled me back up just as my hand grabbed the handle of the door. The pain of Bob's fingers was creasing my neck and driving me forward.

My body nearly crashed through the glass door as it gave way. I tumbled into the darkness and kicked at the door even as I went flying beyond it. Two rows of cheap shelving crashed beneath me and the exposed bone in my chin caught on the lip.

Darkness, true mental darkness, enveloped me immediately as I succumbed to the pain, terror, and exhaustion that had chased me inside this dim shop.

CHAPTER FIFTY-ONE

More than one day passed as I lie across the overturned shelves. I didn't notice them pass, nor did I care. I was just happy to be away from the long and painful fingers of light just outside my small haven of darkness.

When I finally shook free of the unconsciousness that gripped my soul, I realized that I was hungry. Starved, in fact. No, starvation had passed long behind me now.

In my semi-alert state, I laughed at my empty stomach. It hurt to laugh, but it hurt even more to be starving while I lay there surrounded by bags of food that I would have eaten as a human. But that was my curse; that was my cross. I couldn't have stomached the bags of chips now any more than I could have chewed on a beating human heart when I'd been human.

Neither option sounded entirely enticing any more. In fact, nothing sounded appetizing at the moment. I would starve for the lack of imagination; surrounded by food that would probably sustain my life but rot my gut.

Move.

The voice was low and commanding. The emptiness of my gut didn't matter; not even the emptiness of my soul mattered any longer. What mattered was that I kept moving; that I kept pushing further.

Slowly, I rolled from the tossed shelves like an old man rolling out of a lumpy mattress. I hurt. Everything within me hurt. My bones, many broken or bruised, seemed unwilling to guide the loose flesh where my mind told them to go.

Move.

Okay, okay, I'm moving. I willed my body to stand, but it seemed to have found the pleasures of mutiny more satisfying than those of obedience. I felt my body roll off the shelves and drop to the floor with a strange and discomforting *smoosh.*

I lay there wondering what would make that kind of strange sound when I heard another. This sound wasn't so strange, though. This sound was both familiar and frightening.

Footsteps.

My empty stomach dropped even further as I lay face-down on the service station's dusty floor. Questions filled the voids of my skull as I listened. Human or other? Friend or enemy? Do I hide? At what rate did dust accumulate on an empty floor? Do I attack?

Does it matter?

No, I agreed with the voice resonating through the recesses of my soul, not really. None of the answers really mattered, though I did have to wonder how long it had taken for the thick coat of dust to amass. Human or zombie; friend or enemy. None of it mattered because they were both friend, just as they were both enemy. Neither would greet me with friendly head nods, though I couldn't be so sure if either would kill me onsite as the abomination that I had become.

Then move.

Yes, yes, quite yelling at me. My body rolled to one side and then the other, feigning any true desire to get to its feet.

Move.

Okay.

Move!

Okay, okay!

MOOOVE!

As if my body obeyed the voice and not my mind, I felt feet move beneath me and was quickly standing. Just to confirm who was the master and who the slave, my body rattled across the floor and pushed its way into a dark corner of the dusty station.

Mutiny. There were no other words to describe what my body had just done. Sure, listen to *the* voice but not your *own* voice. This ship seemed to be getting a bit crowded now.

I wasn't even bent to my knees before the footsteps rounded the outside corner of the building. Dropping like the ragdoll I had become, my back leaned against the corner and my legs jutted out at weird angles. I wanted to adjust myself, but I didn't have time as a pair of human eyes peered through the glass front.

Terror gripped my black heart as I froze in the strange position. The gas station's silent lobby quieted even further as I squatted between the freezer windows and an ATM which would never dispense cash again. Dust swirled in the hot air, the tiny bits making floating waves that swelled delicately in the bright streams of light.

The front door of the station creaked open slowly before nearly flying off its hinges. I couldn't see anything in the brightness of the door other than a thick-barreled shotgun that wavered left and then right. The human holding the shotgun didn't chance a step in as Bob's glare cleansed my darkness.

The light hurt the leathery lids of my eyes, but I forced them to stay propped open just a hair. In that sliver of light, I saw the barrel pan the room as the human stepped closer.

Hunger tore at my gut. It was the heavy feeling of true starvation; the belt clenching my stomach compressed one more notch as the human's scent preceded its body.

Mmm, human flesh. I could nearly taste its heart as Bob's light streamed around the shadowy figure. With every breath the human exhaled, I felt my stomach clench even tighter. It took every ounce of strength and even some encouragement from the mythical voice to keep my body still. The shadow took another short step further into the service station, but the human was still little more than a blurry figure that smelled like uncooked barbeque.

The human stepped in slowly, the shotgun barrel getting even bigger as the human leveled it on my chest. I couldn't breathe as I played possum in my dim corner. Though I couldn't see the human's face, I could feel its eyes scanning my body, questioning whether I was dead or really dead. There hadn't been any real difference before the disease—dead was dead—but the infected had changed that equation, my kind were mostly dead even before we got really dead.

Another tentative step forward.

Just a few more steps, foolish human.

For once, I actually agreed with the voice. Just a few more steps. The barrel still looked like a railroad tunnel staring straight back at me, but I knew the human would have already pulled the trigger if it had thought I was still a threat. No, the human thought it was safe to come into my retreat. It thought that the crumpled zombie in the corner was mere death-decoration.

It thought wrong.

I waited.

And waited.

The shadow materialized into a full human form as it moved into the station. Only a dozen steps separated us now. I could feel my muscles tensing as the shotgun swept the room before returning to my chest again. The human was careful, even as its carelessness led it into my claws.

I counted the steps; planned the attack. Three more steps, that's all I needed. I would roll to my weak side and use the counter just above me to stand before coiling my legs against the base of the wall and springing onto my prey.

Another step.

Just two more.

The shotgun swept the room again. My body nearly launched itself prematurely, but the voice steadied it and I regained control before the barrel returned.

One more step.

My breathing was shallow and quiet, just enough air being exchanged to sustain my pitiful existence. The human's scent filled my nose and swooned my head. My stomach erupted in a long and low growl that wouldn't have been heard in anything but complete silence.

But the human heard it.

The human froze in place. It sensed the danger and I could see the finger tightening on the trigger. I had to move quickly or I would die in the somewhat unfurled position I was now in.

Ready?

I was ready. I sucked in the scent again.

Go!

My body tightened into the edge of a knife and then exploded outwards. In an instant, I was flying across the gap between us. My mind lagged behind my body in some sort of hungered delirium, but it was unnecessary for this business. This was killing and I didn't need brains to do that, just instincts.

The human stood frozen, her feet wide and flat as I sailed towards her. There were no sounds that filled the station's lobby as I landed and then launched again. The shotgun never wavered as I bounded towards the human, kicking up clouds of thick dust into the still air.

My nose sucked at the air as my legs uncoiled one last time. The human's scent filled my nose like a smoky barbecue, but I barely noticed it as my hand clawed ahead of me.

And then I was on her. The shotgun barked out uselessly beside me as we tumbled towards the open door. She kicked and swung, but I was already digging my claws into the tenderness of her throat. My feet wrapped around her legs and we bounced across the empty floor.

Bob's light torched my back as we rolled into the light, but my legs spastically kicked out and the two of us bounced past the open door and back into the darkness beyond. The woman fought, but she was weak without her shotgun and I was even stronger for my hunger. My teeth, loose and cracked, flashed towards her neck as my excitement peaked.

That scent.

My teeth were nearly at her neck as my legs constricted around her waist and my arm wrapped around her chest.

It was familiar.

I ignored the voice and the smell as I fought to control the human's body. We were going for the eight-second rodeo and I would lose my meal if I didn't get it dead quickly.

You've smelt it before.

Our bodies rolled over and back towards the light. A pistol barked out in the human's hand, but it only shattered a window high above our heads. My legs flexed backwards as I pushed on top of the human. With my arm pulling upwards, I flattened the human out beneath me and stretched her for the kill.

You smelled this human recently.

My teeth closed on the human's neck, my nose buried right behind her ear in an intimate embrace.

The woman.

Exposed skin broke beneath the gnawing and gumming of my jaw. I tasted the first dribbles of her blood just as I finally recognized her.

Yes, it was the woman I'd seen only days before; the woman who had shot my Zoe. Rage filled my eyes with a crimson filter. I stared at the woman through lidded and enraged eyes. I would kill her. I would kill her slowly. I would enjoy killing her for more than just the simple nourishment her body might provide. I would enjoy killing her for the pain she'd inflicted upon my innocent Zoe.

But the rage passed just as quickly as it had come over me. My heart raced as my nose drew in another scent, one more familiar than my own.

Zoe?

CHAPTER FIFTY-TWO

Rage. Panic. Sorrow. Anger. Terror. My emotional rollercoaster was flying down its tracks so fast that it would soon depart them. I didn't know what to think; I didn't know what to feel. My teeth were frozen just inside the woman's tender skin as I soaked in my Zoe's scent and my soul tried to settle on one emotion.

But it already had. I felt every emotion that I could name and some that I couldn't, but there was one emotion that was as unwavering as the gravity I could feel weighing on my shoulders.

Curiosity.

I had to know. I had to see my Zoe; had to know whether she was still alive.

But you already know.

Yeah, but...

The voice was right. I knew it was right when my argument began so convincingly. She was alive. I knew she was. I could smell it. I could smell Zoe's blood. I could feel her weakness; her pain.

I should go to her. I should be with her. I should save her.

Save her?

Yes, save her. She was my charge. She was my responsibility. She was my child. I knew she wasn't any of those things, but I also knew she was much more than that. That weak and dying little human was everything to me now; the only connection to my own humanity and to my own soul. I had to keep her safe.

Safe from what?

From what? From everything. Anger was beginning to well within my belly as the woman was nearly forgotten. I had to keep my baby safe. End of story.

You can keep her safe from everything?

Yes.

Safe from zombies?

Safe from everything.

You can keep her safe from yourself?

Everything!

So, you weren't going to drain her body of blood recently?

No.

You weren't going to eat her?

No! That wasn't true, though. I knew it wasn't true. I didn't want to eat her; didn't want to pull out her heart or suckle at her brain pan. But I didn't control those urges, at least not always. Tears forced their way into my eyes as I held the woman firmly beneath me. She was still struggling, but my weight was crushing the very air from her lungs and I could feel her convulsive fight quickly dying.

And you can do better than this woman?

Yes, I nearly grunted out my furious response. I could protect my child better than this fool of a woman who'd already shot her. Rage began to cloud my eyes as I lay motionless and struggled to win the battle within my head. Yes, I could protect Zoe from the zombies; from the humans; from everything.

Everything but yourself.

I tried to argue, but couldn't. The voice was right. I could bluster my way through the debate, but I could never convince myself that I was right. This woman might have been a bit careless, but she was protecting herself and my child. Zoe deserved that. She deserved a chance and I couldn't offer her that chance. I couldn't offer her any future because I wasn't of her kind any longer. I could barely offer her a chance to make it through each night alive and weeks, months, or even years weren't within the scope of my prospects. I couldn't truthfully tell myself that Zoe would be better with me tomorrow or next week. I couldn't honestly say that the disease wouldn't drive me to eat her before Bob dipped into darkness again.

I couldn't say any of that because I wasn't human any longer. I could play human, but I still wasn't one and I could never be one again. I was condemned to live as one of *them*. I could argue with myself and try to believe that I wasn't infected any longer, but I was. I would die of this infection, even as I lived through it. Hot, copper death still soaked through my skin and swirled around the remains of my nose. It was unmistakable—the acrid smell of death that didn't seem to take away the spark of life within. The darkened zombies who huddled together through the night were my kind—dead but still walking.

That was my future. I was nothing more than the undead replica of my former self now. That was all that I could offer my little Zoe, a lifetime of hiding from both sides of the war.

Yes.

The voice only seemed to echo the pain in my wilted heart. Yes, I was undead. Yes, I wasn't anything more than a distorted shadow of the human I'd once been. Yes, Zoe was better with her own kind.

The woman's struggles had ceased beneath me and I could feel the calm of unconsciousness soak over her mind as her body shrunk into the dusty linoleum beneath. I was still wrapped around her, but my teeth had left her neck and my nose sniffed at her hair. I could smell Zoe in her hair. I could taste Zoe on her skin.

Tears hit my eyes, hot and unexpected. They rolled from my cheeks and burned as the salty substance soaked into the gaping hole that had been flesh only a week before. The pain sharpened my thoughts, but didn't stop the true pain. The true pain was buried deep below the broken surface of my skin. The true pain was buried too deep for even me to see.

I was alone.

I would always be alone now.

I would never see Zoe's smile again.

There would never be any more smiles again.

There would never be anybody to hold me again.

And I would never hold anybody again.

I was alone.

CHAPTER FIFTY-THREE

The truck engine had disappeared many hours before, but my brief flashes of sorrow and loneliness still clung to my mind like the sickness that owned it. The voice was right, I knew it though that knowledge did little to ease the emptiness of my soul. I had set the woman free. I had let her drive into the oncoming sunset.

And that had been my final traitorous act. I was no longer a part of zombinity any more than I was a part of humanity. No zombie would *ever* set its meal free just as no human would eat another.

So I lay there in the darkness, a half-dead pink-clad ex-zombie who missed his human. The fact that I was more than simply 'half' dead didn't matter any more than the fact that zombies still didn't wear pink. The fact was that I was Zoe's pet; I was her 'widdle puppy' who playfully allowed her to pet its belly but would snap at any other hand that approached.

Yet, I hadn't snapped at the woman.

And she hadn't snapped at me, either.

Had she recognized me? Had she known that I had come to retrieve my daughter? I doubted it. Even in my pink executive shirt, I was sure that we all looked alike to the uninfected. In the heat of that mad moment, I was sure that the woman couldn't have known if it was her own father attacking her. Yet there had been a moment of something. I don't know what that *something* was, but I had felt it.

And so had the woman.

I could have crushed the life from her body. Only a few more seconds in my grip or a few more millimeters of my bite and she would be rotting in my gut rather than speeding away. But I hadn't squeezed her to death nor bitten through her throat. Instead, I had released her like a trout too small to eat.

And the woman knew it. She knew she'd been dead. She knew that I had beaten her and that her life had been mine to take. And she knew I hadn't. I'd seen that knowledge in her eyes when I'd pushed her towards the door. Even with her shotgun back in hand, she'd known that I'd let her live.

But she hadn't shot me. She had done far worse than shoot me. She had taken the small remains of my heart from my withered soul and driven off with it. I suddenly knew how my wife had felt and why she'd cried on the first day of school. I'd thought it silly then, *you'll see Zoe Jane in just a few hours* I'd told her. *Ridiculous*, I'd thought to myself. But it wasn't simply the physical absence of our only child which had driven my wife to tears, it had been the knowledge that everything was different now. Our baby had been 'our child' when she stepped onto that bus and she'd taken a seat on that very same bus as 'her own child'. From that simple and almost overlooked moment on, our Zoe Jane was no longer ours alone. My wife had recognized that moment for what it really was, a monumentous occasion of change and growth. It was the first wheel to roll; the first step on the moon. I'd never realized the importance of that solely and completely human moment while I'd been human.

Or was I *more* human as a zombie than I'd been as a human?

Yes.

Thanks. My thoughts were filled with sarcasm for that arrogantly omniscient voice, yet I finally recognized it as my own voice. It was nothing more than my own voice filling the expanses of my noggin like a critically manic inpatient in a booby hatch.

Then what do I do? I asked the question as if I expected some sort of miraculous answer that would solve all of my problems.

No answer. Anger, soft and subtle, began welling within me. I could feel its cold, red hand pass over my heart as I waited for an answer I didn't expect to ever get.

What do I do?

What did your wife do?

She cried.

Did she?

Even as the voice asked its rhetorical question, I knew that wasn't what she'd done. At least, that wasn't all that she'd done. She'd cried, but not until after she'd followed the bus to school and watched our little ZJ get off the bus and march triumphantly into class. My wife had watched the transformation from baby girl to big girl with the fear that only a mother—and now a zombie in pink—could understand. She'd watched and made sure her baby was safe, then she'd broken down and balled like the baby *her* baby had been.

CHAPTER FIRTY-FOUR

I didn't wait for Bob to park his bright ass over the horizon. I didn't have the time to waste; I had to ensure that my baby was safe. Safe from what, I wasn't sure. What I *was* sure about was that I could feel the universal pain of motherhood driving me on, my own pain forgotten as I fretted over my baby girl.

Like my own wife, I would follow my baby and ensure that she was safe. She didn't need me to protect her any longer, I knew that was true, but *I* needed to protect her. *I* needed to know that she was safe. *I* needed to know that she wouldn't forget me; that she wouldn't move on into adulthood without knowing that she was loved.

That she was cherished.

That she was needed.

Tears stung at my face as they rolled into the broken recesses of a mask that had once been strong and handsome. That was all gone now. I was stripped of the masks; stripped of the humanity. All that was left was love. Pure, simple, unashamed love for a girl that I called daughter but hadn't fathered.

I stumbled out of the service station and into the bright light of late evening on the desert plains. I didn't know where I was; I didn't care where I was.

Bob burned my flesh.

Bob stung my muscles.

Bob tore at my insides.

I ignored him.

Only one thought prevailed within my head now. Not because I wasn't capable of thinking, I was past that now, it was because there was only one thought worth filling the empty spaces.

Zoe.

Zoe Jane.

They were the same.

They were my daughters.

They were all that mattered to me now. I had to make sure that my daughter would survive; that her new guardian was worthy of *my* trust. I had to ensure that the woman would keep her safe.

Broken asphalt passed behind me unseen. I cared not for the ground beneath or for Bob above, my only concern was for the small trail of blood-tinged air that I was following.

The truck's path was easy to follow, I could smell Zoe's flesh on the small breeze that passed over the littered road. I dodged around the cars and the remains of humanity as we delved deeper into the city together.

Houses began appearing to my left and right, occasional at first but soon more common than the emptiness between them. We were working our way into the framework of human civilization that had been lost long before I had even met my new child. There had been battles here, I could see their signs in the roadblocks and bodies littering the carpet of this town. Army upon army—zombie upon human. The battles had changed the entire face of this town and taken away everything that had once attracted people to it. There were no sights to visit, no stores to shop, or restaurants to eat within. No subways travelled beneath the streets or cars upon them. This city had died in those battles, yet there was still life here—both infected and uninfected.

The woman's truck tracked through the maze of other cars and I knew I was beginning to close on them. I could smell Zoe's blood now—not just the small florets of her dandelion-like body, but the blood that soaked her clothes and clotted her wounds.

I could smell her now.

And so could the others.

The infected were beginning to stir in the buildings around us now. I could sense them preparing for the night. I could *hear* their thoughts—simple, yet deadly.

They would soon follow her scent. They would soon chase after my Zoe. They would soon try to feast upon her innocent flesh.

Red.

That was all that I could see as the night began to take over. The red of rage was so thick over my eyes that I couldn't even see the road I walked upon or hear the cry of the others around me.

But the rage wasn't directed at the others. It wasn't even directed towards the woman who had brought my daughter back into the zombies' grasps. The fury and hatred was directed with laser-beam accuracy inwards. It was focused at only one soul—my own.

I was the one who had let my Zoe down.

I was the one who had let my Zoe be shot.

I was the one who had let her be taken.

I was the one who hadn't taken her back.

I was the one who had trusted the woman.

I was the one...

who had failed.

There were no others to blame, I was the one.

My feet moved faster in the dim light. I could smell the humans now. I didn't follow Zoe's scent as I ran through the dead streets. I didn't have to. I knew where the woman had taken my Zoe; I could see where they were now.

CHAPTER FORTY-FIVE

The lights were on.

There was someone home.

How silly they were.

How ridiculous.

How arrogant.

The humans thought themselves stronger; thought themselves better.

They were not.

Yes, they could think. Yes, they could plot. Yes, they could even intelligently defend themselves. But hadn't they thought that they didn't have to? Hadn't they thought it would be safer in the open plains of the desert surrounding this city? Hadn't they realized that my kind couldn't survive the miles of openness? Hadn't they...

No.

The arrogance before me redirected the rage towards the bright lights and high walls. There, in the remains of this city, was a modern compound designed to protect the remains of the human population. They weren't hiding here, though. They weren't huddling together and praying that they couldn't be found. Here, behind the muddled defenses that could be scraped together, these humans were flaunting themselves and tempting the zombies to attack.

And my kind would attack. I could hear their thoughts in the shadows now. I could feel their plots. I could sense they were no longer blindly attacking the humans. They had learned. They had grown.

I slowed until I was nearly stopped in the middle of the wide road that led straight into the humans' new castle. It had been the city's courthouse before the disease, but no trials were heard there now. It had been rebuilt by the humans. Its massive brick walls and tall stone pillars formed the inner base that the humans thought would protect them. A tall crane sat abandoned to one side, its work already completed. Stacks of dead cars stood as the exterior walls to surround the pillars of the courthouse like the outer walls of a medieval castle.

At the base of those cars, piled stack upon stack, were the dead and bloated bodies of my kind. They had been there for time unknown and I could see that each night probably laid a new layer to the wide stack nearly encapsulating the human fortress.

Atop the massive courthouse, I could already see the humans moving into position for the night. The snipers were well placed; their long guns probably capable of picking off the individual fingers from my remaining hand at this distance. But they didn't see me; they weren't worried about my kind yet because Bob hadn't abandoned them yet.

I could feel the movement behind the tall wall of cars, the battle for the night would soon get underway and the humans knew they only had a few minutes of peace left before the zombies attacked.

War?

The final war.

Yes, that was what my Zoe was trapped within. The final battle of the final war for humanity's survival. She was stuck dead center between the clowns to the left and the jokers to the right. The last battle and there would be no victors. We would all perish in the fire that surrounded the fight; we would all surrender to the hell that would be unleashed on this valley.

It sounded somewhat surreal; somehow overdramatic.

It wasn't.

The call of my kind echoed through the dead city. It rose and fell, cackled and crackled, before finally falling silent. I didn't join in; I didn't want to. Had I finally broken the spell of my disease? Had I finally regained control of my body? Of my mind?

No.

I nodded my agreement even as an army of zombie foot-soldiers gathered in the semi-darkness behind me. I could feel their breathing behind me as if a great breeze passed each time they inhaled. Their numbers were countless; their rage limitless. With each step forward that the zombies took, the humans' chances took one back.

I stood in the growing darkness of the world that had once belonged to man, knowing that nothing belonged to man any longer. Nothing belonged to man and nothing belonged to me. We were both dead. The time of man was done. I could feel it in my heart that the war for humanity's future was already raging at its climax. We were both dinosaurs that didn't yet know we were extinct.

And, at the center of that climax, was my beautiful and innocent Zoe. The zombies had her trapped with the other humans, corralled like cattle awaiting the slaughter. The humans, though their intentions were probably honorable, had brought my Zoe in to their battleground and had stamped *Moo* across her wounded body.

The footsteps of my kind grew in the darkness behind me. They marched the dead streets like undead soldiers on parade. There was a calmness to their echoed steps that terrified me. They had grown beyond the fevered kamikaze pilots and had learned that their headlong attacks would not succeed against this enemy.

What else had they learned?

Panic set into my bones with the realization that my Zoe would soon die; her weak body caught between the two warring armies in the final battle for this town.

Generators hummed to life somewhere behind the wall of cars.

Feet pounded the city streets behind me.

Stadium lights sputtered to life above the courthouse. I could hear the dim buzzing of the lights, but the sound was eclipsed by those footsteps behind me.

Drag...

Drag...

Drag...

Drag...

It was terrifying. An army of undead was descending upon the fortress and my Zoe was caught in the midst of this battle. I was caught in the midst of this battle. I was just as much of a bystander as my Zoe now; a non-combatant glued to the stadium seating mistakenly placed upon the demarcation line.

The lights brightened, though only enough to cast a ghostly pallor over the streets. I looked back towards my brethren. Only the first few rows were visible now, their lines as straight as Jong-un's armies and just as brain dead. They marched slowly, their bodies hungry but not hurried. Their faces said that they would soon feed, maybe not tonight, but soon enough.

The zombie army marched onwards, never breaking stride or ranks as they approached the human encampment. They were patient. They had been planning. They had been plotting.

As they approached me, I tried to read their eyes; tried to read their thoughts. I couldn't. There weren't any thoughts and there was only death in their eyes. They marched together as a school of fish controlled by some inertial guidance and programming.

I had to step back from the slowly advancing horde. My feet backed up a stone staircase until my ass was edged into the front entryway of some business long closed.

Line after line of zombie soldiers passed my position—none turning; none noticing me. I was invisible to them, just as I was invisible to the humans. I was nothing more than a spectator, an unseen and unwanted witness to the final battles between man and zombie.

The lights finally flickered to full brightness, but the light couldn't illuminate the darkness now surrounding the humans. An ocean of zombies, so wide that even Moses could not have parted them, floated in the open streets surrounding the humans' final bastion.

The slowly moving mob seemed to filter into the opening unguided, yet they were guided. By what hand, I wasn't sure, but the zombies before me seemed to share one mind; one command. Their feet moved as one, a continual grinding of the bare streets beneath as some stepped while most drug along. The sound, deep grunts and heavy feet, bounced off the high-rise buildings and echoed so loudly that it shook my loose guts.

Humans scurried atop the courthouse walls. I could see them behind the glare of the lights, but they were tiny and inconsequential ants compared to the army of giants before me. Again, the red of anger clouded my mind as I thought of my sweet Zoe trapped behind the thin veil of gutted cars and human guns. They couldn't stop this mob. The humans would be lucky to slow them enough to survive the night. Panic quelled the red as I searched for a way to stop the attack. But I couldn't stop the attack any more than the humans could. I was just as powerless as they were now.

The rear lines of the zombie army finally passed and the air around me expanded with a fresh breeze that nearly tossed me into the road. I watched the backs of my brethren as they filed into the lights; none turned and none stepped out of turn. They were an army, as well trained as any the world had ever produced, but I knew that even the best armies needed leadership. I searched for the hand who guided them; the mouth who issued the orders.

There were none.

Surely they needed a general to develop their plans; a sergeant major to implement them.

There were none.

I searched my own mind, there must be some magnetic guidance tugging me onwards. Surely there must be something written into my zombified genes that would trigger an obedience to this mob's command.

But there was none.

I was alone again. I was a single spectator to the two forces as they prepared for battle.

The two armies stared at each other through the gloomy light. Neither spoke; neither moved. They simply stared at each other as the hands of some unseen clock slowly ticked away the moments. The tension built until it nearly boiled over and then it built even more. A standoff, as historic as the Earp's and as ancient as man's first hunts for mammoths, was developing in the streets before me.

It was terrifying.

It was amazing.

It was enthralling.

I couldn't avert my eyes as I watched. I couldn't move as I stood only an arm's throw from the hellish army before me. I couldn't even feel my body or blink my eyes. I was a statue; a chipped and broken gargoyle staring from my small perch as the actors in the greatest human tragedy met on the stage before me.

But this play's opening night results were more important than a simple review by an overrated critic. The playwright had already written the first scene and the director had already cast his actors, but nobody upon this cement stage knew what would happen after the first lines were spoken. They merely knew that only one army would see the curtains close and that the reviews would be written in the vanquished army's blood.

CHAPTER FIFTY-SIX

The first shot rang out across the night air. It cracked through the streets and the echoes whipped over the angry masses before me.

I didn't see the shooter nor did I see the target, but I saw the effect that single shot had upon the zombie army. They shook and revved like an idling big-block finally allowed to mix air and dinosaur blood. I couldn't feel the hand which held them fast, but it was there and it was strong enough to restrain their thirst for blood and the insanity of their minds. *That* I could feel. The insanity within their heads seemed to seep over the cement streets and somehow turned the peace of the quiet night into the first moments after Fat Man had hit the air above Nagasaki.

Another shot rang out.

Then another.

And another.

I could see the shooters now, small blips of light behind the mask of stadium lighting shining down at us. I didn't look for their targets; I didn't care about the empty-headed zombies falling before the mob. They were simply fodder for the other soulless animals.

Then they were released. It was so sudden that it nearly sucked me forward with it. One second, the mob of zombies was held at bay and the next it was rushing forward with the speed of a Lexington thoroughbred released from the starting gate.

Not a single zombie foot seemed to drag pavement beneath them. I would have doubted that simple statement if I hadn't listened and watched to confirm it.

Step...

Step...

Step...

Step...

There were no sounds of dragging, only steps and the occasional cracks as the few unable to sprint forward were trampled beneath those who were. The zombie army rushed forward with only one target in their minds—the total annihilation of the humans who hid behind the wall of cars and the flurry of bullets.

Screams rose from the zombies; powerfully guttural screams of an inhuman war cry. Those who fell dead from the human bullets or the boots of their kin did not scream—they simply fell in silence and disappeared beneath the wave behind them.

I watched the assault in pained fascination. My body tried to remind my mind that its allegiance lay with the undead assaulters, but my soul held my feet from rushing on with the others. My soul still remembered my humanity and it reminded my mind that I had been a man *long before* I'd become a zombie and that I'd been a better father than I was a blood-sucking brain-eater.

But you're not human any longer.

The voice. The quiet reminder that I *was* insane. The singular voice of the other being in my head; the lunatic; the pink ticket to the crazy bus.

I laughed. I heard the laughter. It was in my head, yet it wasn't. It escaped my lips. It shook my chest. It warmed my soul.

Yes, I was crazy.

Yes, I had someone in my head that wasn't quite me.

Yes, I wasn't human any longer.

None of that mattered now. I didn't owe allegiance to my zombie brethren any more than I owed it to my lost humanity. I owed only one living soul my loyalty now just as I owed only one lost soul my love. The Zoe's, the one I had adopted and the one I had fathered, were my soul's only supervisors now. They were the only ones who could tell me what to do and where to go.

Take that, weird and obnoxious voice.

The laugh shook me even harder now. It was a crazed sound; a cackling of fools, yet it was the most rational and human sound I had made since the sickness had warped my weakened mind. It felt good. It felt free.

I was free.

I stood there on the abandoned cement stoop of an abandoned store in the center of an abandoned town in the middle of an abandoned world. There was nothing left but the few survivors fighting for the scraps of life that dwindled with each sunset. And what little still remained would be gone after this battle was won.

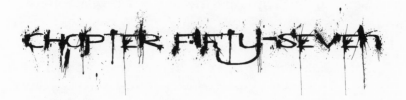

CHAPTER FIFTY-SEVEN

Hundreds of zombies fell to the constant rain of bullets, but those were a mere fraction of the whole that descended upon the human fortress like locusts upon a wheat field. Their bodies littered the ground behind the advancing army, but the remainder only tightened their ranks into a fearsome spearhead that hit the outer wall with such force that I thought they might topple the high wall of cars without even breaking stride.

Terror gripped me again.

Somewhere behind that wall was my Zoe. Somewhere in there was the only piece of my soul that still mattered. Somewhere in there was *all that mattered.*

I stepped into the street. I didn't feel my feet move and I didn't order them forward. Yet they moved me forward as if I were dreaming it all. I felt my body sliding over the pavement and weaving through the small stacks of dead and dying zombies. I had no control of it, nor did I want any. I let my body move forward as my mind quietly watched the great battle rage on.

The wall of cars did not topple, but that hardly slowed the masses beneath it. They climbed the cars—thousands of faceless infected pawing upwards with scary speed. In only a span of a few quick moments, the wall of multi-colored cars turned into a liquid form as the zombie army stretched towards its crest. The sight was spectacular in its horror. The zombies didn't even seem to pause as they scaled the fifty foot wall.

I wanted to stop them.

You can't.

I didn't need the voice to tell me that I couldn't stop them. I was one being—neither human nor zombie—and I was enemy to both sides now. Neither side would understand my motives or offer me any quarter.

But, again, that didn't matter. I moved forward without thought or plan. My body coasted across the battlefield while my mind simply watched the warriors battle before me.

The zombies covered the wall of cars like a thick coat of ivies, but I knew their goal wasn't to crest it. I could feel the hand that controlled them now; I could hear the whispered orders that now tickled their ears.

PULL IT DOWN. That was the command. I heard it in the recesses of my drunken mind. The order was not to climb over the wall or to find a way around it. The master wasn't interested in simply assaulting the human's wall, it wanted to tear the wall down; to make the humans watch as their final defenses were ripped from them.

Pull it down. The order was hardly more than an imagined lullaby as it was repeated over and over again.

Yet they obeyed.

I watched as the thick coating of zombie flesh covering the wall stopped their climb. They were only moments from the top, yet they stopped and rocked.

Back and forth.

In and out.

East and West.

Pink and Floyd.

I watched the zombie multitudes obey, but what master they obeyed or what devious and hidden plans lay buried within that master's mind, I did not know. There was a plan, though. I could see it in the steps those unthinking zombies took; could feel it in their clear paths. They didn't climb the wall like a hungry mob, they surged up it with the defiant obstinacy of a well-trained militia. They did it despite their many disabilities; despite the continual barrage of human guns barking out from the darkness above them.

I was in awe of this zombie army. It was nearly impossible not to be. I hated them and prayed that each would fall in turn, but I couldn't ignore the odd grandeur of their attack. Each zombie had its assignment. Each zombie either accomplished that assignment itself or fell dead and was replaced by another who was equally devoted to that assignment.

They scaled the wall of cars with the ease of wild spider monkeys despite their many missing or impaired parts. I couldn't have climbed the wall with such speed and grace sans my missing arm, yet I saw many one-armed monsters mount the sides as if they were Olympic competitors. It was difficult, despite my hatred for my own, not to cheer those broken fools forward.

Then join them.

No. That wasn't my calling any longer. This wasn't even my war. I had one assignment here and it hadn't been given via some telepathic connection to some invisible master. My orders were to save one little girl and I could feel *my* master beating within my chest. Forget the humans, forget the zombies, I was after Zoe.

Then go and get her.

The voice sounded irritable with exhaustion. What could I do, though. Even if I could have weeded my way over or around the other zombies, I was fairly confident that the humans of Zombiville wouldn't be overly amenable to simply handing over one of their own.

Then just sit here and watch.

I could feel the voice throwing its hands into the air with frustration. Yet, that was exactly what I was going to do—sit here and watch.

The wall of cars was now covered like a hive beneath the swarm. Hundreds upon hundreds of decaying bodies clung precariously to the many stacks of cars, but not a single one of them crested the top.

Discipline. One single word seemed to encapsulate the zombies' attack. Each creature knew their duty and they did it. Even the humans atop the courthouse wall weren't as disciplined as the mindless creatures they shot at.

Hope began seeping out of me. I felt it leave just as if it were my body heat escaping in a frozen lake. It was the zombies' discipline that depressed me. Discipline, honor, thought, love—those were trademarks of the humans; those concepts were humanity's only hope for survival. If the zombies adopted even one of those traits, humanity would never defeat them.

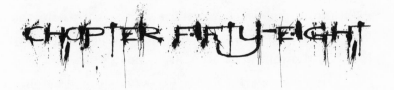

CHAPTER FIFTY-EIGHT

A strange silence enveloped the streets. It came on suddenly and with no warning. One moment, the guns were firing away sporadically and the zombies were crying out with rage and hunger. Then silence—eerie and ominous. No guns fired, no zombies cried out. Just quiet, heavy and blanketing.

I could feel the humans' fear. It hung even heavier than the silence. They knew something was about to happen. They could feel the foreboding in the darkness that could never be lit by mere lights. Human thoughts filtered down through the night. They knew this was no ordinary assault; they knew that this night would change their lives—or end them.

Then the silence was over. A single shot rang out again. One single shot that cracked through the night like a starter's pistol and then the war was on again.

The swarm of zombies coating the wall of cars began rocking again. The tall fortification of metal which had held steady during the first attempts now rocked with the zombies' cadence. It twisted and turned, one side of the long and tall wall coming out while the other went in. Inches at first, barely even noticeable, and then feet and then meters. It was a slow tempo, but it grew with each beat.

The human-built wall of cars, which had looked so steady before, now waved with the strength and weight of the attackers.

Back and forth.

In and out.

The wall waved like an ocean swell, the zombies leaning in with their weight and then stretching out to pull it back. The tall line of cars swung like a whipped rope.

East and West.

Pink and Floyd.

Then the wall crumbled. First the right side and then the left, with a small pillar in the center holding steady. The right side crumbled towards the courthouse while the left fell back into the crowd of zombies beneath with a satisfying crunch of bodies. Like Berlin's physical wall or Roger Waters' metaphorical one, humanity's final wall fell before the onslaught.

Shrieks of metal against concrete filled the entire town and shook me to my soul. Clouds of dust filled the sky, but it was the blood that flew from the zombies caught under the collapsing wall that interested me for the moment. I could see the blood, black and inhuman in the bright stadium lighting. It flew out and covered the crowd around them as hundreds of bodies were caught beneath the heavy wall of metal.

The gunfire went silent again, only for a moment as the humans on the courthouse above gaped in shock. Then they opened up with a ferocity that was nearly as impressive as the collapse of the wall. Small pops of light flashed all across the courthouse roof as dozens of rifles spat out death for the zombies below.

It wasn't enough, though. I knew those guns wouldn't be enough to stop the multitudes of zombies pouring through the gaps now. Another hundred guns wouldn't have been enough even. The zombie army had smelt the humans' blood now. They wouldn't stop until they tasted it.

I watched the wave of zombie flesh empty out of the streets and into the basin that remained between the collapsed pile of cars and the stairs leading up to the courthouse's main doors. They were gone in only seconds, thousands of bodies moving as a single flood. In one moment, I could see them all and in the next they were gone. Beyond the single remaining column of cars, I could see the zombies rushing up the stairs as they spread their deadly darkness onwards. Above them, the humans still fired away, but their greatest defense, the wall of cars, was gone and they were only taking potshots at the enemy.

My feet were moving quickly. I had to see more, I had to be in position when my opportunity finally arose. It took me only moments to get to the base of the wall. What looked like a simple wall of cars from my old vantage was much more. The wall was impressive from its base upwards. Two cars wide at the foot, it had tapered upwards as the lower levels were crushed by the sheer weight. I stood at its base, watching the backs of the charging zombies. Beside me, broken limbs stuck out from the collapsed wall like the Wicked Witch of the East's feet from under Dorothy's house. Some moved; most didn't.

My arm reached up and my hand found its way into the wheel well of a second-tier car. I was already past the third-tier before my mind realized that I was climbing. The other zombies had climbed the wall with a strength and elegance that I didn't possess. Though my movements were rough and clumsy, I climbed quickly enough. I had been afraid of heights as a human—deathly afraid. The fear hadn't changed as my body had, but I fought to ignore the heights and the ground steadily shrinking below me.

The wall tipped back and forth as I climbed, the strength of this small section stolen by its lack of side-support. I ignored the wavering of my metal ladder and focused upon the climb. Only halfway up, my gimp foot missed a toe-hold and I slipped out and away from the next handhold. My body dropped and I only managed to keep from falling the other thirty feet by wedging the stump of my missing arm in between the roof of one car and the bottom of another.

Crack!

I felt the shortened bones in my stump break with a sickening snap. It had been broken so many times now that the pain wasn't as great as the terror I got from the drop beneath me.

The ground was so far below me now. My head swooned and my stomach loosened. The thought of falling was enough to freeze the small drops of blood still flowing through my diseased veins.

Not the fall that gets you.

The voice was light and wispy, its tone mocking as it waited for me to keep falling. I felt the skin of my stump stretch and tear as the wedged bit tried to hold up my dead weight.

It's the sudden stop at the bottom!

I barely even heard the voice's laughter. The knot in the pink shirt's arm hung up for only a moment as the skin of my stump ripped clean. The pink darkened into crimson and I felt my body begin falling again.

My hand gripped the A-pillar of a big Dodge truck as my body began plummeting downwards again. It gripped tightly, but my fingers were slowly pried open by the pull of gravity against my ass. I was about to fall again when the voice spoke up.

Gonna give up that easy? Guess pink was the right color for you.

I looked up at my single hand as it desperately tried to hold me up. My eyes traced the arm down until they hit the white cuff of the pink shirt sleeve. In a moment of instant clarity, I saw the pale little Zoe handing me the dreadful pink dress shirt. I saw her eyes, so full of hope and love for the man—the monster—that she thought would save her. I felt those eyes upon me now, though I knew the whole world was watching the war raging beneath me.

No! I felt the word scream through the cramped confines of my skull. The word, so strong and hard, bolstered my body and tightened my hand. I wore pink because a little girl *loved* me. I wore pink because that little girl *needed* me.

In only seconds, my feet found purchase in the metal wall and I was climbing with a strength I hadn't ever felt before. The cars fell below me as my three remaining limbs dug in and up.

I didn't see the other cars until I was above them all. I stood on the tall wall, only thirty feet below the level of the courthouse wall. It swayed fore and aft as I stood on its slender top—only one car thick and four long. I spread my legs as if I were riding a surfboard and then chanced a look down.

My head swooned again as vertigo gripped at my skull. Vomit burst out from my mouth and shit leaked from the nearly matching orifice beneath. I tipped back and forth as the wall tipped with me. My legs buckled and my body collapsed on the roof of a long Cadillac.

A pink Caddie.

What were the chances that a pink Cadillac would top the mast of cars? The worn pink was only a shade off my shirt as I lay there in a pool of my own bile. Only a shade off of the shirt my Zoe had picked out.

The color cleared my eyes enough to settle my gut, but not enough to let me look down. Instead, I looked out at the humans on top of the courthouse walls. They leaned out and fired down at the zombie army far beneath. The pops of their rifles seemed so small in my head, but I knew they were steadily clearing the ground beneath them.

I tried to move; tried to gain the guts to look down. I couldn't. All of my remaining strength had been used up in the dangerous climb upwards. I was left with just enough strength to keep my eyes propped open and my heart pumping.

#

I lay there silently as the battle around my tiny metal bastion raged on. Above me, the high-rise buildings surrounding the courthouse seemed to frame the moonless night with ghostly edges. The buildings reflected the stadium lights dimly, but it was the pinpoints of light above the earth that I couldn't stop staring at.

Those stars seemed oblivious to the battle that surrounded my small pillar of metal. This struggle for life was so miniscule and insignificant compared to the great worlds that existed all around my own.

Yet this struggle was everything to the relatively small number still involved. It was the end of everything for one side—life or death. The victors would celebrate by either eating the losers or by sweeping them out and continuing the endless struggle for life.

Below me, the zombies battled to enter the building as they tore at the steel and wood barriers.

Beside me, the humans' battle to stop them was wearing down as their ammunition began to wane.

Above me, nothing but silence.

I wanted to go into that silence; to slowly let my body die atop this tall mount and disappear into the dark quiet above. I was tired. Not just physically tired, but emotionally and spiritually. I had nothing left to give; no hidden wells of strength to tap into. I was ready to go; to meet my maker or to simply slide into the still nothingness. I didn't worry about what came next or who would be there to greet me on the other side. I only wanted to go; to be done with this world and this body.

And Zoe?

And then there was Zoe. The one thing that still tied me to this world; the one well of hope that I could still see.

I didn't want to move, but I did.

I didn't want to fight any longer, but I would.

For Zoe, the pale reminder of my chocolate bear, I would move and I would fight.

I rolled onto my stomach, careful not to sway the wall any more than I had to. Looking over the edge, nausea clutched at my gut again. I gripped the pink Caddie's roof and focused on the slight difference in shades between my shirt and the car.

The vertigo passed after only a few sweaty and dizzying moments. I opened my eyes slowly and focused on the courthouse wall before dropping my eyes to the immense pillars and the tall stairs leading up.

The stairs were littered with bodies, both dead and undead, but it was only the moving mass of undeads that I cared to see. They pushed and pulled at the top of the stairs with an intensity that was born by their knowledge that Bob would soon be coming. The black throng below moved in small waves that made it look like a carpet of black insects were crawling across a dying carcass. Of course, that was exactly what I was seeing below me, the evil remainders of humanity attacking the final living limb of their forsaken relatives.

The zombies would break through the doors and pour into the courthouse soon, I could see that even from this distance. The humans had piled heavy debris high upon the entrances to their castle's inner sanctums, but most of it had already been pulled away and the zombie army would only need to gain one tiny opening to empty the stairs.

I couldn't do anything to stop them, though. I was helpless atop my tall pinnacle. The feelings of despair and failure began welling within me again; pushing hope back out to jump off the precipice in a lonely suicide swan dive.

My tall pillar sat alone at the base of the tall stairs leading up to the stone pillars that formed the front of the courthouse. The stone walls of the main building were only a dozen steps beyond those pillars. The walls had two windows on either side of the two massive wooden doors. Above those windows were four more windows. In those upper windows, I could see the humans pouring out their final bits of ammunition. They were dropping the front line of zombies who were still working on the final layers of protection around the two doors, but those zombies were replaced just as quickly by the hundreds still lining the stairs behind them.

I had to do something to protect Zoe. I didn't know what I could do, but I couldn't lie down to die until I truly knew that my baby girl would be safe. My knees pushed under me slowly. I could feel the last wisps of strength moving my arm as it pushed me to my knees. I would climb down and stop them with the last bits of strength I still had. They would kill me before I stopped even one of them, but I had to do it.

My feet finally fell flat on the Caddie's roof and I steadied myself as the stack of cars shifted and wavered. I splayed my legs out again, trying to ride the pillar like a tipsy surfboard. It shook and swung through the sky.

Back and forth.

In and out.

East and West.

Pink and Floyd.

I felt it moving even faster as I tried to gain my balance. Terror gripped me as it kept swaying and then I realized that *I* was making it sway. Something within me was moving it without my knowledge or consent. I watched the walls of the courthouse get closer and then drift away. Suddenly, I knew what was happening and what I needed to do to stop the zombie army and to protect my Zoe.

I turned slightly and began shifting my weight back and forth. The wall of cars came in and then went back out like an ocean wave lapping at the silent sand. Eyes watched me as I shuffled my feet on the Caddie's roof and tried to balance myself. Human eyes tracked me as I leaned far into them and then rode the wave back out again.

There would be only one chance to make my wave crash in. I fought against the weight of the cars as the wall drifted out and then leaned towards the courthouse. I leaned with it, pushing out slightly but leaning in to the building as far as I dared when it was coming back in.

Back and forth.

In and out.

The human eyes watched me with confusion as my pillar came closer and closer to them. Their guns tracked me, but none pulled the trigger. They might have been empty, but I had a feeling the humans were hoping for some sort of miracle savior and they weren't about to shoot the one chance that might still be out there trying to save them.

Further and further I went. I felt like I could nearly touch the courthouse walls as I came in and then I felt like we would topple over backwards as I went back out. Below me, the battle raged on with no attention given to my struggle above them.

East and West.

Pink and Floyd.

Metal shrieked in surrender below me. A car near the base shifted and gave way. I was as far from the courthouse as I could get when it moved.

I was going the wrong way! Panic tore at my chest and I nearly fell dead right atop the pink Caddie's roof.

Be patient.

The wall of cars twisted and shifted even further out. I felt the cars moving below me, leaning even farther away from the courthouse as it began wagging like a pleased pup.

Just wait.

The Caddie's roof was angled so far out now that I had to reach down with my remaining claw and grasp the window frame.

Then it happened.

Slowly and laboriously, the wall started leaning back up to vertical. Before it was there, the wall was moving so fast that I had to drop to my belly to keep from being thrown out.

The wall of cars sped towards the courthouse pillars and then it began breaking apart. The cars at the base leaned in and then turned onto their sides. It collapsed from the very base and threw the top cars forward with such ferocity that I couldn't hold on any longer.

My wall collapsed inwards like Berlin's and Floyd's. I could feel every car come loose from the spine of the wall as they shifted outwards.

Below me, the mass of zombies never bothered to look up at their oncoming death. Metal screeched heavy against concrete as car after car rained down upon the hundreds of attackers which still survived.

I didn't see those below me any longer. I wasn't worried about them as my pink Caddie was tossed downwards. I rode it like a scared cowboy, barely opening my eyes to watch the fall progressing even faster.

Not the fall that kills you, though.

The voice filled my head, barely even heard over the terrified screaming within my skull.

The middle of my wall was crashing down now. I could hear the surprised grunts of the zombies crying out as they were crushed beneath the tons of metal.

The cars just below my Caddie crunched to the ground. I could feel the zombies' bodies beneath me now. I could feel the heat of their bodies rising up, I could smell the stench of their bodies wafting upwards, and I could taste their blood as it was smashed from their dying bodies.

I had a moment of sheer victory as I thought about the many dead beneath my wall. But the moment was only that, a brief second that came and passed before my Caddie finally touched down.

I was only meters from the courthouse's pillars now. My Caddie would smash another couple dozen zombies as it tumbled up the last stairs, but it wouldn't be enough. Still separating me from the courthouse doors were another hundred diseased bodies that were just breaking through as I came down behind them.

I had failed, but I might have given the humans a chance to fight off their attackers and protect my Zoe. I didn't have another opportunity to think of her chances, though, as the right wheels of my Caddie touched down.

My body was thrown off the pink roof as the side hit the top stairs. More than thrown off, I was catapulted off. I heard the Caddie roll over, squishing more bodies before it bounced into the pillar and spun around twice.

I was in the air, my body twisting on its axis as I performed some perverse sideways triple salchow. My gimp leg bounced off a zombie's head, taking both my foot and its head in another direction. The violence of that collision sent me flying like a rag doll into the backs of another line of zombies.

We all toppled into the courthouse wall like a bowling ball and eight of the ten pins. I spun off of them and then planted myself heavily into the wall more than a few feet from the marble ground.

It's the sudden stop at the bottom that kills you!

The stop didn't kill me, though.

Neither did the mass of zombies that surrounded me.

I lay on the ground, my back planted painfully against the stone wall of the courthouse as dozens of zombies rushed through the doors. Feet kicked me. They stepped on me and stomped me further into the marble, but they weren't concerned about me. They had gotten inside and they could smell the human blood they would soon taste.

I lay there wishing that the stop *had* actually killed me. Everything within my body felt broken. The bones felt as if someone had tenderized them with a heavy mallet and my innards felt like that same someone had run them through a large blender.

I was done.

I was ready to die.

I had done everything that I could do.

I had killed dozens, maybe hundreds, of the zombies.

I had given Zoe a chance.

And you still have more to do.

No, I screamed back at the voice. No more! Let me die in peace. Let me lay here and drift off into the darkness now trying to take me.

Get up.

Please, no.

Just let me die! I pleaded with the voice, but a scream inside the courthouse emphasized the voice's order.

I can't.

Get up. You still have more to do.

Another scream, this time a girl's.

Please, let me die.

Move your sorry ass.

The voice sounded like a drill instructor I'd known in another life; in my other life. I obeyed. Not because I wanted to. I obeyed because I had to. Somewhere in my genetic markings was some form of defect that I couldn't ignore. It made me do the right thing even when I didn't want to; it made me fight for those that couldn't.

It would make me die fighting for the love of that one little girl.

I made it to my knees, but that was the furthest I could go. I crawled over the dead bodies littering the doorway and pulled myself through with my limp arm. My body tumbled into the courthouse and splayed itself just inside the doors.

Two hallways led to either side, but the view from the front doors was dominated by long, wide stairs that led up to the second floor. The hallways were empty, I didn't even have to look to know that. Every zombie had gone up the stairs in chase of the humans who were firing away with the last bits of their ammunition.

Let me die, I pleaded to the voice which now sat quietly in the back of my skull. Let me lie here and die.

The voice stayed silent, but it didn't matter any longer. I knew what I had to do and where I had to go. Up the stairs, that was where I could fight and die. Up the stairs and after my brethren, then I could pass into the next world with at least some splinter of dignity.

I pulled my body forward until I was at the base of the carpeted stairs. It took several long moments to get my knees back under me and then even more before I could make it to my foot. I nearly passed out as I remembered that my other foot was lying forgotten somewhere outside in the piles of diseased members.

The stairs passed beneath me slowly. I took each one with great care as if I were an old woman scared of falling and knowing that I would never get back up. My single paw grasped at the railing and pulled me up carefully.

The gunfire was slowing as I got closer to the first landing. The screams of women and children could be heard above me, but they were the screams of terror, not of pain.

My foot and stump pushed even harder; my body straightened more with each step. I passed the wide landing and turned right to continue up the next marble staircase. Dozens of zombie carcasses littered the landing, but they were only pebbles across the beach of my consciousness.

Top of the stairs, I told myself. Top of the stairs, kill a few more, and then die in peace.

I reached the next landing as the gunfire stopped in a sudden and painful scream. The man had held out as long as possible, but he'd finally fallen. More screams behind him, but muffled by a door. The humans must have been at their final defensive stand, I could picture them bundled by the dozens inside the single room as they waited for the diseased to break through.

I turned right and climbed the last stairs to the second floor. When my foot and stump flattened on the marble floor, my body wavered and I felt the darkness taking me.

Let it come, I thought.

It wouldn't, though. It couldn't. I had to finish this. I had to save my baby Zoe.

The world spun around me and I felt my body start over the edge and back down the stairs.

Finish it.

Yes, yes. I steeled myself against the dizziness and leaned my arm against the wall. It helped, but only after I stood still and let the nausea pass over.

Using my shoulder to steady my body, I limped down the long hallway towards the screams of terror. My foot was leaned out so far that a single slip would send me down to the hard floor as I wriggled and rolled forward. I could see the mob of my kind at the end of the stairs, their backs to me as they fought to get through the final door separating them from the humans behind.

There weren't as many now, maybe three dozen of the diseased left. I limped towards them, unsure of what I would or could do when I got to them.

The door at the end of the hall broke open under the sheer weight of the zombie horde and they piled into the room beyond. I started forward and nearly fell as I saw the door spring open. The end, I could feel the zombies' excitement build as they poured into the room.

Disappointment. The zombie horde glowed with disappointment as they raged into another empty room. But they didn't despair for long as the scent turned through another door.

I made it into the room and could almost reach out to grab the back of the crowd as the second door crashed open. A thin staircase led up from behind the door and the zombies were distracted just long enough for me to sink my claws into one of their throats.

I was still weak and ready to collapse, but my claws were still sharp and my hand gripped tightly onto the exposed neck. The zombie kicked and spun, but I rode him around the small room like a professional bull rider.

It took several long seconds for my victim to fall and the rest were already filtering up the stairs towards the roof before he was finally dead. I didn't wait for the coroner's report before I stood back up and hopped after the crowd again.

I would pick them apart one by one if that was what was required to be free of this world.

#

I didn't get the chance to catch them in the stairwell, though, as they shot up the narrow stairs leading up to the roof like a reverse luge.

I caught the last in line as the others rushed through the broken door at the roof level. I nearly ripped his neck clean out as the others continued obliviously on and up. The zombie's surprise didn't last more than his final breath, but his strong back bounced me against one side and then the other before we both tumbled down the three steps he'd managed to climb.

The zombie collapsed on top of me as we both flew out of the stairwell. His kicking body crushed the cage of ribs around my lungs and drove the last bits of air from them. I threw him off of me, but I couldn't manage to collect any air as I thrashed on the ground in pain and panic.

Screams of terror funneled through the narrow stairs and down to me. A gunshot sounded out, weak in its loneliness.

Get up!

It wasn't the voice that ordered me up now, it was my own mind demanding me to push forward. I obeyed, knowing that this pain was temporary; that all pain for me was now temporary. That thought—the knowledge that all pain and all loss would soon be over—gave me strength.

I rolled to my knees, pulled myself to my foot, and then bounced gingerly up the stairs. One by one, then by twos, I took the long stairs up towards the dark night which wasn't as dark now.

Bob was coming.

Bob would soon be here. He would cleanse this rooftop if he made it in time.

One look at the chaos erupting on the roof and I knew Bob wouldn't clear the skyscraper horizon before my diseased brothers cleansed the long stone and pebble rooftop in their own way.

The humans were trapped atop the only structures on the otherwise flat roof. The two massive air conditioners stood barely taller than the zombies surrounding them and the humans clung together atop them like animals two-by-two on the Ark. Around each of the powerless air conditioners were a dozen or more diseased bodies reaching up to grab at the legs of their meals.

I searched the humans, hoping beyond hope that I could find my Zoe in there. My foot pulled the stump of my other leg forward and I waddled angrily towards the closest group.

The humans were fighting back, but the broom sticks and mop handles were little defense against the dangerously famished zombies just below them. They wouldn't last long.

I didn't see Zoe as I approached the first battle zone. Searching the faces, I knew I couldn't move on, though. I wanted to. I wanted to keep moving until I found my Zoe, but that defective gene was taking over and my foot wouldn't turn until this small island of humans was safe.

Just steps from the first air conditioner, I saw a zombie reach up and grab hold of a woman's leg. She struggled, tipped, and grabbed out at the others. A man beside her tried to get her arm, but missed it and nearly fell into the sea of zombie sharks himself.

Time slowed as the woman's body leaned out over the edge, her foot pulled down towards the roof. I could see her eyes wide in terror and her mouth screaming out, but it was her hands that horrified me. One hand was clawing out at empty air, but the other was full. A small bundle of cloth and hair filled that hand as the woman leaned even further out.

Her child.

She was clutching her baby and dragging it down with her. I watched the woman's terrifying struggle with horror as she screamed and kept reaching out with her empty hand for the man above.

My hand reached out and the clawed fingers sunk into a zombie's eye sockets. The infected beast twisted and tried to throw me off, but it never turned from the woman's fall. It smelled its meal, it knew it would soon feast, and my gouging fingers were nothing more than small spikes thrown in its road.

I pulled back and used the zombie's skull to propel me forward. The woman was already beyond saving, but her precious package wasn't.

More hands—zombie claws—grabbed onto the woman as she plummeted even faster towards them. The flesh of her leg was already being torn apart as the zombies mindlessly surrounded her. I wasn't focused on her legs, though. Every bit of me was watching that small package of swaddled cloth and hair.

My hand tossed the zombie's skull behind me as its neck muscles fought to keep the head attached. I was flying through the air; a missile targeting the woman's package as I tracked her downward path. I reached out with my single arm and felt the soft cloth in my hand. Ripping at it as she fell into the crowd, I felt her determined arms collapsing around her baby as her final motherly instincts fought to save her child.

I sympathized with the woman; knew that she was surrendering her own life in hopes of saving her child's, but she would be dead in only moments and her child wouldn't last many more beyond that if she didn't give up.

Tugging at the cloth, I felt it begin to rip and give way. The baby popped loose and I nearly dropped it as I rolled past the quickly gathering zombie crowd.

Without waiting even a moment, I reached down and gathered the baby into my arm like a running back protecting the football. The infant was squawking in pain and fear, but I ignored it as I rushed back towards the air conditioner.

The woman's screams fell silent as the zombies wrenched the life from her. For a brief and horrific moment, the roof seemed deadly quiet. Then my football gathered air and screamed out again.

Eyes, terrible in their diseased death, turned back to me as those not already eating searched out their next meal. Bodies turned towards me and I saw three zombies aiming at me like defensive linemen guarding the end zone. They stood between me and the humans, but I was aiming for the touchdown as I pushed off heavily with my stump of a leg.

I didn't get much air as I leapt out, but I got enough. My outstretched arm was only inches over their heads, but I gathered the baby's arm in my paw and tossed it out.

My body collapsed heavily into the three zombies who were searching the air for their squealing meal. They couldn't find it, but I watched the baby arcing up and out as it made a languid approach towards the human's outstretched arms.

She wouldn't make it, my mind shrieked out as I ripped and tore at the zombie flesh beneath me.

She would.

I didn't want to trust the voice, but I had to. I felt claws tearing at my own throat and I had to turn my eyes to those trying to end my own life. I couldn't let them win. Not now. Not before I found my Zoe.

Flesh tore—mine and theirs—as the four of us rolled along the roof top. I was weak with pain and exhaustion, but I was on a mission and I knew that all of the pain would be over for me as soon as I accomplished that mission.

We rolled towards the edge, closer and closer. I used the stump of my leg to hold myself from going over as I muscled one and then two over the precipice. They grabbed at me as they went over, but only took chunks of flesh and fiber from me.

The third zombie stood no chance as I brought my good knee up into its chest and then drove my clawed hand into its face. It dropped dead even before I could finger its spine.

I pushed myself to my knees and then stood over the cloth that had swaddled the baby only moments before. Terror ripped at my gut again as I searched the roof for the child. Looking up, I saw the man holding the bare baby in his arms.

There were still several more zombies surrounding these humans, but I didn't have time to clear them all as I moved towards the next air conditioner.

CHAPTER SIXTY-TWO

I didn't see her.

I didn't see my Zoe.

She wasn't here. She wasn't with the humans.

Terror gripped my throat again, but it quickly settled into a rage so red that I could barely see through it.

The humans had done this to her. They had brought her to the middle of their war and *left* her to die.

My Zoe. They'd done this to her; they'd killed her!

I felt my legs stiffen and the ice of anger pump through my veins. It strengthened me; it pushed me on even faster. I suddenly found the power to push myself to kill them all.

But it was no longer the zombies that I was after. I would kill the humans for what they'd done. I'd murder them all—not for their flesh, but for taking my Zoe from me and then letting her die.

My foot pounded the rooftop while my stump thudded behind. I was twenty steps from the second group when I spotted the woman who had taken my Zoe from me; the woman who had shot her; the woman who I should have killed.

The rage, as icy as the winter winds over Lake Michigan, turned hot and pointed. Red laser beams couldn't have been a more precise targeting system than my anger as it pushed me almost to a flat run.

I jumped into the air, my leg stump digging into the back of one zombie while my foot pressed into another's shoulders. Pure fury drove me forward as my hand gripped into another zombie's skull. I ripped at the head as I jumped forward.

My feet would have made the top of the air conditioners and I would have been onto my human targets before they could have seen me. I would have had the distance and the height, but my fury fell from the leap even before my foot left the other's shoulder.

I felt my body stiffen and watched as my leap quickly turned into a pitiful tuck and fall. My body would have barreled into the air conditioners if it hadn't piled a half-dozen zombies into the roof first. I felt their bodies crumple under my weight as I bounced and rolled across them.

My foot pushed me up as I sniffed at the air again. Was it her? Was it my Zoe? I sucked in large snootfuls of her scent as a hand reached out and pulled me back down.

I barely felt the hands tearing at my flesh as I searched above my attackers for any sight of my baby Zoe. They were going to rip me into a thousand pieces, but I was still so shocked by the thin wisp of Zoe's blood perfume. It hung in my nose as a hand reached in and tried to rip what remained of it off.

There!

I saw it. Just a tiny glimpse of her pale face, but she wasn't imagined. I'd seen her.

The fight returned to my body in a flood worthy of Noah's great one. The power nearly tossed me onto my back as I felt the strength of a thousand armies fill my body.

My foot found purchase on one of my attacker's chest and I heaved him into the air and off the side of the building like he was a wide kite in a stiff wind. The hand on my face was nearly ripped off as I grabbed and twisted it away from me.

Rolling away from my attackers, my knees bit into the pebbles and I launched myself right back at the zombies. I was a flurry of arm and hand as I hit them at chest level. Two of them fell beneath me and I drove the broken spike of my missing arm through one of their skulls as we bounced across the roof.

The other two quickly fell to my angered attacks, but a scream brought me back to the humans. Nearly a dozen zombies still surrounded Zoe's last pillar of hope and two humans had already been pulled down and into the crowd.

I saw Zoe's face splintered in panic and it drove me back to my foot. The roof disappeared under me as I dove like an eagle at its prey.

But I didn't make it to them. In fact, I barely made it into the air before my body was slammed back to the ground with the weight of a heavy hammer. I bounced off the ground and skittered a few more feet before I felt that hammer slam into my back again.

The air escaped my lungs and I rolled onto my back just in time to see two huge hands knotted together coming down at me. Those hands were possibly the strongest set I'd ever seen—or felt—as they became one immense anvil being slammed into my gut.

My knees nearly bounced off my skull as the zombie's hands collapsed the space between my belly button and my spine. A shot rang out in the early morning, but I wasn't sure if it was a pistol firing or my spinal cord breaking.

I doubled up in pain as the creature reached up to bring those meaty paws back down on me again. The pain was so extraordinary that I could see everything around me with an intense clarity that I'd never experienced before.

The creature above me was calm and relaxed as he aimed his next strike at my skull. He wasn't a man or even a zombie, he was something so much more than either. Nearly seven feet of thick, angry muscle, the creature must have been an NFL lineman before the disease had drafted him to their undead team. His thick neck tensed as he brought death down at me.

I rolled away from the beast, not enough to miss the meat of his strike, but enough to keep from having the squishy parts in my skull from being smashed out.

My gimp arm, already broken and mushy, was ground into the roof top as the monster's hands seemed to shake the entire building. I rolled even further, my body still struggling for air as I tried to separate myself from the deadly blows that this immense zombie was trying to offer me.

I got to my knees and then to my stumped leg as I tried to push myself up. I was almost to my foot when the monster was on me again. He picked me up and drove me forward like a tackling dummy.

Zoe's face watched me from the air conditioner as I was carried away. I could see the recognition in her eyes. I could see the terror in her face, but it was the sadness in her eyes that hurt more than the crushing arms wrapped around me. She wasn't sad for herself; wasn't sad that death would soon be upon her. My little Zoe was sad for me; for the death that was only moments away for me now.

Memories flooded through my skull like a strange black and white film in reverse as I floated along in the beast's arms. I remembered watching Zoe as she was shot. I remembered running from her when I thought I would eat her. I watched as she skipped along the deserted streets. I felt the pink of my shirt as I could see her ordering me to put it on. I remembered the boat rides and the deaths of her family. I saw the booted man's shotgun in my face and then I felt the bite of my hand and the weakness it had caused. Every moment since I'd first heard Zoe's tiny scream was remembered as she slipped further away.

We were only steps away from the edge of the roof when the huge creature spun me in his arms and lifted me higher. He was going to throw me over the side. I kicked and struggled, but his meaty paws held me steady as he slowed.

You were weak when you met her.

Seriously? Now the voice was going to taunt me with his words?

Weak.

She made me strong.

You were weak!

I was, just as I was weak now. I was ready to die, ready to move on. My body rose up even higher as the monster got closer to the edge. We were less than a half-dozen steps away now.

Not like now. You were weaker then.

I was.

I was!

Of course I was! I'd bitten down on my...

I didn't even wait to finish the thought as I reached down with the stump of my crushed arm and pushed it into the monster's grunting mouth. Blood still soaked my stump, hot and black, and it filled the zombie's face with its putrid taste.

The reaction was almost instantaneous as my body bounced from his arms and onto his head. He tried to throw me over the edge as he ripped my stump out of his mouth, but I only crashed heavily onto the roof and rolled towards the edge.

My body was nearly broken and ready to quit, but I couldn't leave this world until my Zoe was safe. I pushed myself up even as the monster of a zombie swung down at me. He was slowed by the mouthful of my infected zombie blood and I easily ducked the mammoth paw as it blasted the roof and sent pebbles into the air around me.

The monster was off balance and only a step from the edge when I launched myself into his chest. It was like running into the stone walls of the courthouse, but I felt him step to the side and then stumble once before going over the edge.

 CHAPTER SIXTY-THREE

My body felt like a slow ribbon of muddy water sliding through a shallow cut in a deserted section of Hell. Every piece that had been picked off my body hurt like I'd scalded it with the Devil's own flask, but the remaining pieces were even worse.

Much worse.

I lay there as the monster's body disappeared over the edge and I felt the cool hand of death trying to coax me to it. I wanted to go. I wanted to just leave the heat of my dying body and simply ease into the calm darkness beyond.

The big zombie's body slammed into the earth somewhere far below me. I heard it and could almost feel the shake of the world around me.

It was over, I'd defeated him.

I'd slain the zombie's Goliath.

I could close my eyes and slip into death.

No regrets; nothing left behind.

Except Zoe.

She was safe now. I had killed the biggest of them. The humans could finish the others.

But I knew they couldn't. I knew that I was it.

And, even worse, I knew there was another to defeat.

My knees pushed under my broken body for the last time. Somewhere within me, the knowledge that this was the last time I would rise filled me with a strange and wonderful hope. I would never be able to climb off of the ground again. This was it and it filled me with a calm that was both pleasing and scary. This was it because I would be dead the next time I fell. This was it because that was all that I had left. This was it because I was already done.

I wavered to a foot and then to a foot and a stump as I managed a quick look over the edge to comfort myself that the mean bastard hadn't survived the fall.

He hadn't.

My foot stumbled forward. The stump drug behind it.

Step...

Drag...

Stumble...

Drag...

I was done. I had nothing left as I traced the roof back towards Zoe's island of an air conditioner. My foot continued pulling my body on, but I was more zombie now than the zombies ahead of me.

Six. Seven. I could now count them and I realized that Bob was just about to break the horizon behind me.

Eight.

Eight. That eighth one was the one I was looking for. He was the one I'd always been looking for. He was the one like me. The eighth one was the only one with the brain to know what he was doing and the only one not controlled by pure instincts alone. I could see that thought process swilling in his skull as he paced the roof and searched for the humans' weak spot.

I stumbled towards the eighth zombie, my foot barely strong enough to keep me from falling on my face.

Stumble...

Drag...

Stumble...

Trip...

I caught myself just as I fell forward. I weaved and my knee buckled. I was on my way to the ground, knowing that I couldn't ever push my way off it again, when I saw Zoe's hopeful eyes turn to find me.

Those eyes, so innocent and loving.

I loved those eyes.

My knees tightened as I caught my fall.

Those eyes love you.

They did. I knew they did. Something in them strengthened me as I pushed on towards the eighth zombie. Its back was turned to me as I approached. I drug my weak body on, step after painful drag, trying to get to that thinking zombie before it realized that I was tracking it and it escaped me.

I was only a few more steps from it when he turned to me. He knew that I was here to kill him and he also knew that it would only take a small gust of air to blow me over.

But he didn't know what Zoe's eyes did to me. He didn't know how much I loved my little Zoe and he didn't know that I wouldn't pass from this earth until I had taken him with me.

Zoe screamed out as the eighth zombie swung a powerful arm at me. I hadn't seen the creature even move until the fist was already coming at me.

The fist hit me near the base of my jaw and straightened me up, almost blowing me over. It probably would have knocked me out before I'd met his Goliath-zombie, but this smaller beast had nothing on that big monster's fist.

I shuffled to the side and stumbled foot over stump before finally regaining my balance. My head rattled in the dawn's light and I felt my death approaching on four metal horseshoes.

A smile crossed my face. I could feel its pull on the remnants of my skin as I stared at the other zombie. I studied his face as he stared back at me. There was power in that face; importance and authority. The strong jaw and deep eyes hadn't faded with disease, they'd only tightened into a kingly demeanor that controlled all around them. He didn't respond as his eyes glared at me. I felt him staring back at me as if he were trying to speak to me, to remind me of our common enemy. But we no longer shared the same language or even the same enemy.

The remaining seven zombies skittered around behind this one as Bob's bald head began peeking over the horizon. They knew they were close to feasting upon human flesh, but they also knew Bob would kill them before they could get their teeth sunk in. I could see all of their eyes flash to Bob and then over to the stairs leading down. I followed their gaze and then stepped to intercept them.

You gotta go through me, I tried to tell them.

They didn't have to speak my language to understand. Though I knew they didn't fear going through me, I also knew that they *did* fear me. I could see that fear in their eyes, though it was buried under a thick layer of hatred and disgust.

The others weren't my concern, though. They were simple minions compared to this dangerous monster before me. The humans could kill them when I was gone, but this one would take them all with him if I didn't take him with me first.

I watched as Bob's fingers soaked the tall buildings around us. Let him come. Let him cleanse this roof. Let him kill me and let him kill all of the others around me.

The other seven feared Bob.

The eighth did not.

The eighth zombie had been touched by Bob, just as I had been and Bob's molesting gropes hadn't killed the devil before me.

Those touches had made the bastard stronger. Just as it had made me stronger.

So this monster didn't fear Bob.

But he did fear me.

I was here to kill him.

I *would* kill him.

The fist flashed out at me, so quick that I felt it even before I saw it. It didn't have much force behind it, but the next fist did. I saw the second one only a moment before I felt it, a hammer blow from high above me. My knees buckled and then gave way.

But my own fist was fast, too.

It burst out and wrapped around his neck with a blinding speed that I'd never felt before. My fingers dug into his throat and pulled him down as I fell.

We collapsed together, his body landing heavily on mine as he tried to sprint towards the darkness of the stairwell. Others joined the fight as they tried to make it past me.

They couldn't.

I wouldn't let them go.

We would all die together, cleansed by Bob's brilliance.

But this one wouldn't be cleansed before I was. He was still stronger than me, even as my lobster-claw continued to clamp tighter around his throat.

My body twisted and pulled as I inched towards the edge. I used my two stumps, arm and leg, to dig into the gravel of the roof as I used my remaining foot to collect the others. Two of them slipped past me as Bob moved lower, but they fell heavily as I used my struggling nemesis to trip them.

Fists assailed me as the eighth zombie fought against me. His claws dug into my flesh as his nails shredded my body. Pain erupted all across my frame, but I knew that my pain would soon be over. I ignored it as I kept pushing across the roof.

We were all alone now, our fight becoming the single ball of rage remaining upon the bright roof. I heard the screams erupting from the other zombies' vicious mouths as Bob's heat lit their skulls and baked them into a putrid crème brulee.

The fire of Bob's touch began burning at our bodies. I could feel both of us weakening as I kept pulling for the edge.

My claws dug deeper, I could feel the zombie's last breaths tickling at my palm as I squeezed my fingers into his throat. He struggled and fought. I could feel him beginning to wrench free, but I kept squeezing and dragging.

I had to stop him here.

Now.

I pulled the zombie's throat forward, dragging my dead weight closer. I felt my mouth close over his throat, splitting the tube beneath the sharpness of my teeth.

Air bellowed out at me as he fought to pull it into his lungs. I shot out again, grabbing the last of his larynx in my teeth and tearing through it.

Then there was light.

And then there was darkness.

EPILOGUE

Zoe's face appeared beside me.

I stared at her face, so dark and innocent.

My Zoe Jane.

My own daughter, my true love.

I stared at her and ignored the darkness that surrounded me now. Pain drove through my skull as I willed my eyes to follow hers.

"It's okay daddy. You'll be okay."

I heard the words. I understood the words. I tried to answer her, but my throat was tight with dry heat.

My wife's face appeared beside Zoe Jane's. She was so beautiful, I'd forgotten how much I loved her. I tried to tell her, but she just shushed me and pulled ZJ closer.

I wanted to tell them how much I loved them; how much I had missed them. I couldn't speak.

I reached out to them, my hands rising stiffly as I tried to pull them towards me.

My hands?

I tore my eyes from my family as I stared at the two human hands before me. I looked past them and found two feet poking up from beneath a knitted blue blanket.

Two hands?

Two feet?

My mind shuddered as I tried to grasp the concept of a whole body again. Then it clicked.

I was dead.

I was finally free of that world.

Free of the zombies.

Free of the disease.

Free of it all.

I turned my hands over and back, relishing in the return of the pair. I was human again. Whole again.

It felt good.

I turned back to my Zoe Jane.

She was crying. I could see her tears behind a thin veil of plastic.

Why was she crying?

I was coming to her now. I would be with my family again. Death would unite us beyond the pain of life.

But we were separated still. The thin plastic sheet encircled me and kept us from being together.

Why? Why would we be separated?

I tried to reason what I had done to keep us apart. I tried to grasp how we couldn't be together now. In death.

The plastic sheet split us as solidly as if it were the rift between Heaven and Hell. But it didn't surround us all. Only me. Only I was trapped by the plastic sheet. Only I was separated from the Heaven that I could see before me.

I could feel the plastic suffocating me. Though it never moved, I felt as if I were breathing the sheet into my lungs.

"Doctor!" My wife screamed out as Zoe Jane cried.

A white lab coat appeared beyond the plastic. It contained a man, but I couldn't see him as I fought for air.

"Calm down, Ed." The doctor's voice commanded me gently as I struggled for air. "Calm down or we'll have to restrain you again."

Voices spoke in hurried tones, but I couldn't hear them any longer.

I clutched at my throat and tried to breath. The air was there. The tube between the air and my lungs was whole. The lungs worked.

Yet nothing happened. I couldn't get the air and panic took over. I was pulling myself from the bed when two yellow forms came over me.

Men. They were men in full-bodied yellow suits, their faces hidden behind black masks.

I reached out at them. I wanted to tell them that I couldn't breath. I wanted them to help.

Please help!

Please give me air!

I reached out again and then I felt a wasp sting my shoulder. The sting was hot and quick, but I felt myself falling back into the bed.

Air rushed into my lungs as my panic subsided. I felt myself calming and my eyes getting heavier.

What's happening to me?

I tried to speak, but my throat was too hot and dry.

Water.

I tried to ask for water.

I was surrounded by people, but there were no humans nearby. Just black-masked, yellow-suited men who strapped me to the bed and ignored my pleas for water.

What's happening?

But nobody answered.

Why won't anybody help me?

Nobody answered.

Was I crazy? Had I finally lost it? Was I insane, even in death?

But nobody answered me.

I watched as the yellow figures checked the straps binding my arms to the bed and then I watched as they left my plastic coffin.

I saw my Zoe Jane. I saw the fear in her eyes.

"It's going to be okay, daddy." She tried to calm me as I fought against the straps; against the plastic shield between us. "They're trying to help you."

Help me?

I tried to croak out my question, but my throat was numb now.

Water? Please, water.

But nothing came out, the words only rattled in the emptiness of my skull.

My body started feeling heavier as I begged them for water. The sting, something in it had drugged me. I could feel the drugs moving through me as I lay in my plastic hell.

"Don't fight them, daddy." Zoe Jane pleaded with me again. "The doctors will find the cure."

The cure?

My mind was slowing as the drugs took control.

The cure for what? The disease?

I nearly laughed as I remembered the days when doctors actually believed they could cure this damned disease.

"That's right, Edward." The white lab coat spoke in a calm, doctorly tone. "We're working on the cure right now. We truly believe that your blood might contain the key to taming this flu bug."

I did laugh this time, a rough spattering of laughter that shook my chest.

Flu bug?

It hadn't been a 'flu bug' since the very first days of the outbreak.

Give me some water.

I searched the room around me. Sterile, white nothingness. IV tubes fed into my arms and monitors blipped, but everything seemed to melt into the bright oblivion beyond.

The doctor entered my plastic tomb. I felt him whisk in, his white plastic suit differentiating him from the others. I felt him enter; felt his eyes on me.

I searched through the glass mask over his face and saw his eyes.

I didn't like those eyes.

"Listen, Ed." The doctor started, though his voice was distant and muffled by the mask separating us. I hated him for that mask. I hated him for the smug doctorness in his voice. But mostly, I hated him for the plastic sheet that kept me from my Zoe Jane. "You've got to calm down or we won't be able to help you."

Water.

"Nurse, why don't you take Ed's family to the cafeteria for a quick drink while I speak to him?"

Water!

I was burning up now. My throat clenched and spasmed as I tried to tell them that I needed water.

"I love you, daddy." Zoe Jane blew me a tiny kiss from her palm as she followed the nurse out of the room. "We'll be right back."

No!

Please, no!

I needed my baby Zoe Jane. I needed to see her; to hold her; to remember her.

But she was gone.

Rage rose through my body as my panicked eyes searched for my Zoe Jane. I could feel it tickling my toes, bubbling through my knees, spilling my bowels, twisting my gut, filling my chest, clenching my throat, and shaking my skull, before finally escaping my body. Every nerve screamed out with anger as I shrieked out a single word.

ZOOOEEEE!!!

But the word never left my body and I felt my throat choking back the word.

And the tears.

"Ed, Ed, Ed." The doctor's mask shook as his eyes turned coldly down at me. "How many times have we told you to calm down?"

The doctor leaned closer and yanked my eyelids open wide. I felt the light in his hands wave across my eyes and felt my body jerk backwards. I wanted to scream from the pain, but I could only gasp for air as my dry throat clenched even tighter.

My head was jerked back and forth as the bastard patted my face.

"You've got to remain calm and stable long enough for us to find the cure." The doctor turned to face the other doctors who were just now surrounding my bed, but I saw something before he turned.

Something in his eyes.

I'd seen those eyes before.

My blood ran a little colder even as it settled from the drugs that they had given me.

"You think that this patient holds the cure?" A deep voice asked from somewhere behind the gaggle of other doctors.

Cure?

"Yes." The doctor above me answered. He waved his hand over me like a cheap car salesman showing off his prized car. "Somewhere inside of Patient Zero here is an answer to this damned plague."

Patient Zero?

I'd heard all of that before. Those words were deep in my mind, but I'd heard them before. I'd been through all of this before. Before the zombies, before the blood, before the war.

Hadn't I?

Hadn't all of this happened before?

In some dream?

In some nightmare?

Hadn't I made it through all of this already?

"And you've got him quarantined well enough?"

The voice was so authoritative that I couldn't help but search for his face. My eyes were heavy and my mind was reeling from the effects of the drugs. I saw the flash of a six-pointed badge outside the plastic sheeting. A sheriff's badge.

"As well as we can quarantine him and still study him." The doctor's face peered back down at me and his eyes froze my soul again. "Ed's not going anywhere. Are you?"

Study him?

Study me?

Water! Just give me some damned water!

"Not good enough, doctor." The sheriff's voice was angry. "We can't risk this disease spreading through the town. You need to get the answers and then get him gone."

Too late, I laughed. Everything was gone. Your town was gone. You're gone. I must have been crazy, because it was all gone and there were no more doctors and no more cures.

Water!

Didn't anybody want to help me?

Zoe?

Where was my Zoe Jane?

I was crazy!

Bring me some water!

Bring me my baby girl!

"Patient Zero's blood is the key to all of this, Sheriff." The doctor turned defiantly towards the door as he backed over me protectively. "Without Ed, there is no cure and there is no hope."

No hope was right.

I looked past the sheriff's badge and saw the man. He was a huge, hulking man that stood over the others and seemed to stare down at me from the heavens themselves.

"Patient Zero isn't the only one infected, doctor. You can call him Patient Zero, Ed, ZEd, or anything else, but he won't be called our savior. Get your answer and then cleanse the earth of this abomination."

The sheriff turned and lumbered out. I'd seen the slope of his shoulders before. I'd heard his deep breathing and felt those monstrous hands strike my body.

Zoe!

The doctor turned back to look at me. His face came low and his eyes searched mine. I watched his face twist behind the mask as he watched me closely. "ZEd. I like that. Patient Zero. Patient ZEd."

There was humor in his tone, but not in his eyes. They glinted wide and I suddenly knew that I'd seen them before.

No!

God, no!

I'd killed him.

I'd stopped them.

I'd torn out his throat.

I ate the bastard's throat out!

Hadn't I stopped the zombies?

Hadn't I killed this bastard?

My head swirled with drugs and confusion.

Hadn't I saved my Zoe?

Hadn't I stopped him?

Hadn't I eaten this bastard?

My eyes were closing as my body began to shut down. I felt the doctor's hands shaking me and heard the smack of his hand across my face as he tried to keep me awake.

It wasn't working. I was drifting away. I could feel my body dropping beneath me as my soul rose above it.

I saw it all as I continued to rise. I looked down from the ceiling and watched as the doctor leaned in even closer, his hands holding my face tightly. I could feel his eyes burning into my body and I remembered where I had seen them before.

The roof.

I'd seen them both on the roof.

And then I saw it all.

I saw my chocolate Zoe Jane.

I saw my vanilla Zoe.

I saw my mouth.

I saw his hand.

I saw my teeth.

I tasted his flesh—metallic and dead.

I felt the weakness fill my body.

I felt the disgust of the disease twist my innards.

And I felt the final shreds of humanity escape my discarded soul.

Author's Note

Thanks again for reading my rags. I hope it was as fun to read as it was to write. One of the greatest things about being a writer for me is the chance to finally free the little demons crawling through the darkest recesses of my mind. To see the voices sprout legs and run with scissors is a thrill, but to hear what others think of the little buggers is just as exciting. I welcome you all to join my Facebook fan page 'mj Hangge' and to review me on Amazon or wherever you purchased my book. I truly look forward to reading your comments, both positive and negative, and hope that you will keep my zombie hordes well fed with your own imaginations.

Now that we've gotten to the end of the tale, I can finally confess the birth of it all. This story stemmed from my daughter's simple question, "If you turned into a zombie, would you eat your own family?" I hope I could fight the urges, but I've given them explicit instructions to shoot me if I do turn.

So, let's hope I don't get bit and, if I do, let's hope their aim is true...

About the Author

mjHangge is an active-duty aviator with the world's finest Special Operations aviation unit. A career marked by desert wars, he has fought in Operation Desert Shield/Storm, Operation Iraqi Freedom, and Operation Enduring Freedom where he has earned numerous awards for his heroism and valor. He currently lives in Tennessee with his wife and three daughters.

14884663R00172

Made in the USA
Lexington, KY
25 April 2012